Love and a
Bad Hair Day

Love and a Bad Hair Day

Annie Flannigan

AVON BOOKS

An Imprint of HarperCollinsPublishers

HarperCollins books may be purchased for educational, business, or sales promotional use. For information please write: Special Markets Department, HarperCollins Publishers Inc., 10 East 53rd Street, New York, NY 10022.

FIRST EDITION

Designed by Elizabeth M. Glover

Library of Congress Cataloging-in-Publication Data

Flannigan, Annie.
    Love and a bad hair day / Annie Flannigan
        p. cm.
ISBN 0-380-81936-8 (pbk.)
I. Title.

PS3606.L36L68 2003
813'.6—dc21

2003041452

03 04 05 06 07 JT/RRD 10 9 8 7 6 5 4 3 2 1

Chapter 1

"Sometimes, I swear, I feel just like Esther Williams."

"Hairdresser Channels Spirit of High-Diving Movie Star!" Emma Corbett, my closest friend, former sister-in-law and sometimes-weekday-coworker rattled the pages of the tabloid clutched in her manicured hands. Never one to do sarcasm lightly, she crossed her tanned legs, swiveled in her orange faux-leather chair and leaned in toward the open pages, pretending to read on. "Jolene Hadley Corbett, thirty-five, of Verbena, North Carolina—"

"Thirty-four and you know it." I snatched the paper from her and tossed it on the pile of reading material she always carted along wherever she went. Emma was always reading. The tabloids. *Cosmopolitan. TV Guide.* And *Money* magazine. Those, she figured, covered just about every angle of every issue that held any interest at all to her. Friend or not, if Emma were a swimming pool, she'd be 90 percent shallow end.

So, I suppose it shouldn't have surprised me that she

didn't understand the heartfelt analogy I was trying to make here. "When I say I feel like Esther Williams I don't mean literally. I don't mean some old-time movie star."

"Really? Gosh, it just seemed to figure that *you'd* identify with a woman who did water ballet wearing a gold lamé girdle for a swimsuit, then rose up dry as a bone with a headpiece of flaming sparklers!" Her grin revealed more than her eerily over-white bleached teeth. Deep down, Emma held a grudging admiration for my driving work ethic and pursuit of perfection.

I think.

"Not *that* Esther Williams." I finished sweeping up the floor of my salon, set the broom against the wall and went to the front door to flip over the "Yes, We're Open. Walk-Ins Welcome!" sign. "Though I have to admit, it's hard not to envy someone who did most of her work under water, yet still managed to maintain that flawless movie-star-quality hair."

"Oh, will you shut up about hair for one minute?" She swiveled the chair around again and tried to fluff out her bangs by holding up a stick-straight black strand and rubbing it between her thumb and forefinger. "Holy shit, Jolie, you're a hairdresser by practical design, not by divine providence."

"I can't help it." I took the two steps from the door to my work station, yanked up a clean mascara comb and took the spot behind Emma's chair. For fine hair, bangs and wisps around the neck and face, you gotta use a mascara comb or a toothbrush. I've told her that roughly a gazillion times but she never listens. I went to work on her hair, silently pluck-ing out the few gray strays I found as I went along. "I feel like I spend half my days in over my head—"

"You spend half your days under water?"

"Not under water. *In over my head.* In something just as hard on a woman's looks—real life!" I paused in the work and did a quick check for dark circles under my eyes. "And some days it takes all I can do to keep from looking like I got ready by licking my finger and sticking it into a wall socket."

"You always look great and you know it." Emma pushed at her temples for her daily do-I-need-a-facelift test.

I smacked away her hands with the comb. Then met her eyes in the mirror and smiled, sympathetically.

"Want me to do your hair now?" she asked.

I held a shudder in check and did her the courtesy of squinting into the mirror at my head of red curls.

"Kidding," she muttered. "Shit, sugar, there is not a hair out of place or a loose thread or a wrinkle to be found on you. There never is."

It was not vanity that made me agree with her, it was practicality. I held no illusions that I was any great beauty, but as the sole proprietor of The Combin' Holiday, Verbena, North Carolina's only real salon, I had a duty to keep up a certain level of good grooming. And Lord never let it be said that Jolie Hadley-Corbett ever shirked any of her duties!

So every day I crawl out of bed way too early and listen to motivational tapes while doing some Yoga mixed in with a few Jazz dance moves I learned growing up. I call the routine Motivate-Yo-Azz.

Practically nobody thinks that's funny but me, but I don't care, it helps me get down to it when the alarm goes off before 6 A.M. Then it's a shower, and a wash, blow dry and set—yes, *every*day—and then it's time to get my nine-year-old son, Dylan, up and around. One quick phone call to make sure my elderly grandmother, who lives two houses down, is still kicking—and that I'm out of her line of fire when she starts at it. Then it's packing lunches, checking to see who is working in the salon that day and how many appointments are on the books. Finally, a minute to make sure I haven't forgotten some detail of my son's life.

Soccer practice?

Check.

Science project?

Check.

Still my sweet, little baby boy?

Like hell!

He's nine, after all. He may have my freckles and innate sense of responsibility and his father's quick grin and longing to find out how far and how fast he can go in life, but Dylan is his own little man. Divorce and a dad who never settles down at one address long enough to get your letters or keeps a job long enough to afford child support, much less a stinking birthday present, will do that to a kid.

Still, for a few fleeting moments every morning I catch a glimpse of the child Dylan once was. In the next instant I see the amazing adult he will be and figure whatever I go through now for his sake, it's all worth it.

And then he's out the door, me on his heels heading down the sidewalk to my salon. A lot of days, like far too many of us in that self-reliant sisterhood of working single moms, I'm already bone weary before the school bus pulls away. But I do it all because, well, I *have* to.

And I always make sure I look my best because, though

I don't make a point of telling people this, I firmly believe that someday, somehow, something absolutely extraordinary is going to happen to me.

And I dread it with every fiber of my being.

That's why I feel like Esther.

I twisted around, ducking my head low so I could make a point of squinting up at the South Winds Trav'O'Tel sign across the street. Someone long ago, probably long before either Emma or I was born, had named the figure of a woman in a red swimsuit and white bathing cap on the top of the boomerang-shaped sign after the famous bathing beauty. "Anyway, when I said I felt like Esther, I meant *that* Esther."

"A motel icon?" She did not turn to follow my line of vision, but then she didn't have to. Anyone who had lived in Verbena, or even driven down the long, twisting Highway 612 that cut through this corner of the Blue Ridge Mountains knew the sign. "You're saying some days you feel like a motel icon?"

"Yeah. You'd a thought that would be more *your* style, huh?" I always say stuff like that to Emma, but she knows I love her more than my hot curlers, which I cannot live without.

Emma wriggled in the seat and tugged her skirt up at the waist. "Honey, if I was to be the icon for some motel it sure as hell wouldn't be some fleabag dump like the South Winds."

"Oh, don't say that. I love that old place." Twelve bright, white, meticulously clean units with doors painted shades of kelly green, lemon yellow and flamingo pink formed a blocky horseshoe around a rectangular blue pool. It was as much a part of the fabric of my hometown as the A. E. Hadley Auto Garage and Museum that my grandmother had run since the 1960s. It was as important to town lore as the generations-old feud between my family and the O'Malleys, owners of the South Winds, the All Day Break-fast Buffet and general scourge of the tri-county area. "Be-sides, girl, when I say I feel like Esther it has nothing to do with the motel. Just look at her there perched on the very edge of oblivion, and when she's all lit up at night . . ."

Really there were two Esthers. One with her arms stretched high and straight over her head and the second seeming to perform a death-defying leap from the sign into the small, aqua-blue swimming pool at the center of the Trav'O'Tel's semicircular drive. At night the flickering play of the lights outlining her painted metal body lent the air of sure, graceful motion to the image.

I identify with both Esthers, the one balancing on the edge, rigid, unable to propel herself forward, and the one willing to throw herself with absolute abandon into the great dark void. One is the person I am, the person too many people around town and in my own family need for me to be, and the other . . .

"I'm just saying I understand what it's like to stand on the edge and wonder if you'll ever find it in yourself to make that one, meaningful, fearless leap."

"You want to make a leap? Then go to the service tomor-row." Emma's eyes grew more somber than I had seen in a very long time.

My heart practically stopped at what she was suggesting. "Are you nuts?"

"Probably. But that doesn't change the fact that if you

ever want to break free of your family's demands on you and all the old ideas that hold you in place here, you've got to do something bold. Tomorrow seems as good a time as any to try it."

"But go to Howdy O'Malley's memorial service?" I couldn't even imagine it. Could I?

"Why not? You liked the cheap old bastard, didn't you?"

"Yes and no." I clenched my jaw. "I certainly did appreciate how he became like a substitute grandpa to Dylan."

Howard "Howdy" O'Malley had been dead and cremated for two months already, but not a soul among his lousy excuse for a family had come to claim his ashes. So finally a small group of friends and acquaintances had taken it upon themselves to memorialize the man who had at one time or another screwed over almost every person in town. It would be a memorable event, to be sure. Short, probably not sweet, and a small gathering at best—but memorable. And my going would only serve to make it more so.

Verbena doesn't have much to recommend it, I suppose. But we do boast my granny's auto museum, which is a fancy way of saying automobile graveyard, a restored one-room schoolhouse, a mayor who swears he's shirttail relation to Andy Griffith, not to mention our much-ballyhooed Every Second Saturday Flea Market and Jamboree. We have those, but most of all we have The Feud.

The generations-old grudge between my family and the O'Malleys is kind of a poor man's—one with an overactive imagination, if you ask me—Hatfields and McCoys. It all began as a dispute over selling land to the government to build the highway that now divides the O'Malleys' property from what is left of the Hadley land.

Like a lot of folks in these mountains, my great-grandfather was cautious about dealings with the government. Some say that was because he didn't want anyone finding his still, but my grandmother swears that's pure nonsense.

She always adds with a wink, "If people couldn't find his still, how was he supposed to make any money at all moonshining?"

The truth was something far more complicated than that. Or was it far more simple? Anyway, the fact was, my great-grandfather had not acted fast enough because he was waiting for a sign.

All Hadleys believe in signs and divination. Now it's sort of trendy again, linked to New Age philosophy and the like, but for my family it is a much deeper thing. We believe that there is a power greater than ourselves and that we are not alone on this earth. We know in our hearts that if we trust and believe and watch for the signs we will be shown the way.

The O'Malleys have no such spiritual grounding. If that bunch has any kind of roots they are of the "root of all evil" variety—firmly planted in the love of money. That's why whenever my family found an opportunity for financial gain—the answer to our prayers, as it were—some O'Malley would beat us to the draw before we could see it through. Time and time again.

And now here was Emma suggesting that if I really wanted to be like my untouchable ideal soaring above all the worldly nonsense, I had to find it within myself to go across the street tomorrow, stand in the open and—and it knots my stomach to say the words—pay my *respects* to Howdy O'Malley.

"It would kill my grandmother," I whispered.

"Bullshit." Emma rummaged through the pockets of her fake-suede jacket, probably for a pack of cigarettes. "That old gal has survived much worse. She'll get over it."

I took a deep breath and held in the familiar smells of hairspray, shampoo, the heated metal of curling irons and the hot wax tray. Turning, I faced the South Winds, my eyes trained on Esther. "I just don't know if I have it in me, Em."

"What don't you have in you? You just get up tomorrow and fix your hair and makeup like always and go. You just do your hair and go, Jolie."

I raised my eyes to the cross-stitched sign above my salon's door.

A KNIGHT HAS HIS ARMOR, A GENERAL HAS HIS TROOPS BUT NOTHING PREPARES A WOMAN FOR HER DAILY BAT- TLES LIKE THE PERFECT HAIRDO.

Well, *that* I had. Maybe it was time, after all, to take this step, to fight my own battle, to jump, to fly . . . to sink or swim.

Just like Esther.

"Okay," I said much more firmly than I felt. "I'll do it."

"Good." She took out a nearly empty pack of cigarettes. "I think."

"But be warned, this better not completely mess up my life." I grabbed the cellophane-wrapped pack from her hand, tossed it in a long, graceful arc into the trash can and added, "Or my hairstyle."

Chapter 2

"You know what really gets me?" Emma tapped her just-arrived copy of *TV Guide* against my shoulder.

"Besides any man under fifty in the tri-county area?" I had this misguided notion that I could somehow shock the woman into shutting up.

It was a funeral, after all, even if it was taking place behind the barn where they held the monthly flea market. And while (daring leap or not) I could not in good conscience insinuate myself into the circle of mourners gathered by the flower bed, we were not standing far enough away to pull off a conversation without drawing too much attention to ourselves.

"Very funny." Emma peered over the top of a pair of cheap plastic sunglasses. Subtle shadow and smudged liner softened the appearance of her—as she puts it thirty-never-you-mind-year-old—eyes and went right on talking, albeit in a whisper now. "The thing that gets me is this idea that the only people in America having wild, hot monkey sex live in big cities."

I tried to shut her out and concentrate on the semi-solemn—how somber can a ceremony be that consists of scattering a mean old grouch's ashes in a strip of dirt decorated with hardy mums and hay bales?—proceedings before us.

"We won't start for a few minutes, to give everyone a chance to get here." The local lady minister—not that she just ministers to ladies, but female clergy are still pretty rare here so everyone calls her that—began handing out stark white pages to the invited guests. "But I'll go ahead and hand out the program for the service. Raise your hand if you want a copy."

All eight people lifted their hands.

The minister looked our way.

I pretended a sudden overwhelming interest in brushing off my black sweater.

Emma went right on expounding on her opinion about rural verses urban sex lives. "That's just crazy. If all the sex *was* in the cities, then nobody would live anywhere else. I mean, I personally have stories that would scorch a sex therapist's couch. Don't you?"

"No. I don't." I don't even have stories that would warm a church secretary's settee. "I don't want to run your brother down, Emma. But Art and I married straight out of high school barely knowing how the parts fit together and fell into a sex life so routine that I didn't realize the marriage had ended until we missed three Saturday-night lovemaking sessions in a row."

"Oh, please. You haven't been *completely* celibate during these last four years since your divorce and I know it."

"A dozen bad dates and a couple of uninspiring short-term boyfriends does not a seat-scorching love life make."

"What you need is a fantasy man."

"What?" I kept my eyes on the folks shifting their feet as they waited for the minister to begin the service, careful not to make eye contact with anyone who stole a peek at us over their shoulder.

"A fantasy man. The perfect male specimen. Someone to think about to get you revved up when the sex isn't particularly satisfying."

"Oh, I have one of those."

"Anyone I know or may have met, say when we were younger? Tall? Rich? Gorgeous? Totally off limits?"

Ryman O'Malley. It didn't take a genius to figure out who she meant. Howdy's grandson, the only O'Malley who ever showed a lick of consideration for the old fellow and who used to spend his summers working at the South Winds. I heard he'd done a stint in the Air Force and later became a private pilot. I remembered him best from his last summer in Verbena—when he became the first boy, albeit by accident, to touch my naked breast.

I couldn't contain a sigh, just recalling the moment.

Ry O'Malley was definitely the stuff of sexual fantasy.

And not who I had in mind at all—least not that I'd tell Emma.

"Actually, my fantasy man is older, short, wears a uniform . . ."

"A pilot's uniform?"

"Sailor, actually."

"Sailor? You mean we're not talking about—"

"Cap'n Crunch." I cut her off because the last thing I needed today was someone nearby to overhear us and think we had come to Howdy's funeral to gossip about his grandson.

"Who?"

"You know, on the cereal box?"

She shook her head.

"Emma, the only fantasy that has gotten me revved up through my last two brief yet interminably boring relationships has been that as soon as the sex was over I could go eat a bowl of cold cereal."

"Shit, we have got to change that, girl!"

"Shhh. The service is starting. I don't want to detract from it and give people more than is necessary to talk about later." With those words I had to admit that my big splash was, in truth, more of a little toe dip to test the waters. Still, it beat the hell out of the response from the O'Malley family, which was to ignore the old man's death entirely.

"What are you worried for? It's just Norris and Sorrel Wyatt, the lady preacher and a few of the flea market regulars."

"That's enough." I looked away from the knot of mourners to my own home and hair salon across the highway, then down the road to the E. A. Hadley Memorial Auto Museum and Garage. "If one word from them to anyone around town gets back to my grandmother—and it would get back to her—I'll find myself in a world of hurt."

"Don't be ridiculous." She pitched the magazine into her enormous purse. "It won't be a *world* of hurt. A half a block of hurt at the worst. And that's only *if* word gets out."

Word would get out, of course. I could practically hear the buzz working its way from the Sunshine Market to the DB Saloon straight through to the coffee and doughnut fellowship hour after church tomorrow.

When folks heard that the woman whose son represented

the last best hope of reestablishing the Hadley family had gone to the funeral of the lone surviving O'Malley left in Logie County? There would be the devil to pay. The devil, that is, in the form of her eighty-year-old, white-haired, cherub-faced, one-hell-of-an-auto-mechanic, forgets-she's-a-Baptist-if-the-bourbon-is-good-enough grandmother.

The Feud. *Again.*

Every small town in these parts had its share of legends and folklore and even some historical facts tossed in for good measure. They had their monuments and historical markers, their weekend festivals and weeklong celebrations in hopes of drawing the tourists in off the highway to spend a little time and a lot of cash. Of course, in a dying town like Verbena it's the other way around, people could spend all day here and hardly part with a dime.

But every three or four years, somebody around the state rediscovered The Feud and wrote about it in a local paper. Then we'd get an onslaught of lookie-loos coming around expecting to see barefoot hillbillies in one-shoulder overalls toting rifles and taking potshots at one another. Not to disappoint, every local shop sold plastic weaponry, tasteless postcards and T-shirts—with a fake bullet hole through the sleeve—that read: I SURVIVED THE VERBENA FEUD.

The mayor's son even had a painting done—the kind on a big piece of wood with holes cut out for people to stick their heads through—so people could pick a side, Hadley or O'Malley, and get a photo taken. It's surprising how many vacationers stop to do it. And the people who don't want to part with the two buck "donation" expected in order to shove their heads through a hole and say *cheese* just stand in the center of Highway 612 and pretend to look crazed with anger at one another for their keepsake photo of their visit to Verbena.

The locals were just as bad, gabbing about the two families whenever they could, adding to the nonsense of it all. Few ever bothered to learn the facts behind the pain my family endured at the hands of those awful O'Malleys.

The minister launched into a generic-sounding, none-too-personal homily for Howdy, which was probably the most kind thing she could come up with under the circumstances.

I sighed and turned my attention to our surroundings for a moment.

Heavy gray clouds crowded the sun from the early afternoon sky. Dotting the mountains rising all around our small town, I spotted the first hints of autumn. A yellow-tipped leaf here, a pale brown one there. Now and again a flash of orange stood out in the thick greenery, or even an entire limb that had seemed to burst into vibrant red as if suddenly aflame.

Soon all the trees would change.

I hate change.

Not the change of the seasons—I don't dwell on each new season as marking the passage of time. And I truly try to embrace any change for the better, though I am the first to admit the very term "change for the better" is something of an oxymoron for me.

I drew in the scent of damp, earth-scented air and a wave of nostalgia so palpable it took my breath away washed over me.

What I really hated was loss. I have seen far too much of

that in my life. My marriage, which had afforded me some level of comfort and the hope of having a family. And this last year my father, who had died, and my mother, who had moved out of state for a better job.

I focused again on the makeshift memorial service. The cluster of townspeople struggled to find a common tune and cadence for the hymn they were attempting to sing.

I started to sing the familiar old words, softly, I thought.

"Now who needs to be quiet?" Emma reached out and shook my shoulder. "You know that you can get away with a damn sight more than most people want to admit around here as long as you don't hurt anyone and—"

"Hey I know the rules. I practically invented them." I rolled my eyes. "Hear no evil, speak no evil, see no evil. But if you can't help yourself—*don't be obvious.*"

"Don't be obvious," Emma echoed.

I pinched at the sleeve of Emma's baggy men's trenchcoat. "Look who's talking."

"Don't blame this on me." She popped the back of the lapel up and held it closed under her chin. "You suggested we wear disguises."

"I suggested we show some discretion." I shifted my shoulders. I had worn head-to-toe black: sweater, pants, shoes. Understated. Tasteful. Perfect. "It's not these folks I'm hiding from, you said so yourself."

"You talk brave, girl. Yet I notice you've got your hair— which anyone in Logie County could spot from a mile off— covered with some nasty old head scarf dug out of the salon's lost and found."

Any protest I might have made died as I touched the sinfully synthetic fabric of the butt-ugly scarf.

"I thought today was about being brave and independent and leaping off ledges or whatever you called it." Emma raised an eyebrow.

"I'm here, aren't I?"

The group launched into the second verse of the hymn, a little less awkward this time.

"You're here, but you're hiding in plain sight all because you are still frozen in place with fear that you might disappoint your Granny Missus."

For as long as I could remember, everyone in Logie County called Hannah Rose Hadley "Granny Missus." The name came naturally to a woman whose own husband had never been heard to call her anything but Mrs. Hadley. The one person who took exception to that nicety had been Howdy O'Malley. That dearly departed old goat had called his lifelong adversary many things, but never by her name—proper or otherwise.

"Okay, I am not leaping anywhere, but I am so still striking a blow for independence. You'd just have to understand my family to know how much that's true." Not since I defied my mother and went swimming at the South Winds pool when I was thirteen had I done anything so openly against my family's wishes.

Even all these years later the echo of that one impulsive moment struck a chord deep in my being. If I had not gone that day, I never would have been goaded into jumping off the diving board. I never would have ruined my hairdo that day, dragged home looking every bit the raggedy, careless mess. I probably ruined my father's chances of getting the loan he had counted on that day and I lived with the pain of that knowledge forever after.

But if I hadn't gone, if I hadn't jumped that day, I never would have nearly drowned. And Ry would never have cupped my naked breast in his gentle, long fingers. Even if he was just trying to rescue me when my bikini top came off after that disastrous dive.

Still, that was a memory I wouldn't want to wish away in a lifetime. Conflicted about my choices that day? Always. But about the sensation that still gave me a delicious thrill of pleasure more than twenty years later? Not even once.

"Not that I blame you for keeping under wraps, girl." Emma picked a long black hair from her lapel. "Three generations of Hadleys and O'Malleys despising one another is a lot to overcome. Not that they haven't given y'all cause to bear a grudge."

"Time and again." Time-glorified teen lust memories of Ry O'Malley aside, I had no reason to hope for a resolution to things between the two families. In fact, as of today I had more reason than ever to dislike and distrust Howdy's heirs. "Damn arrogant sons of—"

"Let's hear that refrain one more time, my friends," the lady preacher urged her meager congregation. "And as you sing of eternal peace, think kindly of our dear friend who has gone on before us."

"Notice the preacher didn't say *where* he's gone before us." Emma pointed downward.

I smiled more out of habit than to agree.

The sparse chorus of voices rose again in song.

"You know, Em, I can tick off every meanness, every manipulation, and every mischief done against a Hadley by some member of the O'Malley family." I sniffled and touched the corner of the rayon scarf to my eye. "But I can never equate those things with that fellow who became like a grandpa to my Dylan."

"People did marvel at it, I'll give you that. How the youngest of your family and the oldest of theirs got on so well."

"Dylan knows his own mind, trusts his own heart. He would never let a lot of hooey-fied history determine who he could and could not care about."

"Gets that from you, you know."

The cool October breeze ruffled the wisps of hair that had worked free of the scarf. "Me? I've been as bad as any of them about taking this feud nonsense too seriously."

"I wasn't just talking about that." Emma nudged me with her shoulder. "You never once let hard feelings about my shithead of a brother stand between us."

I laughed. "We've been friends since before we even noticed boys—well, before *I* did. I suspect you came out of the womb primping in case you had a cute doctor."

Emma looked at me over the top of her glasses but did not deny it.

"God only made a few men worth squashing your hairdo for and not a one worth frosting a friendship over," I assured her.

"Yeah, but people say . . ."

"People can mind their own damned business."

"Too bad you don't take that attitude when it comes to answering to your family."

"My family never stood between me and a friend."

"*Maybe* not. But they did push you into marrying my brother when you weren't really sure it was what you wanted."

It was true that from the time I was old enough to date I'd heard them say I needed to marry a man who would help out in the family. And Art, with his two-year degree in business, his plodding personality and his big plans for the future seemed the right man for the job. They say there are doers and there are dreamers. Turns out Art was a third kind of person, a dream-doer. In his dreams everything the man did was cause for a ticker-tape parade. Change a diaper—he wanted Father of the Year status. Bring home a paycheck—proof he'd already done his share of work and everything else was my responsibility.

That got old fast, so he followed his "dream job" running a chain of miniature golf courses in Gatlinburg, Tennessee. Then after that, working in a guitar shop in Nashville. A nightclub manager in Memphis. A televangelist's business associate in Tulsa. By the time he set his sights on staging a show in Branson, Missouri, it had become clear to me the man would never settle down and amount to anything, and I'd be better off back in Verbena on my own with Dylan.

I never had any grand illusions about romance. Love to me was what my family knew—an action evidenced by self-sacrifice, by respect and by the commitment to stand firm through anything life threw your way. I thought I had found that in Art, but I learned early and got reeducated often that I had misread him entirely.

"You just try too hard to accommodate people you love." Emma's touch on my shoulder brought me back to the present. "Still, I always thought that where that feud was concerned, you'd have crossed that invisible line if you thought it was the right thing to do."

"Oh, I don't know . . ."

"You put your toe on that line that summer you had such a crush on you know who." Emma held her hands together and mimicked diving into the pool.

"You're saying if I am . . . um, properly motivated, I might actually stand up to my family?"

"If by properly motivated you mean crazed with lust over a prime piece of manhood, then yes, I think so."

I turned my head away. Esther, her paint chipped and faded, loomed high above us just a few hundred yards away. "Gee, you make me sound so shallow."

"Not shallow—human. You've played the part of family martyr so long I think sometimes you forget you're a flesh-and-blood woman."

"And you think it would take the likes of Mr. Too-Cool-for-the-Pool to make me remember?"

"Can you think of a better candidate?"

"This isn't about me, anyway." I tore my gaze from the sign. "Dylan was just plain hungry to have a male role model in his life. Howdy fulfilled that for a time, nothing noble about allowing it on my part. I was doing what was best for my child. Plus, I felt so sorry for old Howdy the way his family treated him."

I glanced over my shoulder at the backside of the Trav' O'Tel and had to fight back a wave of sadness. Without Howdy O'Malley there to run it, the place would surely fall into decay. It had already begun to show signs of inattention in the two months since the old man passed on. And the twelve-unit motel with its adjoining breakfast buffet was not the only victim of that neglect.

Tears blurred my vision as I leaned back to better see

across Highway 612, the road that cut through the hills and divided my family from the O'Malleys in more ways than I cared to count.

My salon and my grandmother's business, each with a cozy home nearby, sat tidy and inviting as ever. It was that empty building and the quiet house between my place and Granny's that got to me. Without the added business the motel had brought in, my mother had had to move away to take a "temporary" job, just until things got better in town, she said. For three generations now, Hadley men had done the same thing time and time again. Except those temporary moves had always come with permanent sacrifices.

"If only one of Howdy's children had stepped in and taken over the motel or at least sold it quickly to someone who would have kept it up." Damn, it galled me just to think about those selfish, heartless jerks.

"Are you kidding? Those miserable O'Malleys spent their time bickering and backbiting over every cent and asset right down to the very last scrap of their inheritance."

"I cannot believe the selfishness of those jackals has deprived my family of the most precious thing we have—the *only* thing they have—each other."

"Amen-n-n-n." The hapless singers managed to end the hymn together by drawing out the closing word until it became a soft, harmonic hum.

I pushed down my burning anger. What did the O'Malleys care? They had what mattered to them—money. And too bad for anyone who stood between them and it.

Howdy's children and grandchildren cared about the motel and about tiny Verbena about as much as they had the old man. It was evident how much they cared for him, given that the funeral parlor had waited two months for one of them to come and claim their patriarch's ashes and no one ever did. "Damned heartless, greedy O'Malleys! Not one lick of loyalty in the lot of them."

In one of those life-goes-on reminders that often add texture to a funeral, a big green SUV roared past on the highway. Maybe a family on a weekend drive or a group of friends off looking for a secluded fishing spot, going along completely unaware of my—of everyone's—brief moment of grief.

The tall woman facing the small cluster of mourners raised her hand in the air. "Ashes to ashes . . ."

"Speaking of ashes, how long do I have to wait after they dump the old boy in the flower bed before I light up a smoke?"

"You know how I feel about your smoking." I smoothed my scarf with my hand.

"Yeah, the smell gets in your hair and you have to stop everything and wash it out."

I gave her a narrow-eyed glare. Why Emma clung to that stupid excuse over the truth—that I loved her and wanted her to stick around as long as possible—I never could understand. But then the Corbett family had never gone in for displays of affection, as I had learned the hard way with her ex-husband.

The lady minister lifted the brass urn in her hands. "We gather here today to return Howard Ryman O'Malley back to the land which he so loved."

"Loved?" Emma snorted a laugh. "The only thing that old goat loved about this two-bit tin barn was the business it brought his motel and restaurant."

The minister knelt by the flower bed.

"Well, they could hardly spread the poor old fellow's ashes around the motel or the buffet house, now could they?" I shifted my weight and cocked my head to try to get a better view. "That would hardly be good for business."

"What business?"

I blocked out the rhetorical question by concentrating on the proceedings. It was a sad spectacle to mark the end of such a long, noted life as Howard's. When I told my son, Dylan, about it after school today, I decided, I'd make it seem like lots of people had come.

I might even invent an imaginary O'Malley or two. Why not soften the situation for my nine-year-old? He simply would not be able to understand the mentality of a person who would forsake their family for anything, least of all material gain, so why expose him to it? "I cannot believe that not a single member of Howdy's family showed up."

The group closed in and I couldn't see what they were doing.

"Why not? They even arranged for the cremation through a series of phone calls and lawyer visits."

"I know, but . . ."

"They were always that way." Emma pulled a bright blue disposable lighter from her purse and waved it as she spoke. "You know that, girl."

The minister bent low over the urn, one elbow thrust out like a person struggling to loosen the lid of a pickle jar.

From the corner of my eye, I noticed the green SUV coming from the direction it had gone a minute ago. If they were lost, they need only stop and ask someone. If it was one thing folks in Verbena loved, it was telling people what to do and how to do it. But the vehicle did not stop, and disappeared over the nearby hill.

Across the lot, the minister had her tongue sticking out of the corner of her mouth.

Norris Wyatt's face scrunched up and he spread his fingers like he was about to get in there and wrestle with the stubborn thing, if that's what it took to get it open.

In the distance a car's brakes squealed.

Before I could look around to see if there was a problem, the urn's lid popped free.

The mourners gasped.

The minister sneezed.

I blinked.

The pot pitched forward, somersaulted and landed upside down in the middle of some wilting sweet peas.

"Leave it to Howdy," Norris muttered, the darkness of his once-flexed hands now a serene contrast to the white of the urn as he righted it. "An irritant to the very end."

His wife, Sorrel, tucked her head down and coughed.

Emma chuckled.

"Irritant or not, I wish just one member of his family had shown up today," I murmured, turning my entire focus again to the South Winds. "But why would they start now? In all our years here have we ever laid eyes on a one of them? Well, on any of them but . . ."

"Ryman."

"I swear, Emma, you've got that man on your mind." I shut my eyes to keep from letting on that the idealized memory of Ry, tanned and lean, with tousled waves of sun-kissed dark hair had crossed my mind more than a few times these last few years. "We haven't brought up that name in forever, but count on you to conjure him up out of the blue today."

"And a damned fine job of conjuring it is, Jolie, sugar."

I indulged in a slow smile. "You can still picture him, too, huh?"

"Picture him, nothing, I'm looking right at the man."

"Emma Jean Corbett, you lie like a rug!" My heartbeat thudded high in my throat as I scanned the handful of mourners shuffling off to their cars in the flea market parking lot. Ry? Here? Impossible. I'd have recognized him, wouldn't I? "You're seeing things, girl. I only wish he was here, though. For the way he treated his grandfather—I'd like to serve him up a piece of my mind."

"Better make that order to go, then, because he is here— and he's standing at your front door."

Chapter 3

"Emma," I croaked out over the slap and clatter of her slingbacks and the steady footfalls of my low-heeled boots as we crossed the highway. "Next time I tell you I feel like Esther ready to throw myself off the high dive, please remind me to check first and make sure there is water in the pool."

"Honey, they drained the pool the week after Howdy died, remember?"

"That was a metaphor, Em. I meant that I need to re-member to think things through before acting, to weigh the consequences, to . . ."

"Look for a sign?" she stretched the word *sign* out long enough to fill three syllables, which is Southern for "insert throwback idiot notion here."

A sign. All the Hadleys believed in them. I did more than anyone since my grandfather, the man who waited so long for a sign that he lost out to the original opportunist O'Malley.

"Hell no. I don't need a sign, Emma. There already is a sign big as life and twice as handsome standing in front of my salon, pounding his big old fist on the door."

In theory facing up to a member of that no account family and giving them "what for" held an empowering appeal. But nothing had prepared me for seeing the object of more than twenty years of fantasies that ran the gamut from revenge to ravishment standing before my eyes. We reached the parking area—a row of faintly marked parking spaces on pour-it-yourself asphalt—and I made a lightning-fast appraisal of the man.

Taller. Of course. Broader in the chest and shoulders than he had been at sixteen. *Filled out real nice* is what my Mama would say. Definitely grayer and decidedly more mature than the teenaged incarnation of my memories.

And yet when we made eye contact . . . my heart stopped. I swear it stopped. My thoughts stopped. Time stopped . . . okay, that was a bit overstated. Time did *not* stop. It went backward and for just one sweet instant, I swear, it felt like I had just seen him, just been touched by him only moments ago.

"Hi! Ya'll wouldn't happen to be locals, would you?" the man drawled as he raised his hand and flashed a smile that was all sex and dimples, a blend of boyish "Aw-shucks ma'am" and yet every ounce all-grown-up-and-able-to-do-something-about-it male. Was it this potent mix of maturity and mayhem in those eyes that had my heart in my throat?

Even his hands were compelling—strong and large. How could I ever get the nerve to confront a man that time itself had not contested? How could I speak my mind to a man who would always be beyond my reach . . . not just another O'Malley, but *the* O'Malley, to my personal way of thinking?

"I was just about to go inside and ask for some assistance." He squinted down at us like he knew something we didn't. "But maybe you can answer my questions."

It was that pause that did it. The way his lips lifted more on one side than the other. The air about his powerful body when he put his hands on his hips and waited just long enough to make sure we all knew who was in control.

Control?

Over me?

An O'Malley? And on my side of the highway?

Oh, I do not think so!

That propelled me out of my daze, and before I could think it all through, the words came pouring out. "I'll answer your questions as soon as you answer a few of mine and not one minute before."

"I beg your pardon?" He said in that way meant to stop overwrought women in their tracks.

I did stop. And as soon as I did it, the oddest sensation came over me, like I'd just been flung out into the street buck naked.

The man on my porch did nothing to dispel that feeling. He gave me a long, undisguised once-over from headscarf to heels and didn't even try to disguise his slow, burning admiration for all the parts in between.

My skin tingled. Actually tingled, they way they say it feels just before a lightning strike.

"I mean it." My voice quavered at first but I took in a deep breath and forced myself to steady it. "You owe me some answers and I want them now."

He leaned against one of the posts that held up the ragged awning in front of the Combin' Holiday. He folded his arms. His grin worked up slowly.

I pressed my lips together.

"Whatever your little heart desires, ma'am." He had draped the smarmy reply in a rich Georgia accent, showing the unmitigated gall to form round sensual words and draw them out like a silk drawn in agonizing slowness over bare skin. "Go right ahead. Ask away."

"I will." I drew another shaky breath and jerked up my chin. "Who do you think you are and where the hell have you been?"

His eyes narrowed. "Who wants to know and why is it any of your business?"

"You said you'd answer my questions first."

"I said you could ask your questions first. I didn't say a thing about answering them."

Emma, dark glasses in place and oversized overcoat swinging around her angular body, came around to stand beside me. She crossed her arms too. "Typical O'Malley arrogance."

He stood up straight and scratched one finger along his bristled jaw. "Seems you already know who I am. I don't suppose we've met before?"

"Oh, we've met." I tugged at the knotted fabric under my chin. A woman is not raised in the South—especially not by a family capable of carrying on a bona fide feud for seventy-five years—without acquiring a certain flair for the dramatic. "But I think it's fair to say we also share a history that goes beyond personal acquaintances."

The headscarf fairly whistled as I whisked it off.

"Why, Jolene Hadley, as I live and breathe." His expression warmed but he did not actually smile. "Am I right?"

"I won't go on record about your living and breathing part. Being an O'Malley, you may have sold your soul to the devil and be one of the evil undead." I tried to glower at him but not having much practice, feared it came off looking like I smelled something sour instead.

"Evil undead." He chuckled.

"Well, maybe that was taking it a bit too far." And with his grandfather having died so recently and . . . suddenly I remembered why I was so ticked off at the gorgeous jerk. "But for the second part, yes. I am who you think I am."

He responded with a flat-out dimple-intensified grin. "And here I'd just said I intended to avoid any of those bad-tempered, bad-risk, bad-mouthing Hadleys at all cost."

"You know what they say about the path to hell being paved with good intentions." I have to admit I was kind of proud to get off at least one coherent smart-ass remark at last.

"But it looks like I've just run headlong into the feistiest—and prettiest—Hadley around." The creaking floorboards under his feet barely masked the low, satisfied chuckle from deep in his chest. "One I do believe has just told me I'm headed for hell? You just going to point the way, Miss Jolene? Or ask me to come along since you're already headed that way yourself?"

My cheeks grew hot. My pulse raced. I placed my fists on my hips. I drew a deep breath and opened my mouth.

He held up his hand. "In the interest of time, let's forgo the tirade."

I felt slapped. I blinked. I ran my hand over my hair to

smooth it, knowing full well it looked fabulous, of course. I may not be the most secure woman when it comes to matters of sex or even verbal sparring with a sexy man, but I do know about hair, and mine always looks great. "Mr. O'Malley, I assure you, I never—"

"Like hell you never." In a heartbeat he stood before me.

I may have stammered a syllable or two.

He took a strand of my hair between his thumb and forefinger.

I wanted to pull away from his touch, from the overwhelming nearness of the man. But . . . you know . . . it would have . . . um, messed up my hair. "I wasn't going to . . ."

He leaned down and whispered, "Don't forget, Jolie, darling, I've been on the receiving end of that temper of yours."

That blew the bouffant out of my beehive but fast, I tell you.

He straightened back up and spoke louder then. "I can just imagine the grown-up version of a patented Jolene Hadley hissy fit."

I wanted to retreat a step, maybe two or three, but Emma had planted herself firmly behind me.

"You'd wag your finger." He demonstrated. "Your eyes would go flinty."

I brushed my fingertip along my lower lashes just to make sure I was squinting at him already.

"My family members' names would be invoked and their reputations discredited."

"Don't think I'd hold out for the chance to pitch a fit to do that," I muttered, trying to regain lost ground.

"And if there were anything cheap and breakable within reach, I'd have seen it flying towards my head so fast I wouldn't have time to duck."

He had me pegged. Except for that bit about throwing things, he had just described the woman I had, in fact, always aspired to be and so often fell short of.

I looked across the street to the South Winds Trav' O'Tel sign, with the diving girl soaring so high above the world that nothing touched her, nothing frightened her and nothing could hurt her.

And I wanted to cuss a blue streak.

How dare Ry O'Malley be the one to invoke my inner Esther, then turn it on me to try to keep me from doing the very thing I'd set out to do! "My actions or would-be responses are not the issue here. I want to know—"

He cocked his head, practically eating me up with his unblinking gaze. "Last time I saw you, Miss Jolene, you were still a little—"

"You'd do best not to provoke me further." My lips tightened, the knot in my stomach grew even tighter. "It's neither necessary nor gentlemanly."

He reached out to tuck back the strand of hair he had fondled earlier. "You were still a little wet behind the ears."

"Get off my property."

"I didn't come to cause any trouble." He smiled in what he must have thought was a soothing way. "I just wanted to speak to someone who could tell me where and when my grandfather's memorial is being held."

"Well, if you want to call the joke of a service a memorial, then you just missed it." Emma gave my back a light shove. "And my friend has plenty to say to you about that."

"I'd like to hear it." He stood there like he actually expected me to keep talking.

Hadn't he heard me order him off of my property? Who did he think he was to just stand there and keep yapping?

"Jolie just wants to say that you may think you're hot stuff but that doesn't mean anything to her." Not a single drop of indignation colored Emma's tone.

I scowled at her, for all the good it did me.

"She knows your type," Emma practically cooed, playing it up big. "The kind that needs to be *taken in hand and taught a lesson.*"

"Oh, shut up or I'll take your neck in my hands." I virtually ground the threat out between my clenched teeth.

"And I was just saying to Jolie that she is the very woman to tend to you."

"Well, by all means, Miss Jolene, go on and tend to me. Take me in hand. Teach me. I'm yours."

It was the kind of invitation I'd heard a thousand times in my dreams, the kind of thing I had longed to respond to with complete abandon. Hearing it now, like this, only made me want to bang my head against the blonde brick side wall of my salon. No, better yet, I would bang *Emma's* head against the wall.

Emma dipped her glasses down at last and looked at Ry like she'd given up candy for Lent and he were made of solid chocolate. "Hi, Ry, honey. Remember me? Emma Corbett? We took driver's ed together at the Vo-Tech the summer we were sixteen."

"Did we?" The warmth of his voice could not hide the tense tick of his cheek. Clearly, he had no idea who Emma was. "Good to see you . . . um . . . again."

Emma giggled like a complete and utter moron.

Ry straightened his shoulders and turned to me. "You say the memorial service is already over?"

I stood rigid on the walkway, doing my icon proud with my immovability. "We just came from it."

He put his hand on my shoulder.

I sighed like a schoolgirl. Oh, yeah, I was Esther-ing the bejeebers out of this situation, all right. Sheesh.

His eyes narrowed but not so much that I couldn't see the confusion in them. "*You* went to my grandfather's memorial?"

"Well, it seemed the right thing to do." I intended to say it softly, nothing like an accusation at all. But it came out smarting of smugness, implying I had cornered the market on ethical actions and that I didn't expect an O'Malley to know the right thing if it bit him on the butt. On the nice, firm, adorable butt.

Ry simply nodded.

"I didn't let people see me." This time I managed to speak with all the sympathy and sadness I truly felt at Howdy's passing. "I promise you that I didn't let my presence detract from paying homage to your grandfather. But I did go."

"Damn it." He rubbed his eyes.

"That's nice talk coming from someone who didn't even show up." Emma edged forward protectively.

"I tried to get here." He said, seemingly to no one in particular. Then his eyes met mine. "Believe me."

I wanted to believe him. Heaven help me, I searched for some reason, anything, to tell me to believe.

"I planned on rolling in midmorning, but I met with a

few . . ." He bent his head and aimed his concerned gaze toward his car ". . . complications along the way."

A slight figure sat up in the truck and pulled her knees to her chest. She lolled her head to one side so that what was left of her hair stuck out the open window. Then she looked directly at me.

I gasped. I should have had more composure but I couldn't help myself.

This poor, delicate waif of a girl with dark shadows beneath her luminous brown eyes had only patches here and there of what I judged to have once been thick, dark, wavy hair, not unlike her father's in his youth.

The teenager heaved a sigh so heavy it must have rattled her to her bones.

"My daughter."

"Your . . . " The man had driven all day with an obviously sick daughter in tow to try to make it in time to bid good-bye to his grandfather, and I had never so much as given him the benefit of the doubt. He was an O'Malley, therefore his actions were always suspect.

"Can you at least tell me where they put my grandfather's ashes?"

I spoke to Ry but continued to focus on the girl. "They scattered them as best they could in the flower bed behind the Flea Market barn."

"Excuse me, did you say flower bed? In the Flea Market?"

Emma jerked her thumb over her shoulder toward the sprawling barn half-covered in signs promising everything from hotcake mix to the state's hottest fiddle-playing.

He stared unblinking. "*That's* where they laid my grandfather to rest?"

"Where your grandfather rests doesn't really matter anymore, but where your daughter rests . . ." I laid my hand on his arm. It seemed important to touch him as I spoke, to interact with him, not as old rivals but as one parent to another. "She looks awfully tired, Ry."

"Yeah, tired of me, mostly."

I saw past the weak humor to the pain beneath. I gave his arm a squeeze and then stepped back.

He shrugged and nodded. "Guess we better get over to the motel and settle in."

"You'll be staying for a while?" I was fishing—and not one bit ashamed of it, I might add.

But he was not biting. "I'll stay as long as it takes."

"To . . . ?"

"Two, three, four, like I said whatever it takes."

"I beg your pardon?"

He dipped his head in a way of saying goodbye, then walked down the porch steps and over to his car. "We'd better get on over to the motel."

I had wanted all my worst thoughts and fears about this man and his family confirmed in this one momentous encounter. But I did not get my wish.

Ry hadn't meant to miss Howdy's memorial. He had tried to get here in time.

If I was wrong about him this time, could I be wrong about my other deeply held beliefs about the man and his family?

I ruffled my fingers through the ends of my hair and watched the girl. "Is there anything I can do to help?"

He looked up at that moment, up to the motionless figure of the diving girl on top of the South Winds sign. Or maybe he was looking to something unseen beyond. Then he shook his head.

"Thank you, but no. I know what needs to be done now and I can handle it all by myself," was all he said before climbing into his vehicle and making that short but significant trek across highway 612 to the South Winds Trav' O' Tel and All Day Breakfast Buffet.

I watched him go, fighting back a new, odd sensation. Seeing Ry and his daughter and knowing that there would be O'Malleys in the South Winds again this very night created a lightness of spirit. Not a full-fledged death-defying metaphorical swan dive—but God help me, at least for those few moments I no longer felt rigidly rooted in one place.

And the man had only been in town an hour.

Chapter 4

⑥ Sometimes I can be such an ass. Really. It's not the kind of thing I like admitting, even to myself, but there it is.

All afternoon, when I should have been concentrating on customers, all I could think of was Ry and his child. The poor, stricken girl had been sitting not ten feet away from me, probably suffering fatigue and who knows what all after their long trip and what had I done about it? Picked a fight with her daddy was all! *Ass!*

My mother raised me better than that, and now, several hours later, as darkness had begun to fall, it still weighed on my conscience. So I intended to do something about it— something helpful and considerate and not in the least bit motivated by my curiosity about what must be happening across the street in the living quarters behind the Trav' O' Tel's office.

I peeked out my front window again. *What the heck was going on over there?*

The lights in the office flicked off, then on.

I hurried to check the contents of the cardboard box in my arms, stepped outside, then paused on my front porch to watch my son heading off for an evening at his great-grandmother's.

Dylan went weaving along the uneven sidewalk toward Granny Missus's house with the game of *Life* tucked under one arm, totally oblivious to my plans. I won't say I sent him down there to ensure the old gal stayed occupied while I crossed over into "enemy" territory bearing Jell-O salad and sympathy. But I wouldn't have the brass to completely deny that either.

Of course I had no idea what I would walk into over there. Would they see my gesture for what it was and welcome me? Or see my gesture for what it *really* was and kick my behind back to my own side of the street?

I looked heavenward. *"This* would be a good time for a sign."

From the growing darkness an old, familiar hum reached my ears.

An electrical pop.

A sputter.

Suddenly a surge of light rose from the base of the fifteen-foot sign to illuminate the night with the promise:

SOUTH WINDS TRAV' O' TEL.
GOOD FOOD. GOOD RATES.
GOOD FUN. GOOD FOLKS!

"Sometimes I think you're just playing with me," I told the Almighty with no small measure of embarrassment as I made my way to Ry's door.

At first I tried to peer through the paper that Norris Wyatt had taped over the all-glass front of the old office shortly after Howdy passed. But I couldn't see a thing. So I knocked—or rather kicked because my hands were full—at the door in hopes someone was close enough to hear me.

"What kind of jerk would come to a closed-down motel with a dried-up funeral wreath still propped up in the window and start kicking at the door?" Ry undid the deadbolt and pulled the door inward. "Where'd you learn your manners? From a jackass?"

"No. I learned my manners from *my* family, not from yours." Seeing that sign lit up like that must have stirred something powerful in me, because I would normally not have been so bold. Or maybe his assessment just hit a little too close to my own description of myself earlier and I snapped out of pure defensiveness. Either way, the look on that man's face when he found me standing in his doorway speaking my mind was too priceless to have missed for all the civility in Savannah.

"Jolene, I—"

I thrust the large, open cardboard box into the man's impressive midsection. "Don't think I'm doing this for you."

"Come in, won't you?" Accepting the box, Ry stepped aside, the door propped open wide against his broad back.

I gripped the doorframe. I'd come on a mission of mercy, a show of good faith and proper manners, propelled by motherly concern for the man's weak, ailing daughter, nothing more. I had no business lingering even a few minutes to exchange pleasantries.

He looked down into the box and put on a big act of inhaling the steam rising from my best blue-and-white stoneware serving dish. "Mmmmm. Chicken casserole?"

"We always keep a couple in the freezer so we can heat them up and take them around if someone should need a helping hand or well . . . you know."

He nodded. "Funeral food."

"I don't know how they do it in all those far-off fancy places you've traveled to, but around Verbena, ham is for funerals." I strained my neck to peer beyond him and into the motel's dusty office. "Casseroles are for comfort."

"Then why don't you come on in? I could really use some—"

"If you dare finish that sentence by saying you want me to come in and give you some 'comfort' "—I said it all smarmy-like, the way I imagined a man with dishonorable intent would—"I'll slap you clean into next Tuesday. And don't think I won't do it, either."

"Oh, I believe ya. I've been on the receiving end of your power punch before, remember?" He balanced the box against his lean thigh.

Remember? Sheesh, not likely he'd let me forget. I glanced over my shoulder at the empty swimming pool illuminated now by the sputtering lights of the motel sign and the office lights.

For one brief moment the memory overtook me of how it felt to be nearly naked in Ry's arms.

I forced the memory from my mind. I could not afford to let some visceral response to our fleeting bit of personal history weaken my resolve. I held my breath and bit my lower lip.

"You'll be perfectly safe inside here," he said, his gaze sweeping over my face. "My family may hail from the wrong side of the highway for your tastes, but we have managed to pick up a few pointers on how to act around decent folk along the way."

I relaxed my grasp on the doorframe.

He tipped his head to silently prod me to come in.

I had wanted to get inside this place for the longest time. Now more than ever I believed that the keys to my future and that of my family lay within the walls of this very room. If I stayed, even only a few minutes, I might learn something about what Ry had in mind for the South Winds.

I touched my toe to a fallen leaf blown against the doorjamb. But did I dare?

"I was asking you in because I could surely use the company."

A plea for some company from a man caring for his ill child all alone. That, with only a minor bit of truth-bending, fit in with my mercy mission just fine. Gingerly, I ventured over the threshold.

He moved away from the door.

It fell shut with a *whoosh*.

And before the metal latch clicked, he placed himself so close that I could feel the fabric of his turned up shirtsleeve brush roughly against my sweater.

I flinched, tense as a cat, claws at the ready to pounce for so boorishly trying to manhandle me. But when I twisted my head around to confront him, I found his interests focused not on my "goodies" but on my good deeds.

My whole face warmed. I pretended to rearrange my bangs with my fingers.

No other man had ever gotten to me like this one. No male ever reached beneath my practiced exterior simply by walking into a room armed only with an unassuming look or an honest smile. I didn't have to see Ry or hear him to know he was around. I could feel this man's presence on my very skin.

It had been like that when I was a gawky teen. That much had not changed. And just as then, the man was totally oblivious to his effect on me.

He peeked under the red-trimmed tea towel that partially covered a shallow, round pan. "Apple pie?"

"Store-bought." I stiffened, hoping he picked up on the implication that the fact I hadn't baked it myself completely distanced me from the intimacy of the gesture.

"Still . . ." He edged closer. "It's the thought that counts, right?"

"Don't flatter yourself too much. I wasn't thinking of you when I picked it up." I slipped away to lean against the front desk counter. At least from there I might spot some clues as to what lay in store for the Trav' O' Tel. "If I had been thinking of you I'd have bought day-old sticky buns."

He laughed. "I like that idea."

See, I *should* have gotten sticky buns! Maybe he hated pie or his child was allergic to apples or . . .

"Yes, I like that indeed." He dropped the cloth covering the pie and lowered his eyelids to hit me with a look that the romance novels Granny Missus favored would call *smoldering*. "You wandering around the good ol' Sunshine Market thinking about my buns."

"Your . . . ?" My gaze just naturally dropped to the backside of his faded jeans. "That's not what I meant!"

He laughed again.

Well, there it was, another big, shining yee-haw donkey-braying moment in front of Ryman.

Suddenly, trying to make my case for the connection between day-old baked goods and the bad taste of the man showing up too late for his grandfather's memorial seemed pointless. This whole visit seemed pointless. "I just wanted to bring by some food for you and your daughter."

"I know."

"Because I knew you couldn't get much in the way of hot food here tonight unless you fired up the Buffet kitchen."

"With me in there, 'fired up' would be the operative word." His smiled invited me to lighten up.

Lightening up, especially around Ry O'Malley, was not on the menu tonight. Though I wouldn't turn away the chance to fish for a little information. "Don't worry, you'll have that kitchen up and running in no time."

His expression went distant but gave away nothing of what was going on his mind or what lay on the horizon for the buffet or the motel.

I sighed. "Like I said, just bringing by some comfort food—"

"And it all looks so good, too." He cut me off before I could wriggle in another not-so-subtle hint about what he might have in mind for the place. "What's this wedged in the corner, between that juice bottle filled with . . . ?"

"Sweet tea." My voice went high and raspy.

"I doubt that you'd make any other kind, Miss Jolene."

I cleared my throat and touched my fingertips to the hollow above my collarbone. Cool and aloof, that's how I would play it. "I'm sure you're accustomed to something a little more sophisticated."

"A man likes variety."

"Then you should love the three-bean salad." I pointed to a sunny yellow margarine tub and the moment his attention wavered, slipped around to the other side of the freestanding counter.

"You didn't forget a thing, did you?" He set the box beside the guest registry and pulled out a heavy plastic bowl with "Hadley" written on the lid in permanent ink. "Jell-O with bits of cut-up fruit and marshmallows?"

I pulled my shoulders up. "*Black cherry* Jell-O with *Coca-cola, cream cheese and walnuts.*"

"Ahh." He closed his eyes—well, he pretended to close them, but I could see that he never really took his gaze off of me. "The good stuff."

"You don't have to make jokes at my expense. I know it's a simple thing, nothing like you're used to, but—"

"You're right about that." He opened the lid on the plastic container.

The rich, fruity aroma drifted through the musty office.

I braced myself to defend my cooking, my adherence to the old-fashioned custom of bringing food to newcomers, heck, even my very way of life, which I feared any O'Malley threatened just on principle.

He raised his gaze to mine. "I am not used to anyone going out of their way for me when they have nothing to gain by doing it."

"Oh."

"Thank you." He extended his hand.

I looked down. My daddy had taught me that you learned a lot about a man by his hands. Daddy's own fingers bore the cuts and calluses of years of hard work. Yet they had the gentleness to caress Mama's hair with great love, the certainty to lift a child in air in play and the dexterity to work a camera in his hobby, creating art from the everyday. My daddy had told me that only Hadleys had hands like these.

O'Malleys' hands, he'd said, were soft and pampered as the people themselves, useless for anything but pinching pennies and signing deals to better their place in the world.

I blinked at the open hand before me. Strong and in the very gesture of reaching toward me, tender in that strength. Toughened, if not actually callused, and nicked just enough on the thumb and around the knuckles to show he didn't mind getting his hands dirty with manual labor. This was not the hand I had expected to see. It made me wonder for the second time today what else I might have gotten wrong about this man.

"Your kindness means more to me than I can say, Ms. Hadley."

I slid my palm inside his and whispered, "Corbett."

"Corbett," he repeated, showing no signs that the significance of her having a different name registered with him one bit.

"You don't have to thank me, really." Damn. I sounded far too kittenish and coy to my liking but with my heart racing at the man's touch, I no longer had much control over my reactions.

He took my hand in both of his.

I wet my lips again, thinking that if he were to try to kiss me now I would have to slap his face.

Good manners would demand no less.

Yes, if he leaned in now and put his lips to mine I'd have no choice but to put him in his place with an uncompromising smack—after he'd finished kissing me half-senseless, of course.

He reached out to take my left hand too.

I took a deep breath and held it as he brushed his thumb over my bare fingers.

He smiled and stepped closer.

I should have retreated, set my feet firm and demanded he behave like a gentleman. Instead I inched forward, my head up and whispered, a little too invitingly, "I was only being . . ."

"Neighborly," he finished for me even as his mouth came lightly over my lips.

I shivered, shut my eyes and slid my arms around Ry O'Malley's strong neck.

He kissed me with the same sweet mix of hunger and tenderness he'd shown so many years ago when he had first touched me the day he dove in to rescue me in the swimming pool.

But this time I responded in kind, not out of fear or embarrassment. Something I'm sure he appreciated on many levels, but most especially that he did not have to fear another knee-to-the-groin, young-girl-defending-her-honor reaction.

I had wanted this to happen. So much so that I had ignored my upbringing, my instincts and my intuition. I had not looked for a sign to urge me into this man's arms. I pressed my body to his, dragged my mouth from his, then flicked the tip of my tongue across his lower lip. And then I kissed him again.

He groaned and fit one hand to the back of my head.

If I needed any portent for proceeding, the building wave of pleasure coursing through me was sign enough, wasn't it?

A set of headlights slashed across the closed blinds of the large windows, distracting us.

I jumped and tried to pull away.

He circled my wrist lightly with his fingers. "Please, don't go."

Even as my pulse beat wildly against his warm skin, I whispered solemnly, "I can't stay."

Tires ground slowly over the uneven pavement of the South Winds' U-shaped drive.

I shifted my shoes on the stained carpet. "You don't understand how complicated my life will get if somebody from town sees me here."

"Complicated?" He laughed and released my wrist. "You're only being neighborly."

"To you it looks neighborly." I wet my lips and listened to the idling motor outside. "Someone else might see it as a betrayal."

"Pretty strong word. Really, don't you think you're blowing this out of proportion?"

"Yes, of course it's out of proportion." I raised my shoulders in resignation. "Out of proportion happens to be the baseline response I'm talking about here, the jumping-off point for bigger—and louder—reactions."

"Jolene . . ."

I held my hand up. This was the last person on earth I wanted to explain my grandmother's silly prejudices to, and the last person who would understand putting a family member's feelings over your own interests. "I just don't want to have to deal with it all right now."

A car door slammed and I nearly leaped out of my skin.

He moved toward me as if shielding my body with his. "Jealous husband?"

I made a lame attempt to push him away when what I really wanted was to curl up close and let him go on sheltering me. "I'm not married—anymore."

He relaxed, but just a little. "A boyfriend, then?"

I tipped my head back to look up into his eyes. "If you must know, it's my granny."

His cheek ticked up on one side, showing off the dimples made even more pronounced by age and good humor. "You're afraid of your *granny*?"

"I am not afraid." I tucked my hair behind my ear and managed a weak but heartfelt smile for him. "And you don't know my granny."

An almost musical series of quick taps on the door took Ry's focus away. If a knock on a door can convey the caller's intent, this one seemed to give off a "happy to be here" vibe.

"Just fooling around with the light. We're not open for business," Ry called out, then fixed his attention back on me. "I'd tell you how silly it sounds, fearing your old granny, but as a man who has conducted far too much of his life according to the whims of his family, I'm hardly one to find fault."

"You?"

"You think my family wanted me to come here for the memorial service?"

"You *didn't* come for it," I reminded him with just a touch less starch in my tone than I'd had when I first saw him today.

"No, I didn't get here for it, but I did come with every intent of attending that service."

"You did?"

"Yes but . . . do you have children?"

"Your daughter." Did I feel like a jerk, or what? I'd come here to help with his daughter and let myself get so sidetracked by him and wanting to find out about his plans for the South Winds that I forgot about his poor, sick child. "I can see how traveling with her would slow you down."

"You can?"

The knocking broke in again. "Hello? Anyone in there? I saw the lights on and had to stop. Hello?"

"That's Norris Wyatt." I wondered if Ry would recognize the name of the man who had single-handedly run the Buffet for more than thirty years.

"*Mister* Wyatt? The man who used to make me scrub pots and pans until I could see my face in them?"

I couldn't help smiling at that. So Ry's time here *had* consisted of more than the glamorous job of lifeguard and suntanned boy-god. "He probably wants to know when you'll need him to get back to work."

"Work?" Ry swore under his breath.

"What? Is something wrong?"

"Hang on a second, please, Mr. Wyatt. I'll be right there." He rubbed the back of his neck and squinted at the floor.

"Ryman?" I ducked to try to maintain eye contact. "What is it? Have you hired someone else to do the cooking when you reopen the Buffet?"

His gaze locked onto mine. "I'm not going to reopen the Buffet."

"Okay. Well, yes, I don't guess anyone around here truly expected you would." I had had my hopes, based on what was best for the community, of course, but Ry's news did not surprise me. I wet my lips and pressed on. "But you might want to consider bringing Norris in to get things in order so when you sell the place—"

"I'm not selling, either."

That unwelcome pronouncement was a verbal shove. I swear I staggered backward just the tiniest bit at the sheer force of it. "You're . . . you're not?"

He moved past me without meeting my gaze.

A knot tightened in my stomach. I wasn't sure I wanted to know the answer, but I had to ask the question. "Then what do you plan to do with the place?"

He rested his hand on the door handle and lifted his head.

From the parking lot, the large sign's unreliable light cast his somber face first in neon orange, then a white glow. Then for a moment it went dark.

"Ryman, what do you plan to do to the South Winds?" I demanded softly.

"I plan . . ." His shoulders rose, then dropped with a heavy sigh. He pushed on the door and a gust of crisp mountain air carried in the once-reassuring scents of autumn.

I shivered.

"I plan, Miss Jolene, to tear the South Winds down."

"Well, hello there, Miss Jolie." Norris Wyatt did not come fully into the office. He placed both weathered brown hands on the sides of the doorframe and leaned forward like a longtime neighbor just poking his head in to chat a spell. "How's that pot-scrubbing arm, young Ryman?"

Ry looked into the hand that only moments ago I had admired, clenched his jaw and gave a curt nod of hello. "Mr. Wyatt."

"Imagine finding the pair of you together!"

"We're *not* together, Norris." I swiped my knuckle under my plumped lower lip, hoping I didn't look like some back hill ho who'd just thrown herself at the son of the town's richest family. It all just had the sting of a bad bluegrass ballad sprung to life.

"Did I drop in at a bad time? Because I can come back later."

"Actually, Mr. Wyatt—" Ry gripped the door handle.

"I was just on my way home." I turned to face the open door.

"Now, don't go on my account. Finding y'all here gave me high hopes all this feuding folderol would finally play itself out. Y'all could end it, you know, if the both of you would just talk to each other."

"That's the problem. Norris, we don't seem to be able to *just* talk." I pinched up something clinging to my sleeve. My eyes grew wide and I quickly let the strand of Ry's silver hair drop to the floor.

"Doesn't do much good to *just* talk, Mr. Wyatt, if no one is listening."

He'd said it to cover my innuendo and I knew it. Ry didn't give a damn if people around Verbena read something into my remarks, but he wanted to protect me from any speculation. The big, dumb sweetie. He was really starting to get on my nerves.

I shifted my weight, stretched my back and laced my arms under my breasts before I realized the blatant sexuality of my body language.

An ass. Really, I wonder sometimes if all the permanent-wave lotion, mousse, dye and hair spray I handle hasn't seeped through my skull and totally softened my brain. Or was it just Ry and his charms that had gotten under my skin? Either way I needed to get ahold of the conversation here and get it focused where it belonged—anywhere but on me.

"I'd come over here tonight to offer some . . ." I met Ry's gaze, then blinked. "Because I thought . . . but then . . ." I shook my head and made a sad, solemn study of the man I had just kissed like a lovesick schoolgirl. "I *was* right all along about you, O'Malley."

"Jolene, I . . ."

"If I spoke out of turn, I'm sorry." Norris straightened up and folded his arms over his crisp blue shirt. "I only thought two smart, young people like you could surely get past all this needless fussing between your families. It just seemed about time for it."

"Time, Mr. Wyatt, is the one thing we don't have. Ryman intends to do away with the South Winds for good. He's come here not to bury Howdy but to erase him—to destroy every last piece of evidence of the old man's life's work."

Lord that was good! Not like me at all to be so brave and articulate at the same time. I felt fired up and strangely sure of myself. And in that instant, staring at the man planning to wreak havoc with what was left of my corner of contentment, I was connected to every Hadley who had ever confronted an O'Malley, and—despite the odds and the fact that they were probably making fools of themselves—stood their ground.

My lips trembled but my resolve rang firm. "I will fight you on this, O'Malley."

He exhaled and looked at an old calendar still sporting the patriotic summer scene from the month his grandfather had died. "There's nothing to fight about. It's a done deal."

Done deal? *Like hell it is*, I thought, even as I gathered my wits to address him in a tone that would have done Julia Sugarbaker proud. "As long as this place is still standing it is not a done deal. I will fight you and I will stop you. You damned O'Malleys will not get away with—"

"Now, Jolene, honey, careful what you say." Norris cut off my threat with a simple hand on my shoulder. "Hard words won't make this any easier."

"I don't want to make this easier, Norris." I can't believe he stopped me when here I was, just one "As God is my witness" away from actually embodying Scarlet O'Hara! "Hasn't his family had things *easy* long enough?"

Ry laughed.

I glowered at him.

"Sorry, Jolene, but easy is not a word I'd ever associate with my family." He turned to the man observing from the doorway. "Can I get a witness on that, Mr. Wyatt?"

"It's God's own truth. Neither of you young ones got blessed with gentle-natured folks for blood kin."

"At least my family tried to make things better for other people in Verbena, not try to suck the town dry for their own profits. That's not something that's going to change with my generation, or my son's." I blinked and suddenly tears washed over my line of vision.

Ry tensed up harder than the proverbial brick wall.

Norris shifted his feet but kept his steadying hand on my shoulder.

The light from the sign flickered, went out, then with a great surge of electric buzzing came back on.

I took a deep breath, put my hand on top of Norris's and met Ry's gaze. "I'll do whatever it takes to try to stop you."

"I know. It might be difficult for you to believe this, but it does my heart some good to think somebody would care enough to stand up for this place."

"Why *somebody*? Why can't *you* stand up for it?" I searched his face for some glimmer of empathy, but saw only resignation and remorse.

"You don't understand, Jolene."

"No, I don't." I shook my head. "But I hope you understand that if there is so much as a hairline fracture in your plan I will find it and use it to save this town."

"Town?" He smiled without mocking me and gave Mr. Wyatt a quick wink. "You seem to have inherited your grandmother's gift for blowing things out of proportion. I'm not doing anything to the town, just taking care of the South Winds once and for all."

"You are such a . . . a . . . such an *O'Malley*."

To his credit, he actually looked like that one zinged him a little.

"Never looking beyond your immediate desires to see how your actions might set off wave after wave of trouble for everyone around you."

"Jolene, I—"

"Save your breath." I held my hand up and gave my head a spirited I-mean-business-buddy shake. One red strand fell across my left eye but the rest of my hair remained as immovable as my attitude. "Or better yet, hold it until you turn blue."

"Jolene, look—"

"No, *you* look." I stepped to the door. With the glow of the sign lighting my back, I spread my arms. "Take a good look around you, Ry. Look into what you're doing and the long-range effects of this shortsighted plan of yours. For once be a person, not just an . . ."

"An O'Malley." He finished for me.

I held my hands up and counted on my feminine charms to keep me from sounding totally disingenuous when I smiled and muttered, "You said it."

He practically scorched me with his gaze, then stepped to the doorway and made a point to look down the silent highway and along the dark, looming shapes of the surrounding mountain. "I'm sorry, Jolene."

"I guess this means the feud is still on?" Wry wit tinged Norris's words.

"Feud, nothing." I said as I turned and headed to my side of the highway. "This is war."

It was at once the stupidest and the most divinely satisfying thing I have ever said. Now all I had to do was find the nerve to actually back it up.

Chapter 5

"Dylan, how many times have I told you not to spin in the stylist chairs?" I collected four shiny quarters from the cash drawer. "I don't know whether to count it as a blessing or a curse that the Logie County School Board saw fit to have the fall teachers' meeting coincide with the October session of the monthly Flea Market."

"I know what I'd vote." My son pressed on the lever at the back of the chair. It squeaked, then sank with a quiet hiss.

"It does free up the school kids to provide cheap labor for the market, but it sure leaves me and you at odd ends, doesn't it, sweetie?"

"Mo-om." The chair ended its descent with a clunk. Dylan just sat there with his arms crossed and his dark hair falling in a tumble over his eyebrows.

"What?"

"Sweetie." He scowled. "It's on *the list*. Remember?"

The list. My son, who did not share my gloomy outlook

about change, had come up with a list of things I could no longer say in front of or about him in public. Cute endearments were at the very top.

"Who's going to know?" I held my hands out. "We're completely alone."

"Yeah, but you always tell me it's how we act when nobody else is watching that shows who we really are."

"Um, yes, I do." I cleared my throat. I clutched the coins in my palm, more than a little self-conscious about my own actions a few days ago. How I had acted when no one was watching was to kiss the daylights out of a man I had no business even speaking to. That was surely *not* who I really was . . . was it?

"I guess it's okay if you call me sweetie when we're alone, Mom." He jumped out of the chair. "Heck, if you'll pay me to work around here today, you can call me anything you want."

"Dylan, about your working here—"

"I'd do a great job, Mom. I can sweep up or make change. Howdy used to always let me make the change. I can count the money backwards even if someone buys an apple fritter and coffee—that comes to two seventy-four after tax at the Buffet—with a twenty-dollar bill."

"Howdy did always brag on what a hard worker you were around the South Winds." I shut my eyes to keep myself from looking across the street. I had not let myself think of that place and that man for three whole days now. Well, not for at least three hours. I sighed at my failed attempt at self-deception. In all honesty I had not gone more than three minutes without that irritating man intruding on my thoughts.

"I'll work just as hard for you, Mom." His tennis shoes scuffed over the worn floorboards.

I sighed. "This is an entirely different kind of business, Dylan. My customers might not feel comfortable talking freely with a little boy around."

Dylan frowned.

"I mean with a young man around," I corrected. "It might interfere with their girl talk."

"Girl talk?"

"You know, beauty secrets, gossip, complaining about men." I had wanted to say bitching about men but I caught myself in time. "Anyway, if the ladies who come to the salon around Flea Market time aren't able to speak their minds freely then, well, their heads might explode."

"You won't get many tips fixing hair in a town full of headless women." Dylan laughed at his own joke.

"You see my dilemma, then, don't you?" I gave my son a kiss on the nose, then dropped the quarters into his outstretched hand. "Go get yourself a soda and some gum from the machine, then go see if you can help your grandma. She's been hinting that she needs someone to pitch in and clean up around the garage."

"Can I work on the Starliner? She says she almost has it running."

"You know how I feel about you working on car engines."

He stuffed his hands into his jeans pockets. "Then maybe I'll go across to South Winds and ask if I can work there instead."

"Don't you even think about it, young man!" It came out too fast to pass off as a simple motherly directive, so I tried to cover. "There's all kinds of construction stuff over there. I don't think they allow youngsters around that kind of thing."

"You won't let me do anything fun."

"Believe me, there is no fun to be had over at the South Winds as long as Ryman O'Malley is there." Now there was a mantra I needed to repeat to myself a few hundred times a day.

"You won't let me work on the Starliner and now you won't let me go over to the South Winds. Why can't I ever do the things I like to do? I'm not a baby anymore, you know." He flung the door open and charged out seconds before Sorrel Wyatt came through the door, humming brightly.

"Bye, sw—son. Morning, Sorrel." I flapped a gold-and-pink plastic cape with a crisp *pop*.

With one well-aimed hip check, I spun around the chair in front of the sink and stood behind it, smiling all the while 'til my cheeks ached. I figured Norris had told his wife about finding me and Ry together the other night. Unless I stayed on top of the conversation I might just find myself the topic of some of the pre–Flea-Market gossip fest.

"Morning, Jolie, honey." The tiny woman stood on tiptoe to hang her purse and sweater on a wall peg. "You have any trouble getting around those trucks over at the South Winds?" As far as snooping for information masquerading as a legitimate concern went, hers was a pitiful attempt and we both knew it.

"No, not one bit of trouble."

"That's good."

Since early Monday morning, trucks and cars and even

delivery vans had come and gone on a pretty regular basis to the business across the street. Not that I monitored the goings-on there.

I didn't stand at my shop door and strain to read the lips of the workmen. I didn't listen for the telltale sound of jackhammers breaking up concrete or for the tortured metal cry I expected when the old sign came tumbling down.

Just like I didn't stand at my open bedroom window at night and try to imagine what Ry was doing in his lighted room just across the way. Like hell I didn't.

It didn't help that Emma teased me mercilessly about finding creative ways to convince Ry to come around to my way of thinking. Or that in unguarded moments, I found myself dreaming about those very things—in vivid, heated detail.

"Looks like your customers are scarcer than hen's teeth today." Sorrel's halting accent always seemed at odds with the decidedly Southern expressions she delivered with the ease of a mountain native. "Right odd for Thursday before Flea Market."

Despite its name, the Every Second Saturday Flea Market and Jamboree actually started on Friday mornings and ran until Sunday afternoon, complete with a bingo game Friday night, music and dancing Saturday night and a nondenominational church service Sunday morning. This meant the regular attendees had to get their hair done up for the big doings a day ahead of time.

Joke was that Thursday before Flea Market was the most chaste night of the month in Verbena on account of all those women refusing to risk having their hair mussed up.

Norris Wyatt must have found a way to cope with that

inconvenience, though, because his wife of thirty-two years had come to have her hair done every Thursday since I first opened shop. Mrs. Wyatt had presented quite a challenge back then as she insisted her stiff, ginger-colored hair was God's doing and not some semipermanent magic straight from a box. Moonlight Platinum 104 applied to the Filipino-American woman's jet black tresses had done the trick, though. I had spotted it right off. Gossip that got all the way back from Asheville, where Sorrel's oldest daughter lived, confirmed the purchase of six months' worth of dye from the beauty supply there each and every time Sorrel visited. To this day I have never let on that I knew.

I keep everyone's trust. In return they usually tell me everything.

The older woman wriggled into the orange vinyl seat and raised her chin to allow me to fasten the plastic drape over her new outfit.

"Ready to get gorgeous?" I snapped the cape closed.

"Oh, forget gorgeous. I want to overshoot gorgeous by a mile and head straight for stunning—maybe even down-right glorious." She removed her large-framed glasses and ran her fingers through her chemically damaged hair. "But if you're short on time I'll make do with a wash and set."

"Short on time? Honey I haven't had nothing but time since the South Winds shut down. Even told Emma not to bother coming in and warned the Bybee girls—you know the ones who pay me for the use of my extra chairs on the weekends?—that it would be slim pickin's today."

"Oh no! You'd better get them all on the phone and tell them to fill up to their eyeballs with strong coffee and get on down here. Today you'll be busy."

"Why?"

"Don't you know what's going on across the highway?"

"Up until two months ago a person couldn't do beans around this town without me getting wind of it." I could have phrased that better but rather than try to clarify I depressed the chair's lever with my toe and tipped Sorrel back to rest her neck against the sink. "But I swear I have no idea what you're talking about."

"If you don't know, then maybe I shouldn't say anything— but I could tell you who to ask."

"Oh, I know who to ask, thank you." I turned on the water and let it run to warm up. "And I'd rather style my hair with a hand mixer set on high than go crawling over there to ask that man the time of day."

"Big changes brewing across the street, gal. You can't hide from that."

"Big changes. Yeah, I knew that was coming." My heart sank.

"They were putting a banner up on the fence when I drove up. Go look."

I didn't want to look. I didn't want to see anything out my window that had not always been there. But Sorrel had a point: I couldn't hide from it for long.

I went to the door in time to see Ry and his daughter tying a long canvas banner to the fence around the pool.

"Open?" The rest of the message flipped up and turned on itself.

"That's not all it says," Sorrel called out.

I whispered, "Please say 'open for business' or 'open under new management.' "

Ry's patch-headed daughter slipped easily under his

arm, snagged the canvas sign by its wayward corner and fastened it to the chain link backdrop.

With both of them blocking the view, Ry finished tying the banner in place, then he stood back.

"Open this weekend only," I read softly.

Sorrel came up beside me and prodded me with one elbow. "Check out the poster under the vacancy sign."

A roll and half of duct tape secured an eye-stinging green poster just under the familiar motto. So now it told the passersby:

GOOD FOOD. GOOD RATES.
GOOD FUN. GOOD FOLKS!
AND GOODBYE.

"We all knew it had to happen sometime, I reckon."

I shut my eyes. "If you don't mind, I think I will call Emma in to work."

"Go right ahead." She patted my back.

I dialed without looking at the numbers. I spoke to my old friend without thinking about what I said. I hung up without using the one word seared into my mind at the moment: *Goodbye.*

"Emma's on her way."

Sorrel crooked her finger to motion me back to the front window. "She isn't the only one."

With one hand on his child's shoulder beside him, Ry was headed across the street.

"Land-a-mercy, he *cannot* be coming over to my side of the highway today." I stepped back, my hands on my hips and my heart in my throat. "Why the . . . How dare he . . .What balls!"

Sorrel blinked at the unvarnished assessment but did not miss a beat. "I haven't ever gotten close enough to the man to make that level of personal judgment, honey, but if you say so—"

"Sorrel! I was not referring to his actual . . ." I ran for the mirror, relying on my horrified gaze to properly chastise my longtime customer. "I mean, I *never*!"

Sorrel giggled.

"Well, that *one* time, of course." Why had I blurted that out? Surely Sorrel had no idea what had happened in the Trav' O' Tel pool twenty-something years ago. "That is, I was young and my top just popped off."

"Oh?" She put her back to the door. "Do tell. I hadn't heard about that."

"Never you mind. Just tell me when he gets to the porch, okay?"

"You have a minute. He's gotten waylaid in the street by someone wanting to talk."

The spray can hissed and for an instant a shimmering haze of hair spray softened my image in the mirror. I sighed in relief, knowing I would meet him filled with the confidence only brains, beauty or a big ol' can of Aqua Net could give a woman.

I tugged at the neckline of my sweater until it showed just enough bosom to get tsked over at a church social but not enough to give the wrong idea down at the DB Saloon. I ran a creamy layer of Not-So-Nude Pink gloss over my lips, pressed them together and then checked my teeth with a grin that exposed my gums.

"I can understand you battening down the hatches with

hair spray, sugar, but what's with baring your teeth? You plan on biting the poor man?"

"When I get through with him he'll wish I had just bit him."

"What's between you two, girl? Honestly."

"Honestly?" I held my breath. Honestly? I'm not sure I had the answer to that. But I came up with the best reply I could under the circumstances. "The only thing between us is the whole wide world, the way we look at it and what we think matters in it."

"That all?"

"Isn't that enough?" I licked my lips and edged my neckline down another centimeter.

"You aren't going to talk him out of it, you know."

"I know that." I did, too. I'd looked into every means I could imagine to stop him and grudgingly accepted that I could not do it. "But I don't have to make it easy for him, either."

"Listen to his reasons."

"Why should I? Has he listened to anyone? Asked anyone about what he's doing and how he might do something different?"

"He doesn't have to ask anyone anything. The South Winds is his to do with as he must."

"To do with as he pleases, you mean. He's going to destroy the Trav' O' Tel. Aren't you the least bit upset?"

"Of course. But Norris and I have talked it over and we figure it's not the worst thing that could happen."

I shut my eyes. Butterflies were doing spiral dive-bombing somersaults in my stomach. Listen to Ry? I could hardly hear above my own heartbeat.

"It's forced us to reevaluate and decide to finally follow Norris's dream. To own our own café instead of him running someone else's."

I whipped my head around. "You can afford that?"

"We have our retirement nest egg. And—I hate to have to tell you this because I know it'll make you madder than a wet hen to hear it, but here goes—Ryman is giving Wyatt every penny they pull in this weekend."

"You're right. I don't want to hear that." I supposed that sticking my fingers in my ears and humming the theme to *Oklahoma* loud and off key to blot out potential praise for Ry would go above and beyond the boundaries of good manners.

"Well, he's doing it. Whatever is in the cash drawers and deposit bags at closing time on Sunday is all ours to keep. Not profit after he pays his bills, but every red cent that comes in. Calls it a severance package."

"I'd like to sever something myself."

"Sometimes you have to lose one thing to gain another."

I didn't think Sorrel meant that in the same context.

"Things change," she said.

"But why does my family always seem to end up paying tenfold for those changes? Haven't I lost enough already? I don't want anything more taken from me."

"Then don't let it be taken." Sorrel shrugged.

I thought of watching my dad drive off to find work in another town, all those years ago. Of Granny Missus raising her daughter and eking out a living as best she could while Howdy made money hand over fist. "There never seems to be any choice for the Hadleys."

"There's always a choice. You can choose to get distraught over this or you can choose to do as the rest of the town has and let it go." The older woman stepped away from the door, opening it as she did. "You can let yourself be knocked on your butt by all this or you can go out there and meet it head-on."

I moved hesitantly to the doorway. I looked at Ry and the young girl at his side finishing up a conversation with two people in a delivery van. Here was a man: a businessman, a gentleman, a son, a father and who knew what else, but I had only seen him as an adversary—as an O'Malley.

I touched my fingertip to my lips and raised my eyes to Esther, poised on tiptoe. Some part of me wanted to do just as Sorrel suggested, just as Esther has always silently urged me to do. Just let it go.

"The things you give freely can't be taken. Give away your desire to save the South Winds and you will always have a part of it with you. Fight it and you will lose on all fronts."

I stepped onto the porch. "Will you excuse me just a minute?"

"What will you say to him?"

I paused.

As they started across the highway again, Ry bumped his daughter lightly and smiled.

I swallowed hard. "Maybe I won't say anything. Maybe I'll try to listen."

Chapter 6

"What do you think?" Ry stood at the edge of the salon's parking lot and waited for me to take in the assorted signs and wonders adorning the South Winds.

I pursed my lips and crinkled up my nose. "You want my approval?"

"Hell, no." He laughed. "I don't need anyone's *approval*."

Men like him never did. They just took charge. Did what needed doing. They did not stop to ask opinions, weigh options, wait for signals from above or support from the person across the way.

"The day I started out for Verbena, I made myself a promise never to let myself get too caught up in seeking anyone's approval for my decisions, actions and feelings."

Somehow hearing him say it out in the open like made me envy—maybe even admire—him a little bit. "If you don't want my approval, then why ask what I think?"

"Because I was hoping you'd take this opportunity to tell me how brilliant I am." He jerked his thumb over his shoulder in a not so subtle hint for me to begin oohing and ah-hing over his piddly little peace offering.

I made a point of not shifting my gaze from his.

He laughed. "However, Jolene, if you don't like this final gift to the town, my way of honoring my grandfather's memory, then you could just kiss my . . ."

"Daddy!" The young lady beside him rolled her eyes.

"What?" He smiled at her adoringly.

I smiled too, damn it. Worse, when I tried to cover up how charming I'd found him, it came out all queit, husky-voiced and flirty-sounding. "I think you've got a lot of nerve, O'Malley, coming over to my side of the street to get a better view."

"Well, maybe *the view* is better over here."

I drew up my shoulders to try to regain some ground. "You mean *from* here?"

"Do I?"

"Stop it, Dad, you're embarrassing yourself." His daughter turned her head away.

"I'm not one bit embarrassed—*you* are." He gave her a wink. "That's a parent's job, you know, to completely mortify their children at least once a day."

"If that's all it takes, then you're headed for Father of the Year." She stuck out her tongue just enough to show her disdain and her silver-studded tongue piercing.

Poor little thing, putting on such a brave face. "Don't listen to him." I moved toward her, carefully, hoping she would see the concern in my approach and not assume my attitude toward her father extended to her. "I would never embarrass my son."

"That can be verified, you know," Ry warned. "Just a few questions to the right people."

"If they are the right kind of people, they wouldn't be talking to you, now would they, O'Malley?" I gave him a sly, sidelong look, then put my hand out toward his daughter. "Hi, I'm Jolene Corbett, you can call me Jolie."

She blinked.

"Jolene *Hadley* Corbett," Ry whispered. He nodded toward the auto museum, where a group of people had gathered to point at and speculate about the goings-on at the South Winds. "So go on and shake her hand, but count your rings *and* your fingers when you're done."

"Are you the hairdresser?" She placed her hand tentatively in mine.

"Yes. Are you . . . is there anything I can do for you?"

To anyone but a rebellious teenage girl, the slight hesitation in the tenderly asked question should have rung clearly with an offer of help—the kind of help that goes way beyond hairstyles and beauty advice—if needed.

She jerked her hand away. "I *like* my hair."

"Oh." I shifted my gaze to Ry.

"She did it herself." He moved behind his daughter and took her by the shoulders. "You can just imagine how proud I am."

A white-haired figure in coveralls broke away from the crowd of onlookers at the museum and started, in a cumbersome, rolling gait, toward the salon.

I fought to keep my attention on the sallow-skinned girl scowling at me. "So . . . so you chose this look for yourself? You're not . . . not . . . sick?"

"Sick?" The girl stepped back so fast her nubby head bumped against Ry's chin.

"I . . . I thought you looked so tired that first day. Then I saw your hair, or should I say your lack of hair?" I sank my fingers into the rigidly tamed curls against my neck. I winced and looked to Ry. "I am so sorry I misread the situation."

"Don't be." Ry shook his head. "You were only trying to be a good neighbor."

"If I'm anything, I'm always a good . . ." My lips rounded to form a silent "oh."

Had he used the same words a few nights ago just before he kissed me.

"Don't feel bad, Jolie. Sugar Anne is just fine."

"Sugar Anne?" I batted my eyes—like that would help me absorb the name given to this dark, moody, shaved-and-shamble-headed girl.

Ry beamed with phony brightness. "Suits her, doesn't it?"

"Very funny, Dad." Sugar Anne threw an elbow but only grazed her father's side. Then she looked at me—and I could have been imagining this—her expression softened. "My mom made it up by mixing the names of two family members."

"Her grandmother Shuggee and her aunt Ann," Ry shook his head and chuckled.

"Grandmother Shugee, Aunt Ann and Mama were all debutantes in New Orleans." Sugar Anne tacked that last part on not in a defensive tone or even the disgusted one that most teens might have about that kind of thing. She simply laid it out there as if it explained everything.

And in a way it did, to me. It also reminded me that Sugar Anne's father was the debutante-marrying kind. It made me feel a bit foolish for all those years dreaming about him, in a prince-saves-the-poor-girl-and-makes-her-his-princess sort of scenario.

"But thanks for your concern for Sugar Anne, just the same, Jolie. It . . . it reveals the kindness of your character that you don't hold the sins of the father and his fathers before him—against the child." Ry moved away from his daughter.

"I am not a child."

"She's seventeen." Ry rubbed his fingers over his forehead, then raked through a shock of silvered hair at his temple. "Finished high school a semester early, flunked out of college by not attending a single class the first three weeks and is now spending the rest of the semester with me as her keeper . . . I mean, teacher."

"Right the first time," Sugar Anne muttered.

"So you see the only thing my daughter is sick of is *me*."

"They must be ice skating in hell today," a scratchy voice cried out not three feet away from us. "Because *that* child is something I never thought I'd live to see. . . ."

"Be kind, Granny Missus!" I said, though I knew I was no better at playing keeper to my grandmother than Ry was with his teen.

"No, I never thought I'd live to see her likes indeed! An O'Malley with a lick of sense!" the old woman completed her thought, her pale eyes still full of ornery glee.

Ry made a quick survey of the woman, with her white hair, acrylic ruby starburst earrings, rosy-rouged cheeks and grease-spotted gray coveralls with a violet-trimmed lace hankie poking out of the pocket.

Dylan, with a shock of dark brown hair falling almost to his eyes, strode up two steps behind his great-grandmother.

He stopped and took a slurp of his soda, like a kid on the sidelines of a promising circus act.

I let out a long, weary breath. After a couple cautious sidesteps away from Sugar Anne, I placed my hand on Dylan's back, then faced Ry as if I were quite literally taking sides.

Granny Missus plunked her fists against her ample hips. Her pant legs rose up to reveal a pair of men's socks on wide feet in thick-soled bulky sandals.

Ry flashed his dimples and stuck out his hand. "You must be Granny Missus."

Granny Missus folded her arms over her grandmotherly bosom. "And you must be absolutely out of your skull showing your face around here."

"His face we could endure, if we had to." I laced my own arms under my own thank heavens-not-so-grandmotherly breasts.

"Thank you." He nodded to me, then narrowed his eyes and added, "I think."

"Even his coming back here might not be so bad. He certainly has every right, obligation some might think, to bring his child here to experience some part of her family heritage." I met his gaze again with expectation more than anger. "To teach her the values we cherish here in Verbena."

"Since you're so concerned about my daughter, then you'll be glad to know I *have* come here to give her a lesson about family and values." He tipped his head slightly to me, held his hand up and touched his finger to count off as he finished. "First I want her to learn that sometimes you have to go against your family's wishes in order to be true to yourself."

I raised my chin just a fraction and hoped he hadn't seen it quiver with held-in emotion.

"Next," he ticked off on his second finger, "I want her to understand that there is a time to build and a time to tear down, a time to hang in and a time to let go and move on."

Let go. I lifted my gaze to Esther and then beyond to the cloudless sky.

He tipped his head and looked upward in kind.

I cleared my throat, shook back my hair and nailed him with a steady glare. "Is that all you want to teach your daughter, Mr. O'Malley?"

"No." He stepped in then, closing the gap between us and squeezing out the influences of the place and people all around. His gaze sank into mine. His jaw tightened. "I want her to come away from all this knowing she doesn't have to be afraid of either of those lessons, Jolie."

Not be afraid? To go against your family's wishes? To let go and move on? The mere thought was both exhilarating and terrifying. "You make it sound so easy, Ry. But I know it's never that simple."

"The only thing constant in life is change, Jolie, if you can learn how to handle that . . ."

"Then what?" I stood back, defiance in my posture. "I won't ever feel the need to stay and fight for anything, to work for anything, to jump in against the tide and struggle for what's right, even if I know it's a lost cause?"

"I didn't mean to turn this into—"

"In other words, Ryman"—I inched backward and, with a tug on his sleeve, brought Dylan staggering back a step with me—"you brought your daughter here to teach her how to be the consummate O'Malley."

"O'Malley?" Dylan slipped away from my guiding hand and approached Ry with open curiosity. "Like *Howdy* O'Malley?"

"Like every O'Malley who ever made life miserable for anyone but themselves in Logie County and all parts south, as far as I can tell." Still flustered by my sharp response to Ry's perfectly forthright explanation of what he hoped his daughter learned from their visit, I couldn't seem to keep from spewing the old-line opinions of my family. All the while, deep in my heart, I ached to applaud Ry's desire to instill in his child the courage to follow her own path.

I needed time to formulate responses to Ry, not to merely react to the man. Heaven help me, I had reacted to him on every level possible so far, and that had to stop. If it didn't, then who knew where it might lead before the last stone of the South Winds came falling down?

"I hardly think it's fair to claim every O'Malley has made everyone in Logie County miserable, Jolie." He stood tall against the backdrop of the old motel and motioned toward his daughter. "You can see that Sugar Anne is a veritable ray of sunshine to all she encounters."

The girl frowned and scratched a patch of shaved scalp.

He crossed his arms. "I've dealt fairly with everyone here, but that doesn't mean I plan to go around kissing . . ."

"Don't you swear in front of my child," I rushed to warn when what I really feared was that he would hint too broadly about the kiss we had shared.

He met my gaze and in his clear, smiling eyes I knew he was thinking of that fleeting moment of intimacy. He relaxed his stance and finished, "Kissing my best interests goodbye."

I ran my chilly fingertips along the neckline of my sweater. The man shook me to the core mentally, emotionally and, with no effort on his part, physically. How could I do battle with that?

I couldn't. Nothing in my life here in Verbena or my prudent, practical or problematic relationships with men so far had prepared me for dealing with Ry.

I reached out to grab my son by the arm and pull him close so we could retreat to the safety of the salon.

Dylan eluded my grasp. "You know about Howdy and the South Winds, mister?"

Ry bent down, his hands on his knees and spoke directly to Dylan, "Howdy was my grandfather. And I'm the new owner of his property here in Verbena, son."

Son. Coming from this man's mouth the word sent a jolt straight through me. The man had some nerve coming here, tearing apart my town, then acting all caring and kind and calling *my* son "son."

I opened my mouth, not sure of what to say but pretty much hoping nothing too stupid came out.

"Cool." Dylan beamed up at Ry. "Howdy was my friend."

I froze.

"I used to help him out some at the Trav' O' Tel after school and on weekends and in the summer and days like today when they don't hold classes. I did a good job, too. He always said so. I . . . I really liked . . ." Dylan glanced across the street, then pushed both his hands into his jeans pockets and hunched his shoulders up before facing Ry again. "I liked working for your grandpa, mister. I liked it a lot."

The soft longing in my son's voice pierced the protective bubble of self-involvement I'd been living under since Ry showed up. I wanted to step up and fold him into my arms and instantly knew that was absolutely the last thing I should do. It tore at my heart like all the moments do when as a mom I'm forced to choose between what will make me feel better and what will make my child a better person. At Dylan's age, having Mama rush to the rescue was not in his best interests. And it just killed me.

It must have gotten to everyone because even Sugar Anne's expression went from agitated boredom to a kind of quiet consideration.

Granny Missus coughed and shuffled her feet in the gravel, but that did not disguise her quiet sniffles or the subtle sorrow in her eyes as she looked across Highway 612.

"I bet Howdy liked having you help out, too. My name is Ryman, but everyone calls me Ry."

"Huh! Bet that ain't all they call you," Granny muttered.

Ry held out his hand to the boy without so much as a raised eyebrow at Granny's remark. "And you are . . . ?"

"Dylan Corbett." Dylan accepted the handshake like a somber little man closing a deal.

"Good to know you, Dylan." Ry smiled.

I caught myself before sighing like some big old sentimental goober at the scene the two of them made, man and boy, Hadley and O'Malley.

From a shouting match—in which I spouted things out of fear and anger that I no longer entirely believed—to getting defensive over this man calling Dylan "son" to going positively gushy over seeing the gentler side of Ry, I had just run the gamut. If, as Ry said, the only thing constant in life is change, then I was living life to the fullest at this very moment.

Emma, who had gotten out of her truck after a few last-minute adjustments to her hair, makeup and unaccustomed bra, started toward the group gathered at the foot of the salon's front steps.

I waved her on inside. I did not want anything, especially Em's big mouth, to add to my emotional upheaval.

"Nice to make your acquaintance, sir." Dylan released Ry's hand and gave a very grown-up nod.

Suddenly I felt a flash of shame that I had not always displayed the same level of courtesy or maturity. I stole a peek at the man's face and found him looking up, over my son's head, directly at me.

"He's a fine young man, Jolie."

" 'Course he is. He comes from a fine family," Granny Missus announced, her craggy voice just dripping with pride.

Ry glanced over his shoulder at his own child. "We happen to think we come from some pretty . . . tolerable stock ourselves, ma'am."

"Well, I'll tell you one thing. That one there gives me hope you might have a point." With a shake of her finger my grandmother singled out Sugar Anne. "She's got spunk. And smart! Smart enough to bear a little righteous indignation toward a tyrannical patriarch."

"Tyrannical?" Ry's cheek twitched as he repeated the accusation.

"Yeah." Sugar Anne kept her ground but did angle her body to the Hadley side of the exchange.

"Another thing, that child ain't afraid to express some individuality, to think outside the money box, as it were." A person a mile away watching the whole encounter through a toy telescope could have seen how pleased the old woman was at that turn of phrase. "A rare thing among you O'Malleys, I'd say."

"Rare and precious," Sugar Anne mumbled, her eyes narrowed to catlike slits in her father's direction. "Something to be valued."

"That much we agree on, young lady." He touched the underside of his daughter's chin for only a second. "I do value you, respect your individuality and want more than anything for you to understand that not everything can be measured in material gain."

Sugar Anne batted her dark lashes.

I could see the struggle in the girl's face over her father's loving regard for her as his daughter and his unyielding stance that she still had a lot to learn.

I clenched my teeth to keep from mixing in the family matter.

Granny Missus did no such thing. "You really want to instill that lesson, let your girl come work with me for a day. I could use an extra hand around the garage."

Before Sugar Anne could protest, or I could demand to know what my grandmother was up to with this wild notion, Dylan pumped his fist in the air and shouted in triumph. "Yes! If she works for Granny, then I can go over to the South Winds and help *there* just like I used to!

"No!" I cried out.

Every head snapped up in my direction.

I twisted the ends of my hair between my thumb and forefinger and tried to think of something more to say.

Ry stepped forward, his hands raised. That simple silent gesture shifted command of the situation to him.

I wanted to thank him almost as much as I wanted to kick dirt on his boots, cuss and generally pitch a fit at his having intervened.

"Odd as it sounds, I like the idea of Sugar Anne working with you, Granny Missus."

"But Da-ad . . ."

"Would you rather hang around with me?"

I seemed to be the only one standing there who heard the note of hope in Ry's question.

Sugar Anne heaved a sigh.

"At least with Mrs. Hadley you wouldn't be bored." Ry winked at Sugar Anne.

The girl made a quick study of Granny Missus, who studied her right back without one ounce of reservation.

"And you might discover a thing or two about your *heritage*, child." I wouldn't have described the old lady's grin as wicked, but it was hard to dismiss the glint in her eyes. "Most town folks come by the museum on the Thursday before Flea Market to gas up and get the lowdown before the tourists and shoppers roll in."

"Ahh, the ulterior motive rears its head," Ry said, grinning. "Still looking for a way to influence me and my decision?"

"You don't want your child to hear about life in these mountains?" Granny sounded about as sincere as a Sunday school teacher preaching against demon alcohol with gin on her breath. "You don't want her to know where your family's roots begin?"

He turned to me. "My father always said that once you

Hadleys dig your heels in, no force on earth can shake you loose."

I smiled and met his gaze without hesitation. "It's one of our many admirable traits."

Ry cocked his head. "I don't think he meant it as a compliment."

"C'mon, girl, customers coming any minute now. Let me show you around my garage and auto museum." The elder Hadley wobbled her head, and her earrings danced against the soft folds of her neck, snagging on her upturned collar.

"You got any more of these?" Sugar Anne slipped behind me and Ry and took Granny Missus by the arm, in the guise of checking out her coveralls.

"Sure, sure. Got brown ones and blue ones, you can take your pick." Granny turned and began to make her way back to her business with Sugar Anne at her side. "You want a cap, too?"

The girl rubbed her fingers over a random remnant of wispy black hair. "Yeah that'd be good. Thanks."

"Do you get that alliance?" Ry leaned his shoulder in until it touched mine.

I could only shake my head. "Maybe it's a sign of some kind. You know like the lion laying down with the lamb?"

Ry edged in closer still until I could feel his breath on the side of my face. "What? The Hadleys laying down with the . . ."

"In your dreams, O'Malley." Mine, too. But this was neither the time nor place to allow myself to think about that.

"Does this mean I can work at the South Winds or not?" Dylan slapped his hand on his jeans.

"Not," I snapped, knowing more than a little of my agitation was with myself.

Ry made a big show of checking my heels, as if he expected to find them buried up to the anklebone from my stubborn stance.

"There's too much going on over there." I waved my hand in the direction of the motel but didn't dare look at it, my son or the man I was standing there lying to. "I don't want him to get in anyone's way."

"Ah, Mom, I won't."

"Actually, kid, your mom has a point. Mr. Wyatt banished me from the place until it's time to start checking guests in later this afternoon." Ry held his arm up and checked his watch. "He says he has too much to gain this weekend to let a man who spent his days in the clouds or up to his elbows in engine grease get around his pots and pans."

That did it. There were only a few bits of news that had gotten all the way back to my ears about Ry over the many years since he last came to Verbena as a teenager. One was that he had gone to a prestigious college—naturally. Another was that he had married well. Duh. And the last was that he had joined the Air Force and stayed with it until said wife decided it was a waste of said education. He left the military and then the wife left him. The last I had heard he made a living—well, what O'Malley has to work for their living? Let's say he spent his time . . . as a private pilot.

Dylan's eyes grew wide. "You know about engines, mister?"

"A thing or two, yeah."

"Mom!"

"Dylan, he's a pilot, not a grease monkey for old, broken-down automobiles."

"You're a pilot?" Awe and wonder shone in the boy's face. "And you know about engines? Man, I bet you could fix the Starliner in nothing flat."

"The Starliner?"

"A nineteen-fifty-seven Ford Fairlane 500 Starliner two-tone red-and-white hard-top convertible."

"Skyliner, Dylan," I corrected. Then I turned to Ry. "We just got in the habit of calling it the Starliner because . . . well, it just sounds so much more . . . you know . . ."

"Romantic?" Ry offered.

"Cool," I countered, drawing the word out and driving home its double meaning with an icy stare.

"Mom." Dylan tugged on my hand. "Can I show it to him? Please?"

I tried to not let his expression twang my guilt strings but I could not ignore the significance. My son had not inherited my desire to hunker down in a little home in Verbena for the rest of his life. The very mention of things like airplanes and pilots and people from other places made Dylan's face light up. He loved the concept of going places—and nothing symbolized that better than the Starliner.

Ry tousled Dylan's dark hair with his large, gentle hand. "I wouldn't mind taking a look at the car, if it's all right with you, Jolie."

"Well, I had thought . . ."

By now two more salon clients had pulled into the parking lot.

Emma had stuck her nose against the glass in the front door and mouthed the word "help" at least six times.

Sugar Anne had hurried ahead and stood holding the door open for Granny Missus at the auto museum.

Dylan looked at me with so much excitement and hope in his eyes that I felt like a big old puppy-kicker for even thinking about saying no to him.

And Ry . . . Ry was standing there with his eyes on me, waiting and willing to go along with whatever I decided.

I decided I wanted to pull my hair out.

"Mom, you said yourself that it must be a sign."

"Sweetie, I hardly think—"

Dylan put his finger to his lips to shush me. "The list, Mom. Remember the list."

"The list?" Ry whispered. "What does that mean?"

I started to tell him he wouldn't understand but catching a glimpse of his daughter's fuzzy scalp down the way shut me up. I sighed. "The list. It means my son is growing up."

"Cool." Dylan threw his chest out. "That means I can go, right?"

I shut my eyes and nodded.

Dylan hooted. His tennis shoes thundered down the way to the carport behind the auto museum.

I held my breath, listening for Ry's footsteps to follow.

Instead I felt the warmth of his hand sliding into mine. "It will be okay, Jolie."

I wanted to believe him. And I wanted him to hold more than just my hand. I curled my fingers tightly around his and met his steady gaze. "What will be okay, Ry? The car? The kids? The town?"

"All of it. It won't be the same, nothing stays the same but it will be okay. You'll see."

I shut my eyes again.

He kissed my cheek, so lightly I wondered if I only imagined it, then released my hand and started after Dylan.

As I watched my son go off with Ry, and my grandmother pause in the doorway to snag a cap off a peg for Sugar Anne, I could only stand by in helpless awe. If this was a sign, what did it foretell? Would everything really be okay, as Ry had promised? Or was I witnessing the beginning of the end of everything I held dear?

Chapter 7

I have always tried not to be overprotective of my son. Sheesh. Some people might say that I was so busy protecting my heart—and my hair—that I didn't have the energy left over to shelter all the people I love, too. The truth was, I didn't want to shelter Dylan. Well, not *too* much.

I recognized that he was growing up and needed the chance to stretch his wings. He needed some elbow room away from his mom to try new things and sometimes, without me there to rush in and rescue him, he'd fail. I didn't like it, but I knew it and respected it. Doing it—that was not always so easy.

So, with that in mind, I stayed away from the garage for as long as I could. And when I did finally sneak down there it was *not* to check up on my son—I swear on my best scissors!

No, I went down there with nothing but the purest of motives, which had nothing to do with any maternal feelings whatsoever.

I went down there to spy on Ry.

I couldn't help it. Here was a man I had spent more than half my life mooning about and then he shows up in the flesh, moves in across the street and suddenly he's acting like mail-order-catalogue role model to my son. How could I *not* be curious about that?

So there I stood, hanging back in the shadowy doorway, listening in on whatever lessons in man talk, mechanics and malice among mountain families that Ry had in store for my son.

"Get in there and give it all you've got." Ry put a protective hand on Dylan's back to help steady him as the boy stretched his arm down into the crevices of the car's engine.

"This is fun, isn't it?"

Dylan, intent on tightening a hose, couldn't see Ry's nod. "Yeah. Doing a thing for yourself, getting your hands dirty, building something, making something work, that's what makes a man happy."

"You think we can really get the Starliner running again?" He looked up, his eyes shining.

"Having a first-rate mechanic like you on the job sure improves the chances."

Dylan beamed.

My heart melted toward the man for his kindness—just a teeny bit.

Ry stroked two fingers along the bright chrome trim on the side of the old convertible.

I shivered at the unexpected intensity that gesture had for me. It was as if I felt every inch of that long, languid caress over my own body.

"Yeah. She's a beauty all right. Definitely worth whatever extra effort it takes to do right by her."

He meant the car, not me, I reminded myself.

"Mama says we probably won't ever get her running again, but that it's okay to imagine what it would be like to ride in her." Dylan's muffled voice shook me back into reality. Then he sealed the deal by using my jaded opinion practically as his own. "She says it's the kind of car made for dreaming and that real life wouldn't probably live up to those dreams anyway."

"Your mama says that, huh?"

Didn't anyone ever tell you that your mama can be a real ass? I wanted to shout out, but did not have the nerve. I guess I had never realized how much my fears and apprehensions had affected my child. It cut deep to suddenly see how this precious child, only nine years in this world, had learned from the person who should have nurtured hope and faith and innocence in him that dreams don't come true.

Crying is a weakness I have not afforded myself for a very long time. But I had to hold my breath and shut my eyes to keep the tears from spilling over.

"She's special enough to try for, though, isn't she?" Dylan patted the fender.

Well, maybe there was hope yet. Obviously Dylan hadn't given up entirely on the idea of going for his dreams. I took a deep breath at last. There was hope that I could still fix my mistakes. Lord, what better feeling on Earth is there than that?

"Now do I undo that bolt like you said?" Dylan held up a wrench.

"Yeah, get down in there. It'll be a tough one, so go ahead and really use some muscle."

Dylan looked back over his shoulder. His eyes sparked

with pride at being entrusted with this job. "Okay, Mr. O'Malley."

He gave the boy's shoulder an encouraging shake. "Just do your best, pal."

Dylan looked intently down at the engine. He banged the wrench around in a way that might have seemed, to the untrained eye, like work.

It didn't fool Jolie for a moment.

"Did I say something wrong?" Ry asked.

"Grandpa Howdy used to call me 'pal,' " he murmured.

I shut my eyes. I had forgotten that.

"Guess the two of you got pretty close?"

"I went over to see him every afternoon after school." He didn't look at Ry.

"Yeah?" Ry leaned in like he was enthralled with the engine workings and put his hand on Dylan's back. "What did you two get up to?"

"We talked." Dylan gripped the steel wrench in both of his hands. "He let me have a grape or strawberry soda from the machine."

"Did he still use that slug on a string to fool the machine into sending down a can?"

"Naw, he had a plastic card he stuck in like at the bank."

"Modernization comes even to Verbena, eh?"

Dylan turned the tool over, then over again, his shoulders lifting and falling in a half-hearted shrug. "I guess."

"You know, my grandfather would cuss and connive and crab and cry foul each and every time the vending supply man came to stock the soda and candy machines. The old coot tried to get around paying for anything because he felt, just by virtue of being Howdy O'Malley, he should get whatever he wanted for free. Guess he mellowed with age." Ry tapped his finger on the bolt Dylan needed to loosen. "How else did you and my grandfather spend your time together?"

Dylan dutifully went about the task. "In the summer he watched me while I swam in the pool."

"Really?" Ry raised his head and gazed in the direction of the South Winds, though he couldn't have seen past the backside of the auto museum.

I pressed my back to the wall and did the same. I couldn't see anything either, but oh, how I did remember!

"I used to swim in that pool a lot. Even worked as a lifeguard there one summer."

"I bet that was great."

"You have no idea." He leaned against the shiny red fender.

"Cool. Maybe I can be a lifeguard there one summer when I get bigger."

My heart—and the flash of memories that might have been—stopped.

"Dylan, I . . ." Ry looked at his hands.

"What?"

"I'd check the fit you've got with that wrench, partner. It doesn't look like it's gripping right."

"Oh, okay." He went up on the toes of his tennis shoes. His tongue stuck out. He went after the job, armed with nothing but stubborn determination pitted against an immovable object.

Just like me.

Ry looked at his work-scarred hands, then in the general direction of the old Trav' O' Tel. "You really miss my grandfather, don't you, pa—um, kid?"

"It's okay. You can call me pal. I like it."

"Okay."

"I *do* miss Grandpa Howdy. I miss laughing with him and helping him around the motel, and mostly I miss playing checkers with him."

"Checkers!" Ry braced his hand to the edge of the upraised hood. "I'd forgotten how that old man loved his down-and-dirty, show-no-mercy game of checkers."

"Show no *what*?"

"In the four summers I stayed with him and the handful of Christmases he came to our house I never beat him once at checkers."

"I beat him all the time."

"That so?" Ry narrowed his eyes and scrubbed his fingers along his jaw. "I wish I'd seen him at least once more before he died."

Dylan's mouth tightened. He clanged the wrench against the bolt. He said nothing, but then he didn't have to. Anyone who had loved a person the way that Dylan loved his Grandpa Howdy knew Ry had failed the old fellow big time.

"Well, checkers, huh? You and I will have to play sometime."

"Can we?" His head snapped up.

"I'm not exactly in a position to make promises. . . ." He inhaled deeply.

I held my breath.

He sighed, met the boy's hope-filled eyes and nodded. "Yeah. I'll play checkers with you, pal."

"Cool. OW!" Dylan's hand slipped down between the inside of the fender and the engine.

For a split second I thought about rushing to his aid, but Ry already had it covered.

"You okay, pal?" He placed his hand on Dylan's shoulder. "Looks like you scraped your knuckles up pretty bad."

"I'm okay, but it kinda hurts."

I winced but stayed put. What was I going to do, anyway? Rush forward and get myself nailed with a gargantuan "list" violation for asking my son if he wanted me to kiss the boo-boo?

Ry worked around engines all the time. Surely he had a better suggestion.

"Blow on it. That's what I always do." Ry pantomimed doing just that.

I shut my eyes and gritted my teeth to hold my opinion in.

Dylan puffed out his cheeks and huffed on his curled-up hand. "Will this help?"

"Come to think of it, no, it never did a danged thing for me. I just always do it anyway."

If you always do it and it never works, why don't you try something new? That's what I would have told the man—if I wasn't hiding from him. Besides, how could I, the woman who hated change, actually articulate, much less advocate, an idea like that?

"You want me to go get your mom, pal?"

"Naw. She'd probably want to kiss it or something." Dylan made an awful face.

I winced again and held my breath.

"Yeah, I suppose."

"Girls." Dylan rolled his eyes.

"Yeah." Ry eased out a longing sigh and a knowing chuckle. "Girls."

Dylan stopped blowing on his hand. "It's stopped hurting now."

"Dealing with the bumps and scrapes life throws you is just part of the process, pal." Ry held up his hands to show the boy the array of small scars. "You put your whole self into your work, you keep at it and if sometimes you get a little beat up, well, you clean yourself off and go back in. You don't stop, you don't give up and you don't whine about it."

"I didn't cry."

"I know you didn't. I said no whining. When stuff like this happens its okay to cry a little if it hurts, but definitely no whining."

"That's when you cuss instead, right?"

"You know that real men don't have to resort to cussing, don't you?"

Damn straight, I thought.

"Yes, sir," Dylan muttered.

"And I won't have you run off and tell your mama that I gave you the go-ahead to swear your head off when you get a scrape from an engine."

"That's when Granny Missus always cusses. She says it lets whatever is confounding you know who's the boss." The boy reached back into the engine.

Ry leaned in again, too, both forearms on the fender, his eye on the child. "Your Granny Missus is a double fistful of orneriness, ain't she?"

"Mama calls her a ringtailed tooter."

"I wonder how that ringtailed tooter is getting along with my little Miss Mary Sunshine."

"Who?"

"My daughter."

I wished I could just stand in the archway between the tiny museum building and the carport and go on listening in on the conversation. And if I could have contained myself to just listening I might have tried it, for just a while longer. But seeing Ry there, his sleeves rolled up, his expression so intent and his behind in those faded jeans . . .

I fanned myself, steeled my reserves and broke my silence before I got too carried away thinking about a man who was totally off-limits to me. "Any two members of our families getting along might be a bit ambitious to hope for, don't you think?"

Ry jerked his head up so fast it hit the hood with a hollow *whump*.

"I'm so sorry." I covered my mouth to hide a spontaneous grin. "I didn't mean to startle you."

"No harm done." He rubbed his scalp. "At least I didn't hit anything useful."

"No harm?" My grin slipped into a grimace. "You just rubbed engine grease into your *hair*!"

He looked at his blackened fingers, then simply pulled out the rag that was hanging from his back pocket and began wiping the grime off his hands. "All part of the process, right, pal?"

Dylan didn't even look up. "No cussin'. No whinin'."

I cocked my hip. "And no telling how you'll get that stuff out."

"Maybe there's a hairdresser in town who knows a few—" Ry raised his eyebrows and then finished with a husky growl. "—tricks."

Any smart-ass reply I might have made to that died on

my lips when he smiled just enough to make one dimple appear on his bristled cheek.

"Come on into the salon, I'll see what I can do," I whispered hoarsely, though I had intended to sound vexed and motherly.

"I'd like that." His eyes sparkled with more than just humor over my invitation.

I wet my lips. "What I can do about your hair, that is."

"Of course," he murmured.

I moved fully into the cool shade of the carport. "You know, after you're done here."

He tossed the rag into the toolbox. "We're done."

"What about this bolt?" Dylan looked up, the wrench still clenched in his fist.

"I think we need some solvent to break up the rust and dirt holding that on, pal." Ry pushed down his shirtsleeves. "Besides, it's about time I got cleaned up so I can be ready when the guests start checking in."

Dylan grumbled in protest but set the tool aside.

I pointed toward the sidewalk leading away from the carport. "Use the back door of the museum, wash up, then go find Granny and see if there's anything you can do for her, okay, swee—son—um, pal?"

Dylan groaned but instead of reminding me of the list, he looked at Ry. "What did I tell you?"

"Girls." Ry shook his head.

Dylan's whole face lit up and I knew the boy had made a new friend. A short-term, not-going-to-let-a-thing-like-loyalty-stand-in-the-way-of-progress kind of friend, but the boy didn't know that yet.

Deep in my heart, as I watched him trot up the sidewalk to the museum, I didn't fully believe it either.

Chapter 8

Whatever my doubts about Ry, Dylan and the future, I held my tongue and stood my ground there in the cluttered carport.

"Hey, pal?" Ry leaned back to call out to my son's retreating back. "After you get cleaned up, will you find Sugar Anne and tell her I need her at home?"

"Home?" I hadn't thought the man could make my pulse pick up any faster than it was, but his calling anything in town "home" sure did it. I wonder, does that mean that maybe somewhere, deep down, I still think that dreams can come true?

Or maybe I'm just easily excitable these days.

I walked slowly to the Starliner's side, my head bent and my arms loosely folded over my chest—for effect mostly, but also because I didn't trust myself not to look like a puppy hoping for a biscuit around Ry. Casual, all cool-like, I leaned my backside against the closed car door and waited.

Ry shifted his shoulders in his rumpled cotton shirt. He

made a go at tucking in his shirttail, which had not actually worked itself completely out of his jeans. When he finally met my unwavering gaze, he held his hands out. "What?"

"Don't play innocent with me, mister."

"Believe me, acting innocent is the last thing on my mind when you're around, Miss Jolie." He said my name with that honey-dipped accent, low, long and drawn out just for the pleasure of the words in his mouth.

Disarmed but not disoriented, I held my ground. "You called the South Winds home."

His posture stiffened. "It's just an expression."

"*Home.*" I placed my hands on the door behind me and crossed my legs at the ankle. "Admit it, this place is starting to have an influence on you."

"Not the place." He moved forward. "*You.*"

Beyond this spot the glare of the clouded sky gave the familiar settings a depth they did not have in full sunlight. Alone with him in the shadowy, cluttered carport, I noticed that Ry's hard, lean body radiated the power and desire that he kept beneath the surface when others were around. I could never quite escape that potent mix of the forbidden and the fascinating.

"Me?" I whispered, touching my fingertips to the warm skin showing above my neckline. "What kind of influence could I have had? I've hardly seen you this week."

"You have no idea how much and how often you have *influenced* me, Jolie." He inched closer, until he anchored his feet on either side of mine. His jeans rasped against my jeans. His shirt brushed my sweater. "In my thoughts, in my dreams."

Heaven help me, I knew those thoughts, those dreams.

"In my arms when you kissed me, not to mention all

those years ago when, for the briefest and sweetest moment I touched you like this."

He fit one hand to the small of my back. His penetrating gaze sank deeper and deeper into my eyes. His strong fingers became so gentle that they seemed to whisper over my body under my sweater. The hardness of his muscles played counterpoint to the tenderness of his touch. It took no effort at all for him to push his way beneath my bra, and then his large rough palm cupped my naked breast.

Caught somewhere between panic and paradise, I opened my mouth to respond but no sound came.

He kissed me.

Just barely.

On my collarbone.

In the hollow of my throat.

Behind my ear.

At my temple.

Then he pressed his cheek to my hair, and he used his thumb to tease my already-taut nipple.

I leaned harder against the car for support.

He moved the hand on my back lower and with a well-timed push of his hips against mine, nudged me up onto the edge of the convertible's windowless door.

I gasped as my feet left the ground.

He pressed into me and held me in place with one hand, now slid under my thigh, coaxing me to raise my legs until I was straddling his body. He kissed my cheek, my lips, lightly. Then as he fit us together, as closely as two fully clothed people could, he kissed me hard and deep, his tongue searching and sensual.

I curled my fingers against his tight back and wrapped my legs around him.

"Ever make love in the backseat of a classic convertible, Jolie?"

"No." I moaned softly.

"Ever think about it?" He had worked my bra up with one sweep of his hand, my sweater lifted to expose one naked breast.

I should have been shocked back to my senses, but obviously I didn't have one bit of sense left. I looked him straight in the eye and all but purred like some sex-deranged female villainess on the old *Batman* TV series, "I've never had sex in any car before, but if I were ever going to do it, it would have to be in the Starliner."

He kissed my throat.

One word, one movement from me and we would be in the backseat of the Starliner, going at each other like the yearning kids we once were.

"With you," I murmured against the back of his neck.

"Now?" He eased his head up until he looked into my eyes.

I could see the beginning of the five-o'clock shadow on his jaw and that his pupils had grown big and black as if to completely drink me in. I felt heady yet calm, powerful, sexual, silly and sweet, entirely vulnerable but totally in command all at once.

Just as I had felt all those years ago, a young girl in my first bikini and done-up red hair climbing onto the South Winds diving board with nothing on my mind but making Ry O'Malley notice me.

"Now," he said, no longer making it a question. "No tomorrows, no yesterdays. Just you and me doing what we both have wanted for so very long. Here and now."

I dropped my head back, feeling the mental spring of the board beneath me. One step, one fearless upward leap and . . .

He opened the door and started to lower me over into the seat.

I opened my eyes, determined not to miss a single thing.

The tin roof of my granny's garage filled my view. My granny's garage? What the hell was wrong with me?

I just about went through that roof, clawing my way upright. "Oh my gosh! Not now, Ry. Not *here*!"

I would have thrown us both to the concrete floor but Ry stepped backward, still supporting me, and helped me to my feet.

I clutched at his arm, not out of anger but like a drowning woman desperate for air. "What did we almost do?"

"For once in both our lives, Jolie, we *almost* did what we both actually wanted to do." He pressed his thumb and forefinger against the bridge of his nose.

I could feel his body heat. It competed with the ice-cold anxiety rising within me.

The anxiety won.

I pushed at his chest, trying to put space between us.

He angled his body away from me. "We almost did what *we* wanted instead of what everyone expects us to do."

"If everyone expects us to act like mature, rational people who don't put our own momentary pleasures above what's best and what's right, how is it a bad thing that we live up to that expectation?"

He grunted something I could not understand, then

sighed and looked back at me over one shoulder. "You still going to wash my hair for me, Miss Jolie?"

He said it the way he'd address an old-maid school-teacher who had just admonished him to sit up and act right, mocking but with all his best manners.

I shook my head. I tried to clear my throat. An untamed red curl flicked in front of my eyes. "I will lend you my best shampoo, though. I can bring it over to you in a few minutes."

"So, you really are sending me home alone?" He turned to face me again. His cool fingertips glided over my heated cheek before he brushed back the stray wisp and tucked it behind my ear.

"Oh, great, now I need to wash the grease from my hair, too." And everywhere else those amazing hands had touched.

"You lend me your shampoo, I'll let you borrow my shower." He slowly grazed my lower lip with one knuckle.

"Ry, don't start again. I can't."

"But you *want* to."

"Nothing good could come of it."

"Oh, believe me, Jolie, yes it could."

"Let me rephrase that. Nothing lasting could come of it."

He did not argue.

"It just doesn't make any sense for us to let our hormones rule our decisions at this point. We want each other, sure, but what we both want in the long run is so very different." So different that even now, with my head still spinning, fear crept into my senses. Nothing about this was like me, and the very fact that I could act so out of character threatened everything I held dear. If I could change so quickly and for such a fleeting thing as a few moments of pleasure, then everything could change forever.

And I could not stop it.

I tried to act cool and unaffected by neither his touch nor my own responses. I managed an awkward shrug and batted my eyes a bit too obviously. "Why set ourselves up for more problems?"

"But you have fantasized about the two of us now and then, right?"

"Now and then." *And then again . . . and again.* "But it has to stay that way, Ry, a fantasy."

"Yeah." He stroked the side of my neck, then closed his fingers around a strand of my once perfectly coiffed hair. "I've heard it said that a person shouldn't get their hopes up too much because real life hardly ever measures up to the fantasy."

I pursed my lips to tell him how much I regretted that Dylan had taken that particular piece of my personal philosophy so much to heart. Before I could think of a way to do that without confessing I'd been spying on them, the back door of the auto museum creaked open, then slammed shut with a *wham*.

I gasped and put my hand to my chest. My bra was still pushed up and it peeked above the neckline of my stretched-out sweater.

Without my asking for his help, Ry moved in front of me to give me a chance to get myself together.

"It's Dylan," he told me. "Hurry up."

"Ry! Ry!" The boy's arms and legs flailed as he sprinted down the walkway toward the dim carport.

"Slow down, pal, you'll trip and bust your chin open." He was trying to buy me time and I knew it.

Despite all he said about expectations and doing what

we wanted, at the very core of his being, Ry was a hell of a lot more decent and dependable than even he would admit.

I slid my hand up under my sweater and snatched my wayward bra, yanking it back into place as gracefully as one could in those circumstances. Nothing like going from wanting to boink the man for all he's worth to having a moment of clarity when I actually understood his true and constant value as a person.

Dylan's shoes slapped to a halt. He puffed, then started to walk the last few feet, saying, "Granny Missus said I'd better come tell you before the shit really hits the fan."

"Dylan!" Everything in place, including my motherly indignation, I stepped from behind the protection of Ry's body. "Watch your language!"

"It's not my language. It's Granny's." He batted his eyes in that oh-so-innocent way that told me he knew he'd gotten away with it on a technicality.

Ry held up his hand. "Language is not the issue here, you two. What do you need to tell me, Dylan? Has something happened at the motel?"

"No, it's Sugar Anne."

"Sugar Anne?" His broad back went completely rigid. "Is she hurt?"

"I don't know. No one can find her."

"What?"

"That's what I'm supposed to tell you. Granny Missus sent Sugar Anne to make a deposit at the bank an hour and a half ago. It's only a twenty-minute walk, but Sugar Anne hasn't come back yet."

Chapter 9

"An hour and a half?" Ry spoke as he walked fast and yet without any indication of where he was headed.

"Dylan, sweetie, go ask Granny Missus if she called the bank to see if Sugar Anne ever got there." I followed behind Ry while pointing toward the back of my grandmother's house to underscore my directions.

Ry pulled up short and stood stock-still. "If she ever got there?"

I skidded quickly to a halt and had to press one hand against his backside to keep from colliding with him. "Warn me if you're going to do that, will you?"

"I could ask the same of you, lady," he said too sharply, nailing me with a glare over his shoulder.

My hand flitted upward to Ry's lower back, but I spoke directly to my son. "Go on, sweetie, time's a wastin'."

Dylan opened his mouth, an argument brewing in his dark eyes.

I motioned toward the door. "Now."

The boy turned and took off.

"I only thought to ask if she'd gone to the bank yet because if she'd made the deposit, then she could easily have just gone on back to the motel afterward," I said all too matter-of-factly.

"I should never have let this happen. And I don't need you standing there, the picture of the perfect parent, the perfect grandchild, the perfect . . ." His gaze drifted downward. "Look, I've gotten distracted enough already without you sticking your . . . two cents in, okay?"

I tugged at my neckline.

He glanced at the carport, the highway, anyplace but at me. "Look, I feel guilty enough without everyone mixing in."

"Why would you feel guilty?"

"I don't have time to count all the reasons for you." A quiet power filled his deep voice. "The divorce."

"I can relate to that one."

"Not having been a better example to her when it came to dealing with my family."

"That one too."

The October air fairly crackled around us. Or maybe that was the tension of the two of us standing there, close in the physical sense, coming from the same place regarding regrets for our children, and yet in every other way, worlds apart.

A red pickup, its bed piled with produce, kids and a hound dog with his ears flapping lumbered past us down the highway and turned into the Flea Market lot.

"And for not . . . I don't know, making her needs my first priority. That butchered-up barber routine she pulled should have made me realize how unhappy she was to be dragged here."

I groaned and shook my head in total disbelief. "How can a man get to be as old as you are and know so little about women?"

His expression went cold. "I'm talking about a young *girl's* reaction to what she saw as an impossible situation."

"You are talking about a young *woman*, Ry."

His chilly attitude all but iced over completely when I called his seventeen-year-old a woman.

I didn't care. "We're talking about a young woman whom you have raised to be trustworthy and to make good choices, right?"

"Well, *mostly* good choices," he tossed in.

"All right then, let's say you've raised her to make her *own* choices."

"I'd go with that."

"So, first let's establish that it's not time to get frantic over a soon-to-be legal adult being—let's see, subtract the time to walk to the bank and back"—I wiggled my fingers and made a quick calculation considering things like how slow a teen might walk and how chatty the teller might be—"forty minutes late."

"I'm not frantic. But I am concerned."

"And guilt ridden," I reminded him, because I like to be helpful like that whenever I can.

"And guilty." He exhaled between clenched teeth.

"And except for the concerned part, you have no reason to be." I had a bigger point to make here and he needed to hear it.

"Sugar Anne's shaved head says otherwise."

"That? Let me tell you a little something, O'Malley. That was nothing more than your daughter finding the quickest, surest way of grabbing your attention. And as far as I can see, it worked." I cocked my hip and gave my head a shake. My hair did not move. For the first time ever, I found that an unsatisfactory response. Still, I pressed on. "You gave her your attention. You responded in just the right way."

He let out a hard, cheerless, "Ha!"

"I mean it."

"Okay. Okay, then, if my response was so terrific . . ." He held his hands out, open, and made a point of looking toward the highway. "Then where in hell is she? If she wants my attention, then why isn't she here, so I can give it to her?"

"From what I gathered by that pious little speech you may recall delivering to me, you brought Sugar Anne here to teach her about independence." *"Ha!" your own self, Mr. O'Malley!*

He crossed his arms. "Yeah, so . . ."

"So?" Was he really this dense or was he so upset about Sugar Anne's stunt that he couldn't think straight? "So, right now she's pushing you to see if you really meant it. She's flexing her independence muscles a little."

He slowly rubbed the back of his neck. "Could it be that simple?"

"Take it from a daughter who has wanted to push the limits all my life but never dared try it."

"You don't have to tell me. I know firsthand how you shy away from anything that might hurt your family." He held his hand up. "No matter how much you want something."

The man did not have to be pawing me in the privacy of

a carport to make me feel positively exposed before him. I pressed my lips together and pretended to shrug off his assessment.

"But not everyone is like that, Jolie."

"Well, then believe me when I speak from years as a hairdresser and woman who places a tiny bit of importance on my own hairstyle." I pushed and patted at my 'do, secretly hoping to loosen that sucker up a little, but with no success.

"Okay, I'm listening."

I dropped my hand from my hair and planted my feet firmly as I could on the parking lot's buckled asphalt. "What a woman thinks might be one of the world's greatest mysteries."

"I'm with ya."

"What she says is almost always open to interpretation."

"Well, amen and *amen* to that."

"But what she does with her hair?" I snapped my fingers to add a little drama. "What a woman does with her hair is almost always about making somebody sit up and take notice."

He seemed to take a moment to consider it.

Another loaded-down truck went bumping down the highway, followed by a minivan, then a yellow blur of a sports car ignoring the speed limit signs.

I smiled at Ry to try to encourage him to come around to my way of thinking.

The smile he gave back looked weaker than his grandfather's cheap-ass watered-down coffee at the All Day Buffet. "I don't doubt that what you're saying is true for you, Jolie."

"But not for your daughter?"

"My daughter!" He balled his hand into a fist. "Damn it, Jolie, how do you do that to me?"

"Do what?"

"Make me forget everything that matters to me."

She whispered, "I do?"

"Haven't you noticed?"

"Maybe I've been too busy trying to avoid the same fate where you're concerned to notice anything."

"One minute lost in your eyes and I tossed out my plans to get in and out of Verbena without complications."

"*I* looked for reasons to trust you when I swore I never would." I swept my fingertip over my lips.

"I totally ignored my promise to myself not to get close enough to anyone that I might let them take advantage of my obliging nature."

"I find myself saying and doing things I'd never even thought of before you got here."

"It's like I can't stay focused on what I tell myself I must do and who I have to be when you are anywhere near me." He started to touch me, then let his hand fall to his side. "And by near me I don't *just* mean writhing under me in some stolen moment. Simply being in this same town with you has me totally off kilter, Jolie."

"Oh, my word," I murmured. "You could be talking about me and how I act around you. That's why I couldn't go through with . . . you know."

"Yeah. I know." He lowered his chin but did not take his eyes from mine.

"You have way too much effect on me, too, Ry." Waves of emotions surged beneath the surface as I put my hands to my cheeks and spoke with my eyes cast slightly down.

"Your coming here has affected the way I see this place. You've made me question my life and my choices. That's something I never did before."

"Then maybe the smartest thing for us to do is to stay completely away from each other." He turned and headed out toward the highway. "Don't bother following me. I have to go and find my daughter by myself."

I followed him anyway. "Nobody accomplishes anything around here by themselves."

"This is *my* problem. *I* will deal with it."

"Sugar Anne is almost an adult, Ry, and she's only gone missing a short time. It's not like you took your eyes off a toddler in the middle of Highway 612."

"Maybe a toddler would be safer in the middle of Highway 612 than an angry teenager with access to a town filling up with travelers."

Tires crunching in the gravel lots, doors slamming shut and the muted voices of so many strangers gathering at the Trav' O' Tel and the nearby car museum suddenly sounded deafening.

He turned to me, his eyes grave. "Jolie, she could hitch a ride to God only knows where with the devil only knows who."

"Surely she's smarter than to try that, isn't she?"

"You said it yourself, she's nearly grown. She thinks she knows . . . well, like every seventeen-year-old, she thinks she knows everything. Or at least a damned site more than her bumbling father."

When we were clear of my family's property, Ry headed toward the end of the parking lot and the highway that lay beyond it, with me trying to keep up. He fixed his gaze across the way on the All Day Buffet and beyond to the Every Second Saturday Flea Market barn. "This will be all my fault. I fell back into my old habits, trying to please others, when I should be just looking out for myself and my daughter."

"Maybe if we—"

"There is no 'we' here, Jolie." He whirled around long enough to command me to stand still. "Can't you get that through that helmet of hairspray on your head? *I've* got to find her."

"Helmet?" My fingers sank knuckle deep in my flawless red locks.

Ry moved on before I regained my senses and could call his bluff.

"Mama?" Dylan's voice reached us though we no longer stood where we could see him. "The bank says they got the money an hour ago."

"Thanks, Dylan." My heels kicked up the finely chipped gravel behind me faster and faster to catch up to Ry. "See? She made the deposit."

"I don't give a rat's ass about the deposit." He pushed on around a station wagon hitched to a trailer with a dirty tarp thrown over some large woodcarvings.

"But now we know where she was."

"An hour ago. That doesn't tell me where my child is now."

"She's on foot in Verbena. How far away could she have gotten?" I rushed around in front of him, planted my feet firmly and flattened my palm square in the middle of his chest. "Before you call out the CIA, FBI and phone the sheriff's office in Mayberry and tell Barney to put the lone bullet in his gun, maybe we—maybe *you*—should just check over at the South Winds."

"Yeah, that's a good idea." He put his hand on top of mine and nodded his thanks. "It would be just like her to have decided she'd had it with hearing old stories and helping out and just to go to her room, shut the door and zone out."

I squeezed his hand and moved aside. "Bless her heart, the little dear probably never gave a thought that people would worry about her."

"Bullshit, Jolie, blessing Sugar Anne's heart had nothing to do with that remark."

"I didn't mean anything by it."

"You meant that she's *my* daughter. She's not a Hadley, so she must be some kind of thoughtless jerk."

I shut my eyes and sighed.

"Well, at least you didn't try to deny it."

I held my hand up. "Just go across the street, Ry. I have to get back to the salon, but I will tell everyone there to be on the lookout for your daughter."

"You just can't wait to make my child the subject of gossip at your hillbilly big-hair boutique, can you?"

"Now who's slinging bullshit?" My body went rigid. He could insult my town. He could make cracks about my family. But damn it, I would not stand there and let him ridicule my hair salon! "Don't you ever make fun of my work or my hair again, got that?"

"Jolie, I wasn't talking about you. I was talking about the women over there who are going to grab this story and—"

"And find your daughter."

"What?"

"Face it, Ry, she is a nigh-onto-baldheaded girl, who spent most of the day meeting the old guard of Logie County at the side of none other than Granny Missus Hadley—she's a smart-mouthed O'Malley skulking around Verbena. A town so small, need I remind you, that I'd wager at least five people have already called my grandmother to ask her if she knows two crazy people are standing out in front of the A. E. Hadley Auto Museum hollering at each other!"

As if on cue, a white van pulled into the parking lot of the South Winds and came to a halt beside the empty pool. A tall woman got out and waved her arm with all the enthusiasm of a castaway signaling a rescue plane.

"That's the lady preacher from the Methodist church," I said, my body and voice as tight as a tripwire. Still, I smiled brightly and waved back. "She did your grandfather's memorial service."

Ry swore under his breath. "Think one of those five people you suspect have called your grandmother and asked for an emergency prayer intervention on our behalf?"

"Lord a'mercy, I hope not!"

Across the way, the minister lowered her hand, moved aside and pointed toward the van.

"Do you think?" I crooked my neck low and noticed something barely poking above the van's window.

"I don't think it, I'd know that sullen, listless lump of a passenger anywhere."

"What did I tell you?" I waved again to let her know we understood. "It worked out fine."

"Of course it did, and to top it off the woman who did old Howdy's funeral has brought my prodigal child back."

Ry made a half-hearted attempt at waving to the woman, too. "Because everything in Verbena is always connected."

"Why is it such a bad thing for you to have ties to other people?"

"It's not." He shook his head and flexed his hands. "Is this where I say I'm wrong?"

"No, this is where you say thank you."

"Thank you, Jolie."

"Don't thank me, thank the lady minister."

A cumbersome RV came up the highway toward us, followed by two cars and a small bus. We waited for them all to pass before we could cross over.

"And in a way I need to thank the entire town for being the kind of place where this would happen."

"You're already doing that by opening the motel and buffet for one last weekend."

"But you wish it were a lot longer, don't you?"

I tipped my head back and gazed at the diving figure on top of the sign. "*Do* I wish it were a lot longer?"

He leaned down to murmur into my ear. "That's not a question I've ever had to ask a woman before, don't make me say it again."

I laughed.

"Well?"

"I'm thinking."

"You're kidding."

"No. I'm wondering if maybe I've been wrong in all this. Maybe the only thing—and the very best thing—I can do now is to just finally let go of it all and join the rest of Verbena in bidding farewell to the South Winds once and for all."

Chapter 10

"You're saying you *want* me to tear the South Winds down?"

"To the ground. Demolish it. Leave no trace." I flung my arm out in order to look sure and bold and brave and . . . everything I certainly did not feel.

My eyes glued to the figure of Esther poised up there on the edge of what had once been a safe, unchanging world, I raised my chin and moved on.

"I don't believe a word I heard."

"That only seems right. I can hardly believe that I said it." My feet hit the ground with hard determination. "But I did say it and that's that. End of discussion."

"Watch out!" The lady preacher held both hands up.

With the warning still hanging in the tingling air of the autumn afternoon, I swung my whole attention to Sugar Anne, fearing the young woman had tried something outrageous. Then I heard the hum of tires.

Before I could so much as turn my head, strong arms encircled my waist. I gasped. My feet slipped from under me. I was pulled backward. Suddenly my shoulders, back, behind and thighs fit inch by inch to the unyielding hardness of Ry's body.

"It's okay," he said. "I've got you."

A car horn blared.

In the blur of its passing I squinted to try to catch a glimpse of the driver. Three kids pressed their noses to the windows. Two waved at me and the third stuck out this tongue and gave me a one-fingered salute.

I blinked. I looked down to see the faded center line barely a foot away from the toe of Ry's boot.

"I have this to say for you, Jolie. When you want to make a point you don't go in for subtlety."

"Very funny, now put me down!"

"That was awestruck praise, darling, not a putdown." He laughed.

I pushed against this arm. "Let go of me."

He cinched me up higher against his chest and leaned forward to look down the road. My hair fell forward over my eyes. I swore and wriggled to free myself.

"Nope. Not letting you down until I have that lady preacher nearby to keep you on the straight and narrow. If you recall the last time I saved your pretty ass I paid for it dearly."

"Saved my . . . ? You did no such thing, and frankly, with that kind of talk, you are the one who needs a good preaching to put you back on the narrow path."

"Narrow path? Up until a few seconds ago I'd have called that *your* undeniable domain. But now . . ." He pulled back to wait for an oncoming car to pass. "But now I have to ask, what the hell has gotten into you, Jolie? Why the sudden change of heart?"

Your coming here has affected the way I see this place. You've made me question my life and my choices, something I never did before. I gritted my teeth behind my sealed lips. How could I make him understand my point of view? I hardly understood it myself, except that I knew that after my actions today, every day that Ry remained in town I would change a little. My morals, my expectations, the way I saw my family—his presence had affected them all. Hell, he even made me think twice about my hairstyle.

If that wasn't a sign that I needed to do something to stave off his influence, nothing was.

Since the day he'd appeared here, people had told me I had to face the inevitable. So face it I would, but on my terms. I could fight him, but I could not win. I had always known that. But now I also understood that trying to prolong the battle was taking too high a toll.

Perhaps this was my turning point. My leap of faith. I had taken his arrival here as a sign that I must take action.

And take action I would—by finding the courage to let go.

Esther might have chosen something more showy, more awe-inspiring. But for a hairdresser too cautious to put highlights in her own hair it would have to do.

Ry gave a carefree wave as the next car approached, as if to say, "Hey, don't worry, this is how we act every day around here, y'all."

The carload of people stared opened-mouthed at us.

"Just playing out another chapter in the Hadley/ O'Malley feud, folks," he said, though they clearly could not hear him. "Next show in an hour. Bring your safety goggles and binoculars, because there may be pyrotechnics."

"You're promising fireworks? Just what do you have planned, O'Malley?"

"I've given up planning where you're concerned." He lowered his head so that he spoke against the exposed side of my neck.

I shivered.

"But given our encounters to date, it seems safe enough to assume that whenever we are together, there will be sparks flying."

I shut my eyes and fought to ignore the sensation of his chest to my shoulders, his hips pushed hard against my backside. The warmth of him penetrated my clothing as the essence of him—his masculinity, his unerring instinct to protect others despite his resolve to not get involved, and his underlying, undying decency as a human being—sank into my soul.

"Now, why don't you tell me why you're suddenly so hot—"

I tensed, feeling totally exposed to him and liking it a little too much.

"—to see me follow through with demolishing the South Winds?" he finished.

How could I make him see that I had to let go of the old landmark rather than risk losing any more of myself? How could I find it in myself to admit that to a man, even as his very touch threw my whole world off balance? That he frightened me so much I'd give up the fight just for the chance to scramble back to my safe little comfort zone again?

I could hear car doors opening and shutting in the museum parking lot, gravel crunching underfoot.

Across the way, someone with her hair in curlers and a plastic cape still around her neck had come out to stand on the porch of the Combin' Holiday.

Any second now Granny Missus would emerge from the museum and fireworks would be the least of my worries. Suddenly my building awareness of Ry drained from my body.

"Well?"

I took a deep breath and glanced upward.

"Jolie?"

"Don't you need to go see about your daughter?" Better to make this about him again than to stand in the middle of Highway 612 and confess my reasons for wanting him out of town as soon as possible.

"Yes, actually." He set my feet to the ground but hesitated a moment with his arms still around me. "You're right. Of course. I do."

"I thought so."

He released his hold but did not move away.

I pulled away from him so fast that it stretched my sweater all the way off one shoulder. I stopped to fix it, taking the opportunity to steal a peek at the observers on both sides of the highway.

I had made the right decision. I had to get as far away as possible from Ry O'Malley and this unwelcome sway he had over me. I had to stay away from him. I could not dillydally and I could not risk letting him persuade me again. Maybe I could go and spend some time with my mother until the unpleasantness passed. Until the South Winds and Ry O'Malley were just footnotes in local history.

The unabashed interest aimed my way from everyone around us only emphasized the need for me to escape.

I pulled my sweater into place, then smoothed it down. No doubt everyone watching wondered what I would do next. If I ran back to the Hadley part of the street and then took off to visit my Mama the next day, the gossip would quickly grow so wild you could write a country song about it.

"All right then, let's go on across the street, and I'll introduce you to the Methodist minister." I looked both ways, hoping I gave off an air of grace and good manners. And pride. Hadley pride.

Ry made no pretense of checking for oncoming cars. He did not move and he never took his eyes off me. "You don't really have to go with me."

"Like fire I don't." I smiled at the lady preacher and held up my hand. "These onlookers would love to have had another story of how an O'Malley had made another member of my family look a perfect fool. Pardon me if I don't hand that to anyone on a platter."

"I can appreciate your not wanting to make a scene, Jolie." He chuckled.

I bristled. "Then let's go."

"Thanks, but I'd rather handle this on my own, if you don't mind."

"Oh, but I do mind. I've told you I won't stand in your way as you destroy that precious part of my childhood, endanger my town's future and threaten my financial and emotional security." I turned on him, my lips strained in a smile so sweet it could have drawn bees. "The least you can do is quit your bitchin', slap that shit-eating grin off your face, get your raggedy old ass in gear and allow me to showcase my impeccable civility by presenting you to our lovely lady minister."

"Yes, ma'am."

Chapter 11

"Thank you for bringing my daughter home. . . . Um, I know you told us to call you by your first name, Lauren, but are you sure I can't tack on a 'Reverend' or a 'Pastor'?" Ry held the door of the Trav' O' Tel's living quarters open.

He'd started to settle down in the lobby, but Sugar Anne had pushed her way past and thrown herself down on the sofa.

I, for one, appreciated the child's directness and ability to wrest control of the situation from her hardheaded daddy. And not just because I'd never seen the interior of the O'Malley home close up either—though it gave me more of a thrill than an emotionally mature woman should have felt. Like suddenly I'd become a secret agent infiltrating the enemy home camp.

Or maybe the excitement came from finding myself surrounded by things from Ry's family, from his past. Now, that thought scared me more than thrilled me and should have had me running for the door. But I dutifully plodded along behind the others and as I stepped fully into the room, I was glad I did.

"I'm not one for formalities, Ry." The tall woman minister with short salt-and-pepper hair strode into the musty-smelling living room. "If you hang around Verbena very long you discover that people don't have much use for titles. They show their respect with common courtesy and uncommon kindness."

"And you certainly showed both to Sugar Anne today, and I really do thank you for seeing her safely home." He remained standing.

His shoulders looked wider than before contrasted against the outdated aquamarine-and-blue-flocked wallpaper. Among the décor, which seemed untouched by time or human contact since probably the early 1960s, the man appeared oddly at home.

I could picture him having lived here forever. Living here forevermore. That made it very hard to force myself to remember that this image was a once-in-a-lifetime deal.

Sorrel Wyatt had informed him when we all walked in together that she'd already given out the keys to rooms 2 and 6 and marked four slots as filled on the chart of the RV parking lot. Since he'd arranged not to take any money from guests this weekend, the check-in process did not demand he oversee it personally. But this last hurrah was his tribute to his grandfather and I could see he was anxious to be as big a part of it as possible.

Fine. Let him go. Me, I wanted to linger a moment to take in the surroundings for the first and last time ever.

I also picked up that he wanted to get his daughter alone. As a daughter myself, I felt a little protective of the girl, though. So I had my own reasons for staying put despite my earlier misgivings.

"Don't let me keep you ladies." He employed one of the South's oldest accepted phrases for shooing people away. "I have everything under control here."

"Thank you so much for not embarrassing me outside, Lauren." I anchored my feet in the doorway, my arms crossed. "I can't believe you've lived here almost a year and I hadn't learned your first name."

"Why should you, Jolie? You don't go to my church. I don't come into your salon." She raked her fingers through her coarse hair and sat down in one of the autumn-toned wingback chairs.

"The way people love to talk in this town, I'd have thought you'd know her name, her life story—the Sunday-school-worthy *and* tabloid versions—and what's on her list of things to do *instead* of hanging around here." Ry placed both hands on the back of the other wingback. "And vice versa."

I met his broad and blatant hint with wide-eyed inno-cence and a bald-faced lie. "Oh, Verbena isn't that bad about gossip."

"But they do love a good story to share on the front porch or in the church parking lot, that's for sure." The minister wiggled her eyebrows at Sugar Anne. "So the smart ones find a way to keep from drawing too much attention to themselves."

"I wouldn't stand there and take that if I were you, Jolie." Ry stood straight. "I won't swear to it but I think she just called us a couple of dummies."

"She couldn't have meant me." I placed my hand over

my heart with no intention of leaving in my demeanor. "I've lived my whole life by the principle of H-S-S-D-B-O."

Ry scowled. "Hissedba?"

"Hear no evil, see no evil, speak no evil," I said, counting them on my fingers. "But if you just can't help yourself— *don't be obvious.*"

He scoffed. "And running into the middle of the highway to stop traffic on the day before Flea Market wasn't obvious?"

I put my hands over my ears to show I would not hear his evil teasing, then turned to address the minister. "All of us walking in here like a bunch of old pals probably went a long way toward tamping down the gossip, though, don't you think?"

"About as much as spit on a forest fire." Lauren grinned, crossed her legs and wove her hands together in her lap. "But anything to help."

"I guess we've accomplished all we can, then." I sighed.

That was that. Done all I could. No real reason to stay here now. My heart sank.

I took one long look around the room, then faced Ry. "I won't overstay my welcome. We won't be busy again until tomorrow morning, but I really ought to get back to the salon."

Ry sighed. "You don't have to rush off."

I blinked at him.

He smiled. "But if you feel you have to get going—"

"Oh, no! I'm afraid you can't go just yet." Lauren held her hands up and with her calm proclamation became the center of everyone's attention. "Sugar Anne has something to say that concerns you and your family, Jolie."

"You can tell them," Sugar Anne muttered, her head hanging down.

Not a good sign. I pressed my back to the door frame and held my breath.

Ry squared his shoulders, looked me in the eye, then fixed his attention on his daughter. "If you've done something wrong it's *your* responsibility to own up to it, young lady."

She set her mouth in a hard line, and like the archetype for angry adolescents everywhere, she narrowed her eyes. Still, she had enough of the New Orleans debutante training in her to sound petulant, pouty and above reproach when she asked, "Was it wrong to just want to call my mom?"

"Your *mom*?" He shut his eyes.

Speak of the debutante. I knew nothing about Ry's ex, and the whole thing was simply none of my damned business. But I have to admit my pulse did kick up a notch thinking this conversation might give some insight into that relationship. I leaned in a bit.

"Honey, you can call your mom anytime you want." Ry shook his head. His face betrayed nothing of his thoughts or emotions concerning the first . . . that is, the *former*—I mean, who am I to assume the man will ever have another wife, right?—Mrs. O'Malley. "Why throw the fear of God into me by taking off like that?"

The girl said nothing.

We all watched and waited.

"Sugar Anne?" Ry prodded.

"I just . . ." Sugar Anne looked up at him, her eyes wide with both sorrow and surliness. "I couldn't stand it any longer, okay?"

"Stand *what* any longer?" he asked, his whole body visibly tensing up.

"You made me leave my car in Straffer. You took away my cell phone, cancelled my credit card. Since I've been here I don't even have a dollar to call my own."

Well, I'd have been a bit pissed by those circumstances myself at her age. Though, come to think of it, I did not have any of the things she'd lost *but* a dollar to call my own.

At Sugar Anne's age, I had that dollar or two of my own—and all the love the world could hold from my friends and family. Of the two of us, I'd say I got the better deal growing up.

"Are you saying you didn't sneak off to try to call your mother because you missed her? Or because you wanted to get her advice? But because you wanted your cell phone and credit cards back?" Ry dug his fingertips into the stiff upholstery of the old wingback. "You know how I feel about the family's materialism, Sugar Anne. Please, do not tell me that you scared the hell out of me today over something as meaningless as money. Is that what this is all about?"

"It's about . . ." her lips went thin and a tear trembled above her dark lashes.

Whether she sincerely ached over something or merely meant to manipulate her daddy, the girl had hit her mark. Ry released the back of the chair and stepped toward her.

It was the single biggest step I'd seen him make toward her since they'd arrived. And though it had nothing to do whatsoever with me, my heart swelled to see his willingness to compromise even a little.

"What was I supposed to do?" Sugar Anne sniffled.

"Do?" He bent at the knees to put himself at eye level with his daughter on the couch. "About what, baby?"

"Getting out of this town. Getting away from . . ." She chewed her lip and lowered her chin to her chest. She placed her hands on her head. Chopped-up shocks of her shiny black hair stuck out through her spread fingers.

"She came to the church and asked if she could make a long-distance call." Lauren reached across from her seat and placed her hand on Sugar Anne's wrist. "I told her I could only allow it if it was an emergency, which she said it was."

"An emergency, Sugar Anne? Why? Did you not know how to get back to the South Winds?"

"I wanted to call my friend Dee Dee to see if she could come and pick me up. I knew if I called from here you'd find out who I called right away and come after me."

"Damn straight I would have!"

I cleared my throat.

Ry jerked his head up. "Uh, pardon my language, preacher—um, Pastor . . . Lauren."

The minister dismissed his lapse with a wave and a shake of her head.

"Don't you see?" Sugar Anne drew a shuddering breath, then met her father's gaze. "I had to call a friend. No one in this family would have understood."

You sure don't, Dad. The accusation came in her eyes, not on my lips.

"Besides, I felt so guilty lying to the minister about it being an emergency that before I tried to make the call I promised to pay for it."

See, she's a *good* girl, I wanted to say out loud. Almost

did. And that made me realize that I had better get out before I blurted my way into this private moment. I was the
ultimate outsider, after all. Not just a stranger to them but a
Hadley, unwelcome in this home and certainly in this exchange.

"Um, I really don't feel comfortable intruding on this
family matter, maybe I should just—" I inched backward.

"Wait!" Lauren fished around in the pocket of her jacket,
then pressed a handful of something into Sugar Anne's
limp hand. "Before you leave, Jolie, you should see this."

Sugar Anne's already bleak expression darkened.

Lauren nudged her upper arm. "Go on. Show her."

Sugar Anne pushed up from the couch with her shoulders rounded. She made the short walk toward me in slow,
shuffling steps, then held out her hand and unfurled her
fingers.

"I offered to pay for the call with these."

I peered into her cupped palm and my breath caught
high in my throat. "Grudge money?"

Ry closed in on us to peer down at the fistful of dirty
change. "Looks more like sludge money to me."

I took Sugar Anne gently by the shoulders. "Honey, does
Granny Missus know you have these quarters?"

Ry shut his eyes. "Tell me anything but that you stole
money from Hannah Rose Hadley."

"Borrowed," she whispered.

I shook my head. "Granny Missus would have given you
a bucket of twenty-dollar gold pieces before she'd have
turned loose any of her grudge money."

"I intended to pay it back." Sugar Anne's chin quivered.
"That's the same as borrowing."

"You know better than that." Ry put his hands on his hips. "And what the hell is *grudge money*?"

"Every Flea Market weekend Granny Missus paints a hundred dollars' worth of quarters with a swash of nail polish," Lauren volunteered. "Then she tells everyone who gets one as change in the museum that if they come back and spend those quarters at a Hadley business she'll give them a free soda."

Ry rubbed his temple. "Must cost her a small fortune."

"Not as much as you'd think," Sugar Anne spoke up, her voice just on the verge of breaking. "The old lady worked out a deal to get double discounts from the guy who drives the soda delivery truck."

"How could he afford that?"

I crossed my arms, cocked my hip and tipped my head until a single red curl fell over my forehead. "He afforded it by never giving your grandfather any discounts."

Ry laughed. "I don't blame that vending man one bit. Grandpa used to give him grief about everything."

"Besides, the satisfaction was worth ten times the money she invested. Every quarter Granny Missus got back represented a quarter that didn't make it into one of Howdy's vending machines."

Ry eased his breath out and with it some of the tension around his troubled eyes seemed to ease. "We've got some very twisted roots in our family tree, Jolie. You do recognize that, don't you?"

"It doesn't stop at the roots, Dad." Sugar Anne tipped up her nose at him with the kind of innocent indignation only a seventeen-year-old with half her hair shaved off could muster.

"I still fail to see how all this fits together." That could be because this man and this place and my own befuddled emotions had preoccupied me, I know, but that's the kind of thing a girl keeps to herself. "Why would you take this money, Sugar Anne? Why did you want to run away? And why would Granny Missus have still marked up a bunch of grudge money this weekend?"

"She did it to honor Great Grandpa Howdy's memory. See?" Mascara smudged and nose as red as Rudolph's on that famous foggy night, Sugar Anne still pulled off a regal air as she held up one blackened coin. "She used black nail polish."

"Ah, yes. Trashy cosmetics," Ry muttered. "The ultimate tribute."

Sugar Anne and I both glared at him.

"Believe it or not, Ry, that old woman had a genuine, if somewhat acidic, affection for your grandfather." Lauren laid her head back and chuckled softly.

"*That's* why I had to get out of this town, Daddy."

"You wanted to hightail it out of Verbena with a pocketful of stolen vending machine change because Jolie's Granny Missus didn't totally despise your Great Grandpa Howdy?"

That was the kind of sentence a man didn't often have use for in other parts of the country, I decided, as I tried to sort it out along with Ry.

"I wanted to get out of Verbena because all day I listened to these stories about O'Malleys and about the Hadleys. And I met people who had good and bad to say about both, and then . . ."

"What, baby?" He really seemed to want to understand.

"And then I thought about you tearing down the South Winds and I just couldn't stay to watch you do that. It's just so . . . wrong."

I'm not sure, but I think I swore then. Given the company, I decided to pretend I hadn't and just went on staring at the scene unfolding before my unbelieving eyes.

"You are four months away from becoming a legal adult, getting a job or going back to college, young lady. I can't hang onto the South Winds for someone whose future is so clearly someplace beyond Verbena."

"It's not this crummy motel, Dad. It's the memories. I just wish you could save some of the memories so when the motel is gone the town won't seem so empty."

I groaned and covered my eyes. Full circle and all that. I had tried so hard to make this very point—turned it into a replay of the whole ridiculous rancor between our two families, and just as I was ready to concede . . .

"I . . . I didn't mean to hurt anyone," Sugar Anne pushed her ill-gotten stash toward me.

Ry took a deep breath. "Look, why doesn't everyone who isn't a member of my family go on home or wherever they feel they are needed the most and leave us to sort this out on our own?"

Lauren got up from the chair.

Ry backed away to allow my passage to the hallway out of the living quarters.

I put my hand on Sugar Anne's back.

Then the three of us women closed ranks and shut him out.

"Of course you didn't mean to hurt anyone." I pulled Sugar Anne into a motherly hug, laying my cheek against the young girl's fuzzy head.

"Of course not," Lauren echoed.

The coins jangled as I plucked one out and rubbed my thumb over it. "No one who hasn't suffered through a thousand renditions of the countless stories of all the wrongs done against the Hadleys for three generations could ever hope to grasp the significance of these *stupid* quarters."

"They are intended to bear ill will and I, for one, won't have any part of them." The lady minister spoke with the kind of conviction usually the forte of tent evangelists or wronged Southern belles.

"And thank heavens for that. Because if you didn't have such strong feelings about this worthless grudge money, Sugar Anne might be halfway back to Straffer or who knows where with her friend right now." I stared at the coin in my fingers, then lifted my solemn gaze to Ry. "I think it's a sign."

"A sign? Are you out of your mind? What kind of sign could it possibly be?"

"Only the person that the sign was intended for can interpret what it means," I told him, like I had all the answers. "But given the fact that money was the beginning of the bad blood between our great-grandfathers and the end of your relationship with most of your family and now money has brought your daughter back to you, I'd start there."

He should have told me where to put the quarter and my righteousness along with it.

Instead he stared into his big, open hands.

"Maybe you should do some soul-searching about what role money is playing in your life and how you might use it to set right whatever you can." I spoke softly to convey my empathy and encouragement.

He took a deep breath. The lines in his forehead deepened. The silver in his hair glinted in the low light coming in from the lone window in the room.

I hugged Sugar Anne again and said, "Don't worry, I'll find a way to keep Granny Missus from knowing what you did. But that doesn't mean you get off scot-free. Come over to the salon first thing tomorrow and I'll find some work for you—so you can *earn* your own money."

"Thanks." Sugar Anne actually hugged me back.

Then I hugged the minister and thanked her, too. She said goodbye to Ry and headed into the hallway.

Sugar Anne called out another thanks and ran hellbent up the stairs.

Ry looked at me like he wanted to say something, but really, what did either of us have to add at this point? So I pressed the marked quarter into his palm, nodded goodbye and left him standing there to mull over everything that had just transpired and what it all meant for his family and all our futures.

Chapter 12

A few minutes after 6 P.M. on Sunday it was all over.

The last of the RVs that had parked behind the South Winds pulled onto Highway 612 and headed off. No hangers-on or dawdlers that day.

Sorrel had padlocked the Flea Market's barn door.

Shortly after that, Wyatt had refilled the last to-go cup with coffee and closed up the All Day Breakfast Buffet for the very last time.

Even the diehard old-timers had gone already, leaving only their scrawled farewell messages in colored chalk on the backside of the South Winds.

Grease-stained paper napkins and crumpled sales slips littered the empty parking lot. A plastic grocery sack fluttered like a trapped bird against the chain-link fence. A sad but satisfied quiet had fallen over the lonely strip of highway.

Dylan had informed Ry that Granny Missus cooked up a special dinner after the Flea Market ended, but Jolie had stopped him before he could issue an invitation.

Ry wouldn't have accepted, of course. Not unless Granny Missus had asked him personally, and insisted at least three times that he had to come for supper. But I had wanted to spare him the embarrassment of being singled out as the only person still not welcome to break bread in a Hadley home.

Even Sugar Anne would be sitting down to supper across the street tonight—under the guise of working off some of my penance by helping with the meal. An O'Malley at Granny's table.

It was a wonder that I wished Ry and I could observe together—especially since he would be gone soon and the South Winds and Esther forever gone too, in his wake.

"Hey, y'all!" I held up my hand to Ry and the stranger who had a ladder propped up against the big electric sign looming above the motel's empty pool.

"So, did you write something divinely wicked on the back of my building?" Ry called out.

"You betcha." I waved goodbye to Emma, then slapped chalk dust from my hands onto my black jeans. "Something I wouldn't want my grandmother to read."

"Let's see, too shocking for Granny Missus?" He let out a low whistle. "Must be hot stuff. I'll look for the singed spot in the cinderblock."

I laughed in the way women usually do when the last thing in the world they want to do is laugh.

I reached him in time to watch the workman take the last two steps to the ground. "You the demolition man?"

The fellow spoke to Ry. "Wife?"

"Naw." Ry chuckled. "Busybody."

"Yeah." He nodded like Ry had just given him a complete history of his relationship with me.

"Yeah, you *are* the demolition man?" I shifted my weight and my boot heels crunched and scuffed over the uneven surface of the parking lot. "Have you done this kind of work before? Will there be a lot of dust and mess and rubble left behind when you're through?"

The man shook his head, licked the end of his stubby pencil and began scribbling on a notepad. "I can do 'er."

"Sorry that I was busy seeing guests off and wasn't here to talk to you when you first got here." Ry extended his hand toward the man in brown coveralls. "But I do appreciate you coming by on a Sunday, Mr. . . . ?"

"Don't call me mister." The man neglected to say what Ry should call him, just tipped his head back and frowned. "Yeah, it's doable, all right. May take some time though."

Ry put his hand in his pocket and glanced at me. "I don't have time."

The workman closed one eye and fixed the other on Ry. "You got money?"

I don't know what part coincidence, divine coercion or perhaps a conscious choice on Ry's part played in it, but when he took his hand out of his pocket, Ry held the marked quarter between his thumb and forefinger. He flashed it at me and winked. "Yes."

I smiled in earnest and for one second wished it all meant something—and that that something was something wonderful.

The nub of a pencil scratched harder on the pad. "That'll do then."

"Do what?" Ry asked.

The man pointed one blackened fingernail upward.

Obviously Mr. Don't-call-me-mister was a man of few words.

"Are you saying that money can guarantee the job gets done faster?"

"Not faster, but sooner."

Ry scowled.

"Money has a way of bringing things together, you understand?" the man added.

"What I understand about money is that it just as often tears things apart." Ry slipped the quarter back into his pocket, held my gaze a little too long for my comfort and then turned to the workman again. "But I follow your meaning, if that's what you're asking."

"Well, it brought *us* together and I'm gonna tear this thing apart, so I guess we're both right." He laughed at his joke, but didn't seem to mind—or notice—that Ry and I had not found it particularly funny. "Let me do a little figurin'."

He climbed up the ladder just a few rungs and clucked his tongue, then got down and headed to his truck without further explanation.

Without the workman's weight or Ry holding it in place, the ladder began to list drunkenly to one side.

Ry stepped in and braced the heel of his hand against the closest side to keep it from falling.

"So, what's this all about? Is he a demolition man or what?"

"He's an 'or what'," was all Ry said.

"What are you up to?" My heart raced as I tried to imagine what he had in mind for the old place. I know I'd said I wanted him to tear it down, but suddenly, standing here in the dusk on its last night intact, my convictions wavered. And that allowed a glimmer of hope to creep in. "You're going to do something spectacular, aren't you?"

"I don't know about spectacular." He tilted his head back and looked up. "But Jolie, you of all people should know just how good I am at rescuing damsels in distress."

"You're going to save the South Winds sign," I whispered. "Is that it?"

The salvage man reemerged from the cab of his truck, pad in hand. "Only interested in that figure up top." He never looked up from his calculations.

"I'm saving Esther, Jolie. By paying this man to take her off my hands. It's the best I could do."

"Not the whole sign?" It was like he was talking to me in a language I had not quite mastered. I could make out the gist of what he was saying, but I could not make any real sense of it.

The workman snorted. "No resale potential in that."

"But if you take Esther off, it won't light up anymore." I went into a half crouch to try to make eye contact with the man so he'd look up from his notepad.

He didn't pay any attention.

I turned to Ry, pantomiming as I said softly, "It won't look like Esther is diving anymore."

"Doesn't matter." The man's ruddy face scrunched up and he tilted the notepaper toward the last of the sunlight. "I can only use the standing figure. Once I get it down, it's just a matter of a few minutes with a blowtorch."

I felt slapped. "Blowtorch?"

"A little touch-up paint and it'll be ready to go."

"Go? Go where?"

"I reckon I can split her and sell both sides—you know, to hang on the walls of one o' them seven-bucks-a-burger restaurants?"

I felt like the man had just suggested dissecting my mama and selling her off for parts.

"It's the best offer I had, Jolie." Ry gave my shoulder what I am sure he thought was a reassuring squeeze. "Nobody wants to preserve a motel sign that doesn't even light up anymore."

"It lights up!" My voice cracked.

"The words do. And some of the trim—on good days. But Esther's lights have done nothing but flick a few times and then go off and stay off. It's been like that the whole time I've been here."

"That's nonsense. You just have to know how to get the thing working." I pushed at his chest and slipped away from him. "Go flip the light switch."

"Jolie, it doesn't matter, it's . . ."

"May I use your ladder?"

The man poked the pencil back into his coverall pocket and jabbed his thumb toward Ry. "His ladder."

I didn't ask Ry's permission, just started climbing.

"Jolie, don't. It's not safe." Ry lunged to grab the ladder in order to hold it firm against the sign.

"I used to do it all the time for Howdy." I didn't look down. "You just go flip the sign on."

"There's a bank of light switches inside the motel office," Ry jerked his head in that general direction. "Would you mind?"

"Sure. Gonna write up an estimate while I'm in there, okay?"

"Yeah. Good. And try to pinpoint when you can start and how long it will take, too."

A grunt was his only reply.

"Jolie, be careful up there, you hear?" He started to come up after me but obviously realized he couldn't do that and hold the ladder for my safe return.

If he'd known how many times I'd done this without anyone around at all he wouldn't have been so cautious.

"Wait until the electricity gets humming through this baby, then I'll show you how wrong you are," I called down.

He stood back from the ladder, the better to watch me and be ready if I took a misstep. Though what the hell he thought he could do, I didn't know. But I had to admit his being there for me made me feel . . . safer. Well, not exactly safer, but more . . . not alone. No, that's not it either.

Having Ry O'Malley standing down at the foot of this old sign ready to catch me if I fell made me feel happy. Darn, but I hated that feeling.

I turned sideways and edged carefully along the eight-inch width of the top of the sign, moving toward the side overlooking the highway.

"Jolie, stay put! Just . . . just stay in one place, will you?" He swore and moved along the ground below me like he was following me with an invisible net. "Get back by the ladder, where it's safe."

I waved off his concern and stretched up and out, my face toward the town. "The view up here is too gorgeous to miss. You can't see this view without moving away from the safe spot."

"All right but you've seen the view now, come back. Don't take any unnecessary risks."

I looked down at him, my hands on my hips. "It's official. We *have* had too profound of an effect on each other. You're starting to talk like me and I just said something that was pure Ryman O'Malley."

He motioned for me to do as he'd said.

I shook my head, took one last look, then inched along toward the other end of the sign. My shoe must have caught on the side of the ladder because it suddenly slipped and went crashing to the ground.

Ry jumped aside but his gaze never left me.

"Oh, Ry! You still down there?"

"I'm not going anyplace. Not with you up there on that broken light."

"Esther is not broken. She's just . . . temperamental."

Even as he shouted back, "Takes one to know one," a sudden hum of electricity warmed the tubular lights.

The sign awakened slowly.

The metal vibrated.

Soft halo lamps illuminated the painted background.

Then one flash followed another as the words lit up: SOUTH WINDS in vivid neon orange, the yellow blinking waves that outlined the rim, and finally the promises that had outlasted any other O'Malley's promise I had ever known—good food, good rates, good fun, good folks.

Esther, however, remained dark.

"See?" he called up. "I wouldn't consider letting the man dismantle her if she worked. But right now the only light I see is the last bit of the sunset on your hair."

"I'll remedy that if you'll give me a minute."

"I'll give you 'til the moon rises over Verbena."

I placed a hand on Esther's rounded derriere. "Don't tempt me."

He laughed. "But it won't matter. Those lights are gone. They are never going to . . ."

I held one finger up to command his indulgence.

He snatched up the ladder and propped it against the sign again. He placed one foot on the bottom rung.

"Wait!" I shouted. "Watch and learn."

He tipped his head back. "Won't take my eyes off of you for a second. That should be an education in its own right."

"Oh, ye of little faith." I laced my fingers together and stretched out my arms, a maestro preparing to perform.

Ry shook his head. I knew that not because I could see him well but because I caught the movement of his head in the way the garish light picked up the start of silver at his temples.

I wanted to do this for Esther.

Do it for Verbena.

But most of all for Ry.

Hokey as it sounded, even to a high priestess of hokeyness myself, I wanted him to understand that with a little faith and a willingness to hang on even when things looked dark, old things—old ways—could work. They had value. Change was not the only constant he should count on.

I cleared my throat. I blew on my fingertips with all the finesse of a safecracker ready to unleash his skills.

He leaned in to make sure he did not miss a movement.

I licked my lips.

I took a deep breath.

I spread my extended fingers and looked down to him. "Behold!"

"Be faster," he called back.

I gave a flourish of my hand then hauled off and gave the base of the figure one hard, swift kick.

The glowing shape of a woman with her arms reaching up over her head rose up into the darkening sky. The black slumbering mass of the breathtaking Blue Ridge Mountains behind her made the outline all the more luminous, all the more magical.

My pulse hammered in my ears.

I could hardly swallow.

All my life I had thought something extraordinary was going to happen to me, and suddenly I understood why. Because every day I looked up and saw this image. Every day I had a reminder of who I was and who I wanted to be—who I could be if I ever got the chance.

"It works!" Ry called up.

"I told you, didn't I?" I think my smile must have rivaled the brightness of the diving lady.

"You told me. You showed me. Now, come on down from there, will you? We have to talk."

"Talk?" I hesitated, the fleeting thrill of the moment stopped cold by Ry's request.

My plan to stay away from the man had worked this weekend—though working with Sugar Anne at the salon and hearing the worshipful way she talked about her daddy, learning about their lives in Georgia, about Ry's ex-wife and his career in flying, had kept him in the forefront of my thoughts.

Who was I kidding? If I had sat alone in that salon with the shades pulled and my head in the sink I would still have thought about that man.

I looked at him standing there and then at the glowing image beside me. My heart warmed all over again. He was not my enemy. The past, the bad blood between families—those things stood between us, but Ry was not—had never been—at the seat of my animosity. Until he showed up with a plan to tear down the South Winds, I'd hardly given him—the real man, not the idolized ideal of my youth—a thought. And since he'd come back I could think of little else.

And now he wanted me to come down so that we could talk.

"Jolie? Did you hear me?"

"I heard you. In fact I can hear you just fine. If you want to talk just start right in now. I promise I won't up and walk away."

"Very funny, but I was hoping for something a little more intimate."

"Intimate?" I whispered.

"You know. A good old-fashioned heart-to-heart."

"A good old-fashioned breast-to-chest is more like it. Intimate, my ass, I know what you're up to."

His shoulders shook with laughter I could not hear. "Miss Jolene when you—breast, chest, ass and all—are around, anyone with eyes can see what I'm *up* to. It's so bad I'm thinking of taking to wearing my shirttails untucked."

"Your shirt won't be the only thing that will remain 'untucked,' my friend." I lifted my chin and a cool breeze caught my hair and blew it off my neck. I shivered but went on. "In fact, as far as I'm concerned, you can just go right back into the lobby there and find that nice salvage man and talk to him all you want. Maybe he'll appreciate your tucking sense of humor."

"You have to come down here sometime, you know."

I considered threatening to pull one of those stunts that make the last few seconds of the evening news. *Woman lives in endangered tree for three months. Man breaks world billboard-sitting record to draw attention to cause.*

In the end I merely folded my arms and spoke the truth. "I thought we agreed we should keep our distance from each other."

"If we keep our distance, how will we ever see eye to eye?"

"It's not our eyes I'm worried about, Ry." Every encounter with him had left me more uncertain of the things I had always counted as permanent and everlasting in my life. Knowing that he wanted to try to preserve some part of this place I held precious only made me waver more in my convictions. What good could come of meeting with Ry O'Malley eye to eye and heart to heart?

A flash of his hands on my naked thigh, of both of us stripped of all the game playing and every last scrap of clothing filled my mind. I wet my lips.

Where this one man was concerned, could I find a way to accept his kind of compromise without forever compromising myself?

The wind whipped past, causing only the uppermost part of the sign to wobble. Instinctively I reached out to protect and steady Esther. Even as I did it, I realized I had grabbed onto the icon as a means of steadying something deep within myself.

I inhaled slowly, taking in the very essence of the place I loved so much. I would be all right, no matter what. For a woman standing so high up, I did have my roots in this town and my feet on the ground. Not even Ry O'Malley and whatever transpired between us could change that.

Behind me I heard a door slam. A cautious glance over my shoulder told me that people were arriving for the big after-market meal at my grandmother's house.

I sidled toward the ladder. "I can't stay here now, Ry."

"I didn't really expect you to stay up there, Jolie." The unnatural glow of the electric lights brought out the day's-end shadow along his jaw and made the lines around his eyes appear deeper. His dimples flashed. He seemed to create his own light that chased away the grayness of the moment. "Like I said, I'm all too happy to wait for you to come down to talk to me."

"No . . . I . . ." I tested the soundness of the ladder with the toe of my shoe. "I have to go to my grandmother's or—"

"People will talk."

"They do, you know."

He nodded.

"So, that's it, then?"

"What?"

"You aren't going to hear me out because . . . because people will talk?"

I looked at the figure, then at the lights of Verbena. "What are you going to do about Esther?"

"I don't know."

If he had out-and-out lied just to appease me I'd have known it. And if he had lied, I had to admit as I twisted around to lower myself onto the first rung of the ladder, I'd have known what to do next.

"Will you promise to try to save her? *Really* save her?"

"Will you promise to sit down with me and listen to my side of all this?"

"You suggesting a trade-off?"

"No, I'm asking for a favor."

I climbed onto the ladder and watched the figure shift from standing to diving—diving into the night with nothing to catch her. I sighed. "Okay. We can get together—but not tonight."

"Fine. I'm expecting one last vital part for the Starliner to come in tomorrow and I promised Dylan I'd see if I could put it on. Maybe you can come by and talk to me while I work on the car."

I froze on the ladder. The car? Go with him to the garage where we had almost . . . I swallowed and kept climbing down. "Well, maybe . . ."

He did not move away from the ladder.

I moved downward, step by step, right into the circle of his arms.

He smelled of air-freshened cotton and the last remnants of aftershave. He towered over me and yet I did not feel small. With my body fitting perfectly to his I felt warm and woozy and safe. I felt like the whole world could shift and shake itself silly all around us and I would not feel a thing.

Somewhere, deep in the recesses of reason, I knew the sensation was only wishful thinking and would be temporary at best. Right now I did not care.

He kissed me, not hard but thoroughly, decisively.

I eased my arms around him, my fingers curving to draw him closer even as I arched my back to meet him hip to hip, to press my breasts against the unyielding plane of his chest.

Ry groaned. It was that moment where one of us had to take the kiss a step deeper or back off, move apart and let reality sink in.

He eased me away from him.

"I know I shouldn't have done that, but I—"

"Shh. Don't spoil the moment."

"Too bad we can't preserve that, huh?"

"Like a timeless photograph," I whispered.

"Or like a hairdo sprayed into undentable perfection." He sank his finger into my hair, then took it out.

My hair sprang back into place.

He smiled.

I clenched my teeth for a moment, then laughed. "If we ever needed proof we shouldn't be alone together, that was it."

"You're probably right."

My heart sank a little. "I am. We really don't have any business—"

"Hey, buddy!" The workman bellowing from the lighted doorway of the South Winds' lobby cut me off. "I got them numbers for you, but working or not, I can't salvage anything more than I promised."

Ry's gaze fixed in my eyes as he reached into his jeans pocket and called out to the man across the lot behind us. "If I use some more of that money you said brings things together, do you think I can find someone who will take more of the sign and won't slice up the diver on top?"

The man coughed. Or cursed. I wasn't sure which.

"Well?" Ry asked.

"I reckon you rub enough money on any problem you'll find someone willing to fix it for you."

My heart raced. "Ry? Are you saying . . . ?"

He held up the marked quarter I had left for him to ponder over.

"You believe in signs now?" I asked, dubious.

"Let's just say I find myself uncharacteristically receptive to new ideas and philosophies. More so the longer I stay in Verbena."

My breath stilled high in my chest. I could only mouth the words *Me too*.

He smiled. "Tomorrow then?"

"Tomorrow," I murmured.

"Good."

I slipped away with the light of the sign shining down on me and tried not to think about anything but the impermanent promise I had made . . . "Tomorrow."

Chapter 13

The course of true love never has run smooth, but let me tell you, when you live in a town the size of Verbena, the course of a little trifling lust has its own set of unique speed bumps along the way as well!

I suppose that given my personal slant on things like this, I should have considered my grandmother barging in not thirty seconds after I arrived at the garage to see Ry as some kind of divine guidepost. Well, I didn't.

I saw it for what it was. Pure nosiness. And orneriness. And, much as I hate to admit it, more than a little love and concern on her part toward me and wanting to protect me from getting hurt.

"I never thought I'd see the day!" Granny Missus strolled into the far end of the carport. "An O'Malley working in *my* garage. Devil must be wearing mittens today, boy, I tell ya."

Ry had just begun the few final adjustments on the Starliner. Her craggy voice made him pause.

I narrowed my eyes and tried to send him the mental

message to just let the remark go. *Give a grunt. A nod. Then pretend to be so engrossed in your work that you can't stop and shoot the breeze with the eldest living Hadley.* But years and layers of damned hair spray must have hampered any potential telepathic powers I might have had.

He looked up. "Morning, Mrs. Hadley. Or would you prefer that I call you Granny Missus, ma'am?"

"I don't suppose you'll stick 'round long enough for it to matter what you call me, will you?"

He rubbed a rag over the newly installed part.

I cleared my throat to warn him to leave well enough alone. Shut up. Move on. Not to give Granny an excuse to speak her mind.

Of course that's what she wanted to do, or she wouldn't have come out here. But she would never have initiated a bona fide conversation with this particular man on her own. She needed him to pursue it.

Any gentleman raised to revere his elders, all women, and the insufferably eccentric would have taken up his end of the bargain. It would only have taken a word from him and she'd be off and running at the mouth.

Ry did not rise to the bait. He clenched his teeth and wiped off parts of the engine already so clean they practically sparkled.

"No sir." Granny adjusted the red, white and blue beaded brooch that held her lace-trimmed handkerchief to the breast pocket of her coveralls. "It's an old Hadley saying that it doesn't matter what any O'Malley calls you as long as he calls you long distance."

"An old Hadley family saying?" He stopped polishing and reached into his back pocket.

"Yes, sir," she said, firmly but soft.

He took out his penlight and began to shine it into the machinery's crevices. "Or an old Hadley saying you made up just now?"

She pressed her bright pink lips together.

Ry pretended to examine the battery.

She crept closer and stretched herself up as tall as she could to examine his handiwork under the hood.

He twisted his head around and gave her a look that said he knew she approved of what he'd done with the engine.

She looked away, then watched him again from the corners of her eyes. She wrung her hands. Her gold-toned bracelets clattered on her age-spotted arm.

"You know, Granny, I don't see how Ry could be calling you long distance if you insist on hovering over him all day." Okay, so subtle was not a learned trait among the women of my family. I'd made my point and could take some pride that I hadn't resorted to actually chasing the old snoop back into her house with a stick.

Granny Missus patted the wreath of frothy white hair teased into poodle-cut perfection on her head.

What a woman does with her hair is almost always about making somebody sit up and take notice. My own words came back to haunt me. Even at her age, Granny still used the age-old feminine tricks to try to get what she wanted—just a few seconds of this man's time and attention.

How many times now had Ry's presence in town granted me the opportunity to behave like an ass in order to try to get my own way? I should have kept score.

Granny Missus sighed and started to turn away.

Ry clicked off the penlight and gazed grumpily into the

newly outfitted engine. "What did my grandfather call you?"

Luckily, Ry had better sense than I did—or maybe it was a bigger heart.

The old gal paused, turned slowly, then tipped her nose up, exposing the soft folds under her chin. "A lady would never use that kind of language."

"A lady might not, but how about you?" He double-checked an airtight hose connection by pretending to tug on it.

Her eyes sparkled. Her lips twitched into the briefest of all smiles, then she scowled mightily and barked, "Just like your kinfolk. If manners was moonshine y'all wouldn't have enough to get a goat tipsy."

Her indignant act didn't fool him one minute, of course.

"Yeah, that's true, I reckon. But that doesn't matter to me because—any stories you might have heard about my great uncle Ulysses aside—neither me nor none of my kin ever had much use for drunken farm animals."

She stared at him.

He stared back.

Her grin broke slowly over her face, and when it came into its full force it rivaled the lights of the South Winds' old sign for brightness.

He gave her the double-barreled dimple grin that had melted colder hearts than hers. "I have to compliment you on the work you've done so far on the Starliner. You certainly know your way around an engine."

"Had to learn. Lost Mr. Hadley in 'fifty-seven and had two children to feed."

"Nineteen fifty-seven?" He caressed the gleaming red

fender of the tenderly restored old Ford from that same year. "Must have been a hard time for you. Not many lady mechanics and gas jockeys back then."

"Well, I had some experience. You know us gals filled in at all kinds of jobs for the fellas during the war years."

Yes, he definitely had a bigger heart. Damn him. Why did he have to look so adorable standing there catering to my vain old grandmother?

"Besides, like I said, I didn't have no choice. I had to learn to do it fast, and I had to be the best, too."

"Why the best? Did you have a lot of competitors in Verbena back then?"

"I didn't have no competitors, son, I had your grandfather. I had the O'Malleys breathing down my neck."

"But my grandfather ran the South Winds and the Breakfast Buffet—"

"Did you forget that for the longest time it was just a sorry old greasy spoon? It took a while for folks around here to catch on to the idea of eating breakfast any place but at home."

He smiled. "Yeah, the last summer I worked here was the summer Grandpa made the big changeover."

Granny Missus muttered something under her breath. "In fifty-seven it was just the motel, you know. But when I took over here and put in soda and candy machines, he decided to expand into the restaurant business. He couldn't stand for a person to make a dime off something if he thought he could make a quarter off it—especially after he drove that first person out of business."

"He saw you turn a profit and expanded on your idea. That just seems like good business." While the *s* of *business* still vibrated on his lips, the look on his face said that Ry knew he'd said the wrong thing.

I tensed.

Granny drew herself up. "You don't hardly know anything about the history gone between your family and ours, do you?"

"I know enough." In other words, he did not want to hear some long-winded story featuring his forefathers and the evil villains.

Granny Missus did not take the hint. "I've spent the day with your daughter, young man. I know you ain't got all the facts."

I stepped forward. "Granny, hon, why don't we—"

"And I ain't got the heart nor the stomach to go into them proper right now."

I sighed a silent thank-you for that.

Ry stuffed his hands into his jeans pockets.

"But it's enough for you to know how things was back then. From the time your great-grandfather finagled the Hadleys out of our half of the deal selling our land to the government to build this highway—"

"Now, this part I do know. The deal that gave my great-grandfather the money to build his fortune was almost lost because of the Hadleys."

"He moved in and sold them all the land they wanted at a cut rate, undercutting the original offer to sell equal portions of land on either side of the fence where the Hadley and O'Malley land met."

"He only did that because the Hadleys wouldn't commit to contract. They could have shared in that opportunity if they hadn't dragged their feet, waiting for who knows

what. Maybe a . . ." He looked up to the sky beyond the carport, where once upon a time the lights of the South Winds
would illuminate the sky, and finished quietly: "Maybe
they waited too long looking for a sign."

"Maybe they did," she agreed quietly.

I gasped softly—not some big gulping thing—to hear my
grandmother say that. No one in our family had ever admitted that any Hadley had gone awry waiting for the go-
ahead from on high. It staggered my imagination just to
think of such a thing, and in doing so, I think, shed some
new light on the old, dark, back alleys of my mind.

Perhaps it was not always wrong to move swiftly, to rely on
your own instincts and judgments as their own kinds of signs.

Wow. The concept made my head spin.

"I'll tell you one thing, if the Hadleys hesitated that
much"—Granny Missus raised her hand and snapped her
fingers, giving off a muted pop—"you could betcha some
O'Malley rushed in to take advantage. The highway land.
Opening a restaurant."

"That's just two instances," he argued, somehow without
sounding argumentative.

"You know Jolie's daddy asked the bank to loan him
money to build a doughnut shop onto the garage?"

Ry looked at me.

I looked away. I couldn't hear this story without thinking
of my part in it. How I had gone swimming at the South
Winds that day against my parents' direct orders. That was
the day I jumped off the high dive, my new bikini top came
off and Ry jumped into the water and pretended to save me
from drowning, using the time to pull my top into place
and cop a quick feel. It was a generous and sensitive thing

to do, and to thank him in kind I had generously kneed him in his most sensitive area.

Then I'd gone home and embarrassed my family in front of the loan officer. I shuddered to remember it all.

"My son did a study, found out that people were ready to try something new around here. He knew he could employ locals, give work to the bakery, eventually take on delivery drivers and sell to outlying areas. He felt it would have not just been good for our family, but for the whole town."

Ry looked at the back of the small garage-turned-museum, his expression unreadable. "I'm sure it would have done well."

"He never got the chance to find out because the day before he talked to the bank man that damned old Howdy made it known he was extending the restaurant's hours and switching to an all-day breakfast deal. Made it a buffet so he didn't even have to hire anyone new. The whole thing didn't benefit anyone but himself and his own."

"What?" That was the first time I'd ever heard that. "You mean the bank turned Daddy down because of Howdy?"

"Yes, and your father had to leave town to find work. Lots of men did that, but that didn't matter to Howdy. Howdy had a way of rushing forward, chasing the money without ever counting the human costs."

I started to confront my grandmother about keeping this part of the story away from me, but Ry stepped forward, his arms crossed, and spoke first.

"Is this where I get the lecture on changing my ways, Granny Missus?"

She shook her head. "You can't learn from a lecture what you refuse to learn from life."

He met her gaze. "Then trust me that you don't need to say any more. A lifetime of trying to please my family and always failing has taught me plenty."

"Has it?"

He eased out a deep breath. "I thought so, but . . ."

"I know your girl stole from me."

"You do?" I jerked my head up.

"I know you tried to cover for her, Jolie, but I knew it from the start. That's why I waited so long to tell y'all she hadn't come back from the bank. I wanted to give her a chance to come back and come clean with me on her own."

"When a young person is missing you should act immediately. It's hardly the time to wait because you just don't know what she might have done," Ry said, his mouth set in a hard line.

"Isn't that a funny thing?"

"Funny?" He cocked his head.

"That I, a Hadley, had more faith in your daughter than you did?"

His eyebrows squashed down over his deep-set eyes. He stood there with his mouth open.

And it was such a nice mouth. Wide and masculine, and damn fine to kiss, I couldn't help remembering. And his eyes, they were more than passing fair in their own right. Intense but never too far away from sparkling with mischief. Even at a time like this when my old granny's wry observation had left him bereft of anything cute or cutting to say.

Granny Missus patted his back and made her way toward the path that led from the car port to the back of her house. "Nice chatting with you, Ryman. I hope you'll think about what I said."

He shook his head, echoing obediently, "I will."

"Oh, and Ryman?" Granny pulled up short.

"Yes, ma'am?" He stood straight and waited for whatever gems of wisdom the old gal had yet to impart.

She smiled, softly, and her eyes twinkled. "Hannah Rose."

"What?"

Even I cocked my head in curiosity at that.

"You asked what Howdy called me." She paused and looked toward the highway, then sighed. "He called me Hannah Rose—something my own husband rarely ever ventured to do."

We both watched her walk away, her head high, then I faced Ry and smiled. "I do believe you have just about won over my grandmother."

"Guess I have some kind of charm no Hadley woman can resist." He picked a tool up from the workbench.

"Charm, my butt." I folded my arms.

That did not stop him from leaning over and stealing a quick kiss on the cheek. "Charm your butt and all the rest of you too, my dear. Least that's my plan."

I backed away and clucked my tongue at him, though in all honestly there were really so many other things I'd rather have done with my tongue where this man was concerned.

"Hope you didn't leave some poor lady cooking under a hair dryer."

But I had come to *talk* today, to hear his side of the story and bring closure to the tensions between us. The last thing I wanted was for this man to know how wanton I would be with him if only given the chance. "The salon isn't open today."

"Not open?"

Was that concern I saw in his eyes?

He started fiddling with something under the hood.

"We're never open the Monday after market. We need a day to get our bearings back."

"I had no idea this Every Second Saturday gig had such far-reaching effects in this town."

"It's a big deal," I reminded him in a soft but adamant tone.

"Bigger than I realized."

I told you that. I left the comment unspoken but I did not try to disguise the irritation in any other way.

"I had no idea my grandfather hauled in that kind of money over a three-day period." He put the heel of his hand to the fender. "Who'd have thought so many people would flock to this speck on the map in these mountains to buy buck knives, miracle cleaners and magic potions—'as seen on' late-night TV—homemade bric-a-brac and dealer-discounted hot tubs?"

I studied his quiet features. Just days ago I might have misconstrued the grave set of his jaw for a hardness of his heart toward Verbena, his grandfather and the people who spent so much of themselves and their money at the Flea Market. Now I understood he was just trying to make sense of it all. That was a feeling I could most certainly relate to!

"So," I said, trying to avoid coming off like little Miss Know-it-all, "Guess you're seeing this situation in a whole new light?"

"It ain't 'Move-to-Cal'a'fornie-swimming-pools-and-movie-stars' money." Ry set about prodding around under the hood with no discernable objective to his actions. "But the old man did better off at this place than just skimming by."

"Didn't you catch onto that fact after they read his will?"

Metal clanked to metal and Ry let out a curse. He stood for a second staring at the engine, then let out a long breath and held up the scraped knuckles of his hand. "Misjudged the attachment."

"That's always a mistake," I said softly, then moved over to his side and cradled his hand in mine to get a better look.

"It's nothing—just a scrape."

I wet my lips. "Maybe I should kiss it to make it all better."

He looked at me through half-lowered eyelids. "You do, and you'll set a dangerous precedent.

I lowered my mouth to almost touch his skin, then raised my eyes to meet his. "Dangerous? How?"

His chest rose and fell in a heavy, steady rhythm. "You start kissing hurt parts on me to make them better and I'll just become one big accident waiting to happen."

"Is that right?"

"First I'd cut myself shaving." He put a finger from his free hand onto his cheek just above his dimple.

I held my breath.

"Then maybe pull a muscle working on the car." He dropped his finger to his chest.

"Each requiring a little kiss therapy, of course."

"Oh yeah." He traced his fingertip over my bottom lip.

I held in a groan.

"The next thing you know I'd do anything to get a little of your tender nursing. Start walking into traffic, falling down stairs . . ."

"Spilling coffee in your lap."

He only flinched for an instant. But the mental picture of me tending to such a personal injury must have overcome his initial reaction, because he smiled slowly and cocked his head to one side. "Oh, Jolene Hadley Corbett, did anyone ever tell you that you are one wicked, wicked woman?"

I shook my head and tucked my hair behind my ear. "Never."

"Then I am glad I could be your first." He turned over his injured hand and raised my fingers to his lips. He kissed my palm, his gaze never leaving mine.

He was the first boy to ever touch my breasts, the first man to ever see the fearlessness waiting to awaken inside me, and the only person I would ever have defied my family for. That scared the living daylights out of me.

I pulled my hand away. "I thought I came over here so we could talk."

"Would it offend you greatly if I said I had talked enough for one morning?"

Offend me? No. Unhinge me? Maybe.

"Could we . . ." He studied me for a minute. Then slowly, with delicious delight in his eyes, he smiled, just enough to make one dimple show. "Would it compromise your reputation too much if I asked you to meet me tonight?"

"To . . . tonight?" I had come to find closure, I reminded myself. Today. Not tonight. Not alone in the dark with this man. What kind of closure would I find there? A flash of memory of the two of us in this very place, kissing and caressing, blindsided me.

Suddenly, I had the oddest sensation of having the world drop from under my feet, and yet I did not feel anxious or the least bit inclined to try to grab onto something safe and familiar. I did not even look for a sign to confirm my choice.

I just took a deep breath, inhaling the smell of the crisp autumn air and the potent mix of Ry's fresh-soap-and-shampoo scent mingled with car grease. Then, like Esther preparing to make that great leap into uncertainty, I closed my eyes and said, "Okay. Tonight."

Chapter 14

@ "I feel like we're flying." I climbed up on my knees in the front seat of the Starliner and tipped my head back. The air rushed into my face and stole my breath away for a moment. I didn't care. It was dark. It was late. It was secluded and I was alone with Ry.

"Well, you wanted to be discreet." Ry fixed his concentration on the dirt road ahead. "But that doesn't mean you can run buck wild, girl. Sit down and fasten that safety belt."

"In a minute." I shut my eyes and savored the delicious thrill of wind flowing through my hair like a thousand tiny fingers.

Ry had showed up at my house just after dusk with Sugar Anne as a baby-sitter for Dylan and a secret, for my eyes only, hidden in the back lot of the South Winds. Barefoot and wearing only my jeans and a freebie long-sleeve T-shirt given to me by a hot-wax supplier, I had just washed my hair and protested that I had to pull myself together before I could go anywhere.

Then I looked at him, standing in my doorway in a soft gray sweater, a red-and-black flannel shirt and a pair of seat-hugging jeans. He held out his hand. All the mischief of a boy in his dimples and the hunger of a man met in his eyes. He grinned and told me he liked me just as I was.

I put down my hairbrush and just went.

The next thing I knew we were in the old Starliner, cruising the back roads like a couple of crazy, carefree teens.

"Jolie, sit down. Buckle up."

"Shhh, you'll ruin it," I said. I gripped the top of the windshield with one hand and tried to remember if I had ever felt so in control and unconstrained in my life.

Ry had switched off the engine and dimmed to the parking lights to coast down a hill, at my request.

The air smelled of someone in the distance burning leaves. The darkening sky and mountain horizon blended into one and there was only me, free and flying.

"Jolie?"

"When we get to the bottom of the hill, I'll behave. I promise."

"I must be getting old, because that's the first time I ever talked a woman into behaving herself for my sake." He pumped the brake lightly.

At first I thought he wanted to send me a message by slowing the car but then I realized we had neared the bottom of the long, low hill. I sighed.

"You've had your fun." He flicked on the lights. "Now sit down."

"Now sit down," I mimicked his stern command and then turned my face toward him. "Have you started ordering me around already? I mean, I like a man who's decisive and even forceful under the right circumstances, but—"

"C'mon, baby, you know what I want to hear," he growled.

Caught between shock and excitement, I sank into my seat, my fingers pressed to the hollow of my throat.

The engine sputtered, then revved to life.

And I exhaled slowly, glad for the cover of darkness to conceal my chagrin.

"Buckle up, Jolie. I've pulled some stupid stunts in my life and taken some dicey chances, but there is one thing I will not do." He shifted gears. "I will not allow someone I care about to be hurt if I can do anything at all to prevent it. Not on my watch."

"Hurt?" The metal clip of the new safety belt clattered as it slid into place. "How could I ever be hurt?"

"Accidents happen, even with good drivers."

"Yes, but not to Ryman O'Malley. You're not just any driver. You're a pilot. A former lifeguard. A boy-god grown to your full potential. A free agent."

"Boy-god? Lord, tell me that smoke isn't just old leaves because you are high on something, sweetheart."

"High." I repeated. Yes, high, like Esther, above it all. I tugged the seat belt to get comfortable. "I'm just saying you're in control of your fate, Ry."

His laughter at that came just shy of sounding cynical.

"No, I mean it. You're the kind of man who can fix a car or fly a jet, or dive in a pool and save a person's life." I could feel my own heart thudding harder as I talked about the man. "I just don't think anything could happen to us out here that you couldn't take care of."

"An engine or an airplane, or even an underwater rescue, sure, those I can handle." He did not look at me as he spoke. "But there are so many things in my life I've made a mess of, Jolie, the things that matter, like relationships. I don't think your confidence in me is all that well placed."

"You're wrong, Ry. You're much better at those things than you think."

"Yeah . . . well . . . just stay in your seat buckled up while the car is moving, okay?"

"Okay, but I won't get hurt, because I'm with you."

He took a wide curve in the road with just the right mix of skill and speed.

I shook my head and my hair whipped across my face. I laughed and whispered, "I'm with you."

We drove on under a canopy of falling leaves.

He didn't say a word.

He'd asked me to listen to him but he did not seem ready to actually tell me anything. I wasn't sure what to make of it.

He just gripped the wheel and drove on.

To try to loosen things up a bit, I flipped on the radio. Granny and Dylan had installed a new one with an old-style façade, but in these roads tucked into the mountains, I wondered if we would pick up any signals at all. I hoped to avoid hollering preachers or call-in shows where people reported possible alien abductions. When the sweet, unfamiliar notes of a Latin-American radio station filled the night air, I left it there.

I laid my head back on the thickly padded seat and let the richness of the music wash over me.

"You okay?" Ry finally asked.

"Better than okay. I'm free—at least for now."

"Free?"

"Uh-huh." I shut my eyes. "For once in my life I'm doing something I shouldn't, something just for me, and nobody in town is ever going to find out about it."

"You really find it so restrictive to live there?"

"Restrictive? No, I never said that." I lifted my arms up with my hands open. "Small-town life comes with some definite boundaries, but those work to the good more often than they become a detriment."

"Boundaries? Funny you'd use that word."

Just then the car hit a dip in the road.

I opened my eyes and waited for him to say more.

"Isn't that what you've been telling me Sugar Anne is practically begging for with her attitude and actions?"

I sat back again. "Yes."

He took a left at a broad intersection and suddenly we were under a long, low archway of tree branches.

"You don't dive into the pool without testing the waters first," I concluded.

"You did."

"Yeah, well, I could do that, couldn't I?" A shower of red and yellow leaves tumbled downward toward us and I tried to snatch at one, but the car slipped past too fast and the chance had gone. "I could just go on and jump in because I knew the lifeguard had his eyes glued right on me the whole time."

He chuckled. "It was that pink bikini."

I inhaled and stretched like a cat, keeping my gaze on him from the corners of my eyes.

"But seriously, you're saying that because Sugar Anne's

too young to dip her toes in the waters of adulthood just yet, she's pulling these stunts to make sure she has my attention?"

"You know of a better way to feel secure than to push the one person you hope you can always rely on to the very limit and find out for sure that he won't falter or take his eyes off you?"

"Should I feel good that she's testing me? Or bad that I've failed her so much that she feels I have to prove myself?"

"Good. Definitely good. All children test their parents."

"I'll bet you didn't."

"Shows how much *you* know. The day I went over to the pool to show off in front of you it was against my parents' orders."

"Yeah?"

Suddenly I thought of that day, of the misguided belief I had held about it for so long, and my heart grew heavy. "And that one act of rebellion changed the course of my life."

He took his eyes from the road for only a second. "You're kidding, right?"

"I wish I was. But for years and years I thought that my dragging in all wet from swimming at the South Winds just showed the bank man that even the Hadleys would prefer to spend their time and money at your grandfather's place. I always suspected he took it as a sign. I can't tell you how confused and hurt I was when I heard Granny tell the truth of that story."

I'd come out with him for one tiny escape from reality. I had come to listen to him, secretly hoping he would confess something dark and horrible about his family. I knew this would relieve him and that I would enjoy hearing the dirty details more than any upstanding compassionate girl should. What I had not planned upon was disclosing something disturbing about the people *I* loved.

"Ry, I think my family let me feel badly about the swimming pool incident for a reason. They told me it wasn't my fault about the loan, but they never let me forget what a bad impression I made that day."

"All these years you still thought you'd been a bad omen?" he asked.

"No one ever explained it all to me. I always thought the buffet deal came after they turned down Daddy's idea—you know, like they had to choose between the two options and I spoiled it for my family."

"Kids are self-centered in a way that makes them believe they have something to do with the bad things that happen to those they love." He slowed the car. He did not look my way but I could see that he was not only talking about me when he added, "It's only natural to feel like there is always something you could have done to stop something bad from happening."

"And I think my family let me go on blaming myself just a little bit to keep me from trying to push the limits again."

He looked at me, his eyes searching. "And it worked?"

I stared ahead, trying to fit the pieces together.

After a few seconds of silence he asked, "Are you angry about that?"

"Angry?" I took a deep breath. "No. Oddly enough, no. I just . . . I just feel like I'm seeing these people I love in a new light."

"That's how I felt when I finally decided to make a break from my family."

A break?

"Have you really made a *break* from your family, Ry?"

"Maybe I should say I took a stand."

I nodded. That made more sense. I didn't want to make a break with my family. I only wanted to look at their actions honestly for the first time and hope it helped me live my own life more fully.

"And in taking that stand something between all of us was broken, yes." The softness of his confession lent it a poignant power.

"*All* of you?"

"Parents, sister, ex-wife . . . Of course, there wasn't much of a bond left between Cynthie and me except, of course, wanting what's best for Sugar Anne."

"Cynthie?" I stopped myself before chiming in with "Well, isn't that just a *precious* name" in the sickening sweet tone that other women spot as sarcasm but men never seemed to see through. Instead, I shifted in the seat and demurred. "That's your ex-wife?"

He chuckled. "That your way of trying to get me to tell you about her and the divorce?"

"No, I wouldn't presume—"

"Well, I would. I'm curious as hell about Dylan's father." He stared at the winding stretch of road that lay ahead. "Where is he? *Who* is he? Was he such a rotten role model that the kid had to latch on to my grandfather to fit the bill? Do you still have feelings for him?"

"Ry, I didn't come out here to play twenty questions."

"Then just answer the ones I asked. Then you can ask four or five about my past and it will be out of the way."

"Okay." It sounded fair, and if hard-pressed I supposed I could come up with a question or two about Miss Cynthie, New Orleans deb. "Okay, fair enough. Where he is . . . last I heard, Branson, Missouri, but that was two months ago, so he could be in Las Vegas or even Hong Kong by now."

"World-class traveler?"

I shook my head, feeling strangely generous toward my ex. "World-class dreamer."

"Ah. Goes from job to job?"

"To job to job. His name is Art Corbett and he's Emma's brother."

"So I can assume he was a man of uncompromising taste and gentility."

I laughed. "He was . . . a safe bet."

"No such thing."

"So I found out." I sighed. "But at eighteen, a local kid who'd just gotten a promising job in town, who laughed at the same things I did and was cute but not too handsome for his own good seemed a great catch."

"You loved him and thought it would last a lifetime."

"A lifetime?" I snorted. "Hell, at eighteen I thought waiting for my bangs to grow out was a *lifetime*."

"But you loved him?"

"I loved him." I brushed my knuckles along the door handle. "But I didn't have a clue about who he was, much less who he wanted to be."

He nodded. "At that age you don't even know a whole hell of a lot about the person inside your own skin. And just

when you think you've learned a thing or two about yourself, something happens and it all changes."

I cocked my head and just looked at him.

He smiled, slowly keeping his eyes straight ahead. "I
married too young, too."

Not as young as I did, I wanted to say. He was never as
young as I was and that had nothing to do with the fact that
he was four years older than me. He was a worldly O'Malley and I was . . . a big, innocent, small-town goober.

The cold, damp ends of my hair brushed against my
neck. I shivered. "Is that what happened with you and . . .
I'm sorry, did you say her name was Cynthie?"

"You know I did." He made it clear in his tone that he
had decided to take my pretending to not care as the sin-
cerest form of flattery. "And actually, marrying young had
almost nothing to do with our not making it last."

"Do I have to ask the right questions to get the answers
or are you going to explain that?"

"She had money."

"You married for money? I don't believe that for one
minute."

"No, I married for sex."

"Sex?" I murmured. "Oh."

He chuckled. "Cynthia Dixon-Dupree had class, culture
and curves that wouldn't quit. And the minute I laid eyes
on her . . ."

"Laid being the operative word?"

"I had to have her," he finished without comment on my
snide interruption. "But 'No ice, No dice' was her motto."

"You make her sound so mercenary." I liked that in a
man's ex-wife, I chose not to add.

"Hey, she had her priorities. She wanted an eye-popping engagement ring and a show-stopping wedding. I wanted a honeymoon."

"Fair exchange, I guess, if you both got what you wanted."

"We did. And don't get me wrong, I did love her."

"Well, sure." I wish I were a big-enough person not to wish he'd had a loveless, sexless, pointless relationship with a despicable troll. But I wasn't.

"But not in the right way."

"The *right* way?"

"I knew ever since I had the chance to take a good hard look at my own family and their screwed-up priorities that I wanted something else for my own life. Trouble was I had no idea how to go about getting it."

"I don't follow."

"My family fought and undercut one another and never could be happy because they were always focused on money, who had it and how they could get it."

"Preaching to the choir on that subject, my friend."

Silence answered my smart-ass reply.

"But do go on," I urged.

"Okay, so money was the issue that tore apart my family. Cynthie came from money. *Old* money and lots of it. I assumed that meant she had a better handle on dealing with the stuff."

"The 'No ice, No dice' didn't clue you in to her true nature up front?"

"My focus at the time was purely 'up front,' if you know what I mean." He cleared his throat. He gunned the engine to take a crooked incline. "So I married a woman who had all the same attributes and ambitions of the people I wanted desperately to distance myself from."

Of course he had. Ry was and had always been a rescuer. Rescuers were notoriously rotten at seeing the dark side of people, and often hooked up with someone just like those they had most wanted to save—in hopes of succeeding with the new person where they had failed with the old.

"You know, if you were looking for a woman totally opposite from your family, the obvious choice would be . . ."

Me. The unspoken word virtually hung in the crisp air between us.

Great. Volunteerism is alive and well in North Carolina.

He leaned his forearm on the steering wheel.

In the dim light from the dash I could see him smiling. Or maybe, more correctly, semi-smiling, which had a much more potent affect, to be sure.

I tipped my head back. "Gosh, aren't there a lot of stars out tonight?"

He hummed a noncommittal reply.

"So you and Cynthie got divorced."

"We got divorced. Ten years ago."

"And now you're tearing down the South Winds."

"A bit of an abbreviated version of my life, but there you have it."

"Somehow you think that will keep something bad from happening in your family, don't you?"

"I have to get rid of the Trav' O' Tel, Jolie. I have to make it go away so that it will not be an ongoing source of contention. I'm doing this for them, not myself."

"Not the words of a man who has recently proclaimed total freedom from them."

He stopped at an unmarked crossroads and turned toward me, his arm still on the wheel. "I'll never be entirely free of my family. I wouldn't want to be."

I sat back against the new upholstery and gazed up into the starry sky. "Would it surprise you to hear that what you just said has raised my opinion of you a couple more notches?"

"*More* notches? As in, it was already on the upsurge?"

I only smiled, slyly. "Details, man. How is your family forcing you to tear down the Trav' O' Tel?"

"Money."

"No surprise. But *how*?"

"I got the lion's share in the will, and that did not make for cozy conversations around the family dinner table."

"So? Howdy had every right to leave his legacy to whomever he wanted. If it made some folks unhappy then, well, knowing the old man, that probably would have suited him just fine."

"I see your point." He laughed. "The old guy was not easy to work with, and it shows in all the addenda and amendments to his will. They could have written his last requests on Swiss cheese for all the holes in that thing."

"The way you talk it sounds more like rotten cheese."

"Whatever it was, it had my family salivating. They each saw a different way to get themselves a bigger piece of the pie."

"Cheese? Pie? You're making me hungry." I put my hand on his arm and hoped the one simple gesture would tell him he had my total support and understanding. "So, the South Winds got lost in one of those loopholes?"

"Not exactly." The engine revved but he stayed idling at

the intersection. "I couldn't take the bickering and back-stabbing anymore, so I took the South Winds instead. The motel was the one thing none of them wanted to get their hands on."

"Then why—"

"Don't you see, Jolie?" He put the car in park, then took my hand from his arm and turned my palm upward. "I cut a deal. If they'd agree not to contest the will, I'd let them have everything I stood to gain and accept the Trav' O' Tel as my sole inheritance from my grandfather."

"Then you should protect it, honor his life's work by allowing it to go on."

"If it goes on, either because I sell it or run it, it will generate money and that will just generate more animosity among my family."

"Sell it for a loss."

"I got it for nothing. How can I sell it for a loss?"

"Then give it to Norris Wyatt."

He shook his head. "I saw how much money that place is capable of generating—and without any effort on my part. It might surprise you to hear how depressed I was to realize the old place was still a moneymaker, because that sealed its fate. If one of my family ever found out—"

"You're looking for bad news where none exists."

"You forget my aunt and father grew up here, girl. If I gave the place away they'd only be one phone call away from finding out what kind of business it does." He shifted in the seat and traced his fingertip along my cupped hand. "A long protracted lawsuit later, Norris Wyatt could lose everything to them."

"Ry, I can't believe that even *your* family would cause problems for Mr. Wyatt."

"They wouldn't want to, but I can see where they might feel they had to."

"Had to? Why? They have more money than God already."

"I've said too much about that." He closed off to me then just as surely as if he had turned his back and walked away.

I laid my hand on his shoulder, hoping to coax him to open up again. "So, you are really going to let your family drive you to this extreme?"

He snorted. "Said the grown woman sneaking around in the night on back roads to make sure no one sees her and tattles on her to her old granny."

I decided to ignore that remark. Ignoring unpleasantries was a woman's prerogative, after all. "So that's it for the South Winds? You can't keep it open and try to find some middle ground with your family?"

"You saw what happened to my grandfather when he tried to keep his feet in both worlds."

"He had a good life here. He would have loved to have his family come to visit more, but he had people in Verbena who loved him and many more who counted on him for their family's livelihoods. Is that such a terrible thing? To live where you are loved, where you contribute to the community and where your life has meaning?"

He didn't answer.

Of course, that was an answer. I took a deep breath.

The soft, romantic Latin music on the radio swelled to fill the quiet night. I fought to keep the tears from filling my eyes.

"When will the motel come down?" I whispered.

"Bulldozers were set to arrive Wednesday, but I've asked them to wait until further notice. Can't risk the heavy machinery damaging the sign just now."

I bit my lip to try to keep from uttering a spontaneous "Thank heaven." My spirits had lifted and I could not hide it when I asked, "So, you're still going to try to save it?"

"I think I've found a man through the Internet who knows something about salvaging electric signs."

"Wow. So you found someone who might have the answers?"

"Stop that right now."

"Stop what?"

"Don't tell me you aren't sitting there thinking that my saving that sign *is* a sign. Or . . . or that you are telling me that the grudge money was a sign that changed my direction and therefore validates the whole 'wait for the sign and believe' theory for making life choices."

"Did I say that?"

"You don't have to say it. I can actually *see* you thinking it inside that deceptively disorderly red head of yours."

Disorderly? I took that as a personal insult on many levels. Then it dawned on me what he meant. "Oh my gosh, I bet my hair's a wreck."

I tugged on the rearview mirror to check.

"Your hair is perfect, Jolie. It's your thinking that's flawed." He jerked the mirror back in place, only to have it come off in his hand.

"Listen, it's your business." I knew better than to comment on the mirror so I sat up straight and clasped my hands in my lap. "Lord knows I'm not one to interfere in another person's business."

He held the mirror between us and ducked down low in the seat.

"Just what are you doing?"

"What do you think I'm doing? You said 'Lord knows,' then you told a bald-faced lie. I'm trying to deflect incoming lightning bolts."

"Oh, very funny." I grabbed the mirror from him and stashed it in the glove compartment.

"Hey, it's your system, looking for signs from on high." He put the car in park. "Unfortunately, I think it may be too late to save myself from the jolt."

"You talking God's wrath or—"

"I'm done talking, Jolie." He leaned over and kissed me lightly on the lips.

That was more like it, I thought. I undid my seat belt and angled back against the passenger door. My heart racing, I traced one bare toe along the side of his jeans.

He took my foot in his hand and smiled.

My skin tingled at the combination of cool air, hot music and sheer anticipation.

He inched toward me.

I wet my lips. "If you're done talking, what are you going to do now?"

He snagged both ends of my undone safety belt, clamped them together, then slid back behind the wheel. "I'm going to shut up and drive you home."

"I know you're right, but I'm not ready to go home!" I put my hands to the seat belt like I might just undo it and fling it off with no thought for the consequences. "C'mon, Ry, let's stay out a little longer. I don't want it all to end before anything is even started."

This was a side of me I'd never shown anyone. Without my immaculate hairdo to hide beneath. Without makeup and every detail of my clothing in place. Without the refuge of Verbena surrounding me. Knowing exactly what I wanted and having the courage to ask for it outright.

It should have scared the bejeezus out of me.

But it didn't. At least not yet.

"Jolie, we *can't* start anything between us."

"We're consenting adults. Why not?"

"You know perfectly well why not."

"No, I don't. Is it because of generations of family non-sense? Because you may have a hand in dealing the death blow to the town I love? Or because in a few days you will drive off, or fly off or whatever you see fit to do and never look back?"

"All of those, Jolie." Keeping the car idling for fear it would not start again if he shut it off, he slipped closer to me and took my face in his hand. "Because of who we are, where we come from and where we belong, there can never be anything lasting between us."

I laughed aloud at his cornball conclusions, even as the underlying truth of them made my heart ache. I held my head up. I had gone this far. I could not go home without pushing myself to my very limit. "Did I ask for anything lasting?"

He smiled and kissed my cheek. "You may try to fool yourself, but you don't fool me. You are the 'something lasting' kind of girl."

"I can change," I whispered. "You said life is about change."

"Don't, Jolie. Not for me."

"It's because I told you that I feel safe with you no matter what, isn't it?"

"It's because you are and always will be safe with me, Jolie. I'd never put my own needs ahead of what's best for you." He looked deep into my eyes. "How did we ever get ourselves into this?"

"You asked me to come along for a drive down hidden-away roads in a fine, sexy car with music and moonlight and all this pent-up . . . energy between us."

"Is that what this is? Pent-up *energy*?"

"What would you call it?"

He started to speak, then sighed and gave a half-hearted shrug. "Maybe you're just caught up in the moment. Wanting to take it to the next level by doing something so forbidden."

"Why not?" I sounded sincerely like a person trying to convince myself more than my companion. "No one will ever know."

"I'll know."

"But you'll be gone from here forever, so that hardly counts."

"If we make love, my sweet Jolene, I want it to count."

"*If?*"

"Would you rather I said 'when'?"

"I'd rather . . ." I hunched my shoulders and knotted my hands in my lap.

"You're cold." He dragged his flannel shirt off his back.

"Cold is good for a body. Brings you to your senses."

He wrapped the warm fabric around my upper shoulders.

His hair brushed mine.

I raised my head.

Our gazes locked.

"Ry?" I whispered.

"What, Jolie?"

"You *wanted* me, though, right?"

"You tell me." He moved my hand to caress the evidence of his desire even as he pulled me into an unrelenting kiss.

Chapter 15

"So people really came to Verbena, North Carolina, for their *vacations*?" Sugar Anne leaned on the Combin' Holiday's front counter and flipped through the blank pages of the appointment book.

"Back in the day when a family vacation meant just that—spending time as a family—they sure did." I counted out a handful of fives and a stack of ones, then swung my hip into the cash drawer. It rattled along the slides like a tipsy trolley and then slammed shut.

Ding.

I surveyed the silent salon dimmed by the gray autumn sky clouding the windows. "Maybe all this dreariness will compel some woman out there to have her hair done just to lift her spirits."

"Is it always this slow?" Sugar Anne picked up a lime green hair clip and clamped it on a tuft of hair at the top of her head.

I thought the teenager looked like some modern-day

cavewoman using a bone as a hair barrette, but I kept my opinion to myself. "The whole week after Flea Market is pretty much a dud. It won't pick up again until Friday afternoon, when we usually get a rush of ladies who want to stand out at the VFW hall that night or to show off for their friends at the Knights of Columbus Bingo Bonanza."

"Regular Verbena wild party animals, huh?" Ry's daughter grinned without a trace of contempt. "So, what are we going to do today?"

I don't know what you'll do, but I'll probably waste most of the morning sitting around mooning about what might have been between me and your dad. Then a light lunch and back to acting like a sad old mope for the rest of the afternoon.

Were I a woman who held strictly with telling children the truth at all times, that's what I would have said. Instead, I pretended to straighten the products on the glass shelf behind the counter and lied through my big old, phony smile. "We'll get some walk-ins today. Don't worry, you'll get your chance to perfect your shampoo and sweep-up techniques."

"I just hate for you to pay me for not doing anything."

"I'm not paying you, really. You're paying me for smoothing things over with my grandmother on your behalf."

"Seems like I'm getting off pretty easy, though. I bet Granny Missus would have found something awful and hard for me to do."

"I hesitate to even imagine what you two got up to over there."

"She wanted to talk and I wanted to hear all about the things she had to tell me. We made a pretty good team that way until . . ."

I put my hand on her shoulder. If ever there lived an example to disprove every harsh and hurtful thing the Hadleys had believed about the O'Malleys, this girl was *it*. Intuitive, curious and innately kind, Sugar Anne gave evidence to the best qualities of her family. I chose to credit her father for that, but I might be a bit prejudiced in my judgment.

"I shouldn't have stolen those quarters from Granny Missus."

"No, you shouldn't have."

"And I should have told her what I'd done."

"What she doesn't know can't hurt her."

"You mean can't hurt me? We did it to protect me, not her. And for what good? She found out anyway, my dad told me. I don't think anything goes on around this town or in these mountains that Granny Missus doesn't find out about almost instantly."

I shivered.

"You okay?" Sugar Anne tapped my arm lightly to draw my attention. "You know someone said the other day at the Auto Museum that when you shiver out of the blue like that it means someone is walking across your grave. Or, I guess, where your grave is going to be."

"Just a silly superstition." I pretended to do some touch-up work on my hair.

If anyone took a walk over my grave, then they had probably fallen in. Because if Sugar Anne's observation about my grandmother held true, Granny Missus already knew about my sneaking off with Ry. That meant I had pretty much dug my own grave last night.

"Don't you worry about Granny Missus. You've done your penance with her and it's over."

"You don't think she'd have wanted me to keep working for her just to teach me a lesson?"

"No. I think she taught you all she thought she needed to. That woman is like a dog with a bone when she's determined to get things her way." I put my hand on the girl's back, guided her to a stylist chair and swiveled it around as an invitation to sit down. "But she saves most of her troublemaking and meddling for me."

"My grandparents never meddle in my life." She sounded wistful, the poor misguided child. "Did my great-grandfather meddle much in my dad's business when he came here to visit?"

"Howdy loved your daddy. No, that's not nearly descriptive enough—he *adored* your daddy." It nearly killed the old man when Ry stopped spending his summers at the South Winds. Howdy had not been the only one to share in that disappointment. "But he worked him hard and treated him pretty hard as I recall. Let me tell you, if you'd stolen from old Howdy, you'd be working it off from now until doomsday."

Sugar Anne climbed into the seat and spun it to face forward talking to me eye-to-eye in the mirror. "I guess he would have liked the free-labor angle."

"The man never paid for anything he could get for free." I plucked the hair clip from the girl's hair, picked up a comb and started teasing here and covering up there. "If I were half the businessman your grandfather was, I'd call up Emma right now and tell her not to bother coming in. Then I'd handle whatever customers we get through here today by myself and pocket all the day's earnings."

"You'd never do that to a friend." Sugar Anne did not fight the makeshift makeover.

"Oh, you think not?" I tried to arch one eyebrow the way you always read about in books but came off looking like a person suppressing a sneeze.

"I know you wouldn't." Sugar Anne did not seem to notice the awful face I'd made. She just blinked her big, dark eyes, which followed my every move in the mirror and said, "In that way you're a lot like my daddy."

I froze. The bright pink rattail comb made a bold contrast to the fluff of black hair trapped between my fingers. But that was nothing compared to the conflict Sugar Anne's innocent comment set raging inside of me.

Me? Like Ry? In ways so obvious that a sulking teenage girl wrapped up in her own world could see it?

"You know, Sugar Anne, now that I get a close-up look at this, you actually didn't do so bad with your hair." When I change the subject I don't fool around, I *change* the subject—and sometimes my whole way of looking at things as well.

"Ugh." The girl stuck her tongue out and slumped in the chair. "Don't tell my dad, but I really didn't want it to look *exactly* like this."

"It's not that bad." I combed through the fringe she'd left hanging down the back of her neck. "There's a certain artistic symmetry to it."

"Artistic symmetry." She sat up a bit taller in the seat and laughed. "Nice words for 'looks like crap but could have been worse'?"

"At least your mistake will grow out. When I make a mistake it's usually the kind that comes back to . . ."

"Bite you in the ass," she finished for me, her smile a faint facsimile of her father's.

"I was going to say they usually come back to haunt me."

I thought of how differently I'd take this whole conversation if I had succeeded in seducing Ry yesterday. "But your take works, too."

"Is that why you're so afraid to try anything new?"

"Me? Afraid? Where'd you get that idea?" I asked the question even though I could think of a myriad of sources around town who might have agreed with Sugar Anne's statement. "Who filled your head with that nonsense?"

"No one had to tell me anything. I mean, just look at you."

I did just that. Looked straight at myself in the mirror. Hair, makeup, outfit, attitude, all in place just as they should be.

And yet, I couldn't leave it at that. Obviously this girl had an opinion that she wanted to share. "What's *wrong* with me?"

"Nothing!"

"Oh." I should have accepted it for a compliment, I suppose, but the young woman's tone spoke of anything but flattery, so I cocked my head, met her eyes in the mirror and said, "You want to expound on that a bit?"

She shrugged. "Well, other than you look like you stepped out of a time warp there isn't anything wrong with you. Not a hair out of place, not a wrinkle in your clothes. Jeez, Jolie, you look like some Barbie doll mint in package."

I blinked at my image in the mirror and could form no argument. My shoulders stiffened. Anger—with myself, not Sugar Anne—rose up in my chest, but got crowded out by all the other emotions suddenly wedged in there. I could hardly breathe. "Is it so awful that I want to look nice?"

"But you don't just look nice, Jolie. You look . . ."

"Sad? Stupid? Ridiculous? Rigid? What?" I demanded, when she didn't finish.

"Untouchable," she said softly with the wisdom shared only by young, idealistic people champing at the bit to get out into life and unaware of all the dangers and pitfalls it holds.

I thought instantly of yesterday, when I had gone for an impromptu ride with Ry, with all my defenses, all my affectations and even my hair down. "You don't understand."

"But . . ."

"You don't understand," I said more forcefully, and threw myself into finishing up what I'd begun with her hair.

How could anyone so young and sheltered ever understand why I was the way I was?

I was *not* Esther.

I was not powerful and sure of myself. And the times I'd tried to be those things only served as reminders that it was not to be.

"There's another thing you have in common with my dad. When I start making too much sense you stop talking."

"I don't have anything in common with your father, Sugar Anne, and prefer not to talk about him, if you don't mind." Yes, I was proving her point tenfold but I didn't care. I'd made a first-class jackass of myself chasing after a man who was right when he said no good could come from a brief fling. It would break my heart, or worse for me in the long run, embarrass my family if they ever found out. I needed to steer clear of all thoughts and even chance encounters with—

"Hey, y'all!"

The door swung open so fast that the bell did not warn me in time.

"Ry!" I stepped backward, clutching my comb in my fist like some damned dagger in a black-and-white melodrama. I batted my eyes and tried to sound nonchalant as I asked in a high, squeaky voice, "What are you doing in my salon?"

"I just dropped in to say goodbye."

My heart sank. It was one thing to pledge never to see the man again, but it was quite another to have him stick his head into my place of business and so casually announce his leaving. "Goodbye?"

He stood in the doorway, one hand on the knob and the other on the door frame. Even without crossing the threshold his presence filled the room. "I've got to run an errand. Be gone most of the day. Just wanted to let you know."

"There's no one scheduled to come in today." Sugar Anne slid from the chair. "Why don't I come along and keep you company, Daddy?"

He squared his shoulders and filled the doorway with his large, lean body. "Because you gave your word you'd work for Jolie until you paid off the money you took from Granny Missus."

The girl put on a pouting fit befitting any daddy's-little girl worth her salt.

And I should know because in my day I was the princess of pouting to get my way with my daddy.

"I hate to say no, Sugar Anne." It could not be easy for Ry to deny his daughter the trip. After all, he could justify to himself that it would do them both a world of good. "But if

I don't stick to my guns on this issue how will you know when to trust me?"

Her head snapped up. "Trust?"

"Yes, trust. If everything I commit to falls subject to last-minute appeals and the ruling emotion of the moment, how can you have any confidence in me?"

The girl opened her mouth to argue, shut it, then sighed and hung her head, just a little.

I recognized the old "See how you've humbled me, I recognize you're right, so reconsider and give in to what I want" ploy, having employed it with my own father a few times.

"You're a young woman now, and now more than ever, you have to know where your boundaries are and which foundations you can rely upon." He anchored his feet wide and folded his arms so that the open door rested against one powerful shoulder. "You can rely on me, Sugar Anne."

The girl stubbed her heavy black shoe against the yellow baseboard. She kept her head down as she nodded.

But I could see the slight etching of her daddy's deep-set dimples in the girl's cheek as she fought to rein in a smile.

"Okay?" He did not so much ask it as state it.

She nodded again.

I moved forward and draped my arm over Sugar Anne's shoulders and considered it a bona fide triumph that the girl did not shirk away. "You go on and do what you have to do, Ry. We'll find enough to do around here."

Sugar Anne traced her fingers over the buttons on the cash register.

"Believe me, I'd rather spend the day with you lovely ladies."

Sugar Anne lifted her head just a little.

"But I'm afraid there's a damsel in distress who needs me today."

My pulse perked up. "Esther?"

"That fellow I found on the Internet, remember? He does metal sculpture and has a studio in a cabin up in the mountains. I want to drive up and see what he thinks of the project."

"Metal sculpture? What about an engineer? Or a different salvage company? Or . . . or what about a preservationist society?" I had given up as gracefully as I could on saving the Trav' O' Tel or the Buffet. If there was any chance of keeping some part of my precious heritage intact, I wanted to make sure it was done right.

He shook his head. "I've looked at every angle."

"Which is what this 'artist' needs to do, doesn't he? Why are you going to him? He should come here and see the sign for himself."

"He won't do it. Says his time is too valuable. But he did agree to look over some of the old postcards Sugar Anne found around the office last night." He patted the breast pocket of his denim jacket. "I'm hoping to spark his interest."

"You?" I let go of Sugar Anne and walked toward Ry. "*You* hope to convince this guy?"

"I've been told I can be pretty persuasive." His eyes sparkled. He cocked his head and rubbed his thumb along his jaw.

I could feel the blush working like a slow heat rising from just above my breasts but I did not let it deter me. "You need someone who is *already* interested, Ry."

"This man is our best bet."

"*Our* best bet?" I put my hands on my hips, ready to use any weapon at my disposal to make him see things my way. "Why, Mr. O'Malley, that's the first time you've alluded to the idea that you and I are in this together."

" 'Our' as in mine and Esther's."

I folded my arms. "I'd say you two make a nice couple, but you didn't even have a clue how to turn the old gal on."

"Oh . . . my . . . gosh!" Sugar Anne leaned on the counter and gawked at us. "You two are flirting with each other!"

"We're not flirting. We're negotiating," I never took my eyes completely off Ry.

"We're not negotiating. We're through talking about this entirely."

"How can we be through when it's so obvious you have picked the wrong person for the job? And if he is the right person and you really want him to care about this project, you are going about it all wrong."

"Jolie's right about that, Daddy. Those postcards are a nice touch, but none of them really show the sign all that well."

"I know, but what can I do? I left my digital camera back in Straffer."

I rarely have had moments of clarity of purpose so quick and intense that I did not dare question or seek outside confirmation of them. But this was one. I had a purpose and to fulfill it, I had to go with Ry today. "I have a camera."

"Digital?"

"My father's old Canon. It still has a half a roll of film in it."

"Which would take days to get developed."

"Get with the times, pal." I was already heading for the closet where I kept the old camera. "The Sunshine Market has its own one-hour photo now."

"A one-hour photo lab? Here in Verbena?"

"It's not entirely the sticks, you know. They put it in to capitalize on the Flea Market crowd and it's gone great guns every since. That is until . . ."

"Until . . ." His jaw set and he scowled at the floor.

"Well, they'll probably be glad of the business, then," Sugar Anne chimed in.

"Oh, I almost forgot." Ry reached into the pocket of his jacket and pulled out a small plastic object. "Sugar Anne found some of these and I thought you might like to have one as a memento."

I laughed. "I haven't seen one of those in years. You're grandpa used to sell them in the lobby for fifty-nine cents years and years ago."

"Sell? He didn't give them away?"

"Give? *Your* grandpa?" I shook my head and gave the cheap souvenir snow globe a vigorous shake. "Thank you, Ry. Now let me pay you back in kind by taking those pictures for you."

Ry rubbed his finger over the bridge of his nose and relented. "Okay. Fine. Take some shots, I can wait an hour to hit the road."

"Good." I studied the brightly painted plastic landscape under the small dome. "That'll give me time for Emma to get here and me to make arrangements with Granny Missus."

"Emma? Granny Missus?"

"Emma can run the salon and Granny Missus can watch

Dylan after school. That way I can go with you to persuade your Internet metal artist how important this job is."

"If Jolie's going, then I'm going." Sugar Anne stepped forward.

"Jolie's *not* going," Ry told his daughter without meeting my gaze.

But I *was* going. Come hell or high water I would make that trip. No waiting for signs. No weighing pros and cons or worrying over what Granny Missus might say. This was bigger than all that.

This was my chance to hang on to some tiny portion of my past, to do for Verbena what no Hadley had ever been able to do before—rescue it from the greed of the O'Malleys. Not Ry's greed, I understood now, but the greed of his family. In some way, I knew, I had to make sure this small piece of the past got preserved, as much for Ry's sake as for anyone's.

"I am going." I sat the snow globe down with a decisive *thump*.

"You and me running off together?" He chuckled low and gave me a slow, burning once-over with his eyes. "Whatever will people say?"

I picked up the pink comb again and used it to freshen up my hair, speaking to the mirror as I did. "They will say I went along on business."

"Yeah." Sugar Anne hopped up to sit on the counter. "Monkey business."

"Young lady . . ."

"Don't get after her, Ry. She's right. People might just make that assumption." I pressed my lips together and, satisfied with my looks, tossed the comb into the plastic bin by the sink. Then I walked up to Sugar Anne, handed her the keys to the cash drawer and smiled. "But I'm banking they *won't* say it, not loud enough or often enough for it to become real gossip and get back to me."

Sugar Anne cupped the key in both her hands. "Why is that?"

"Because, honey, there are two people in life you do not want to tick off." I inched her chin up. "The person who fixes your meals and the woman who does your hair."

Sugar Anne tipped up her nose. "I do my own hair."

"In that way we are cut from the same cloth, Sugar Anne, darling." I gave her the quickest of impromptu hugs, then moved around to the other side of the counter. "I do my own hair too. That's one of the things my life's experiences have taught me. Never leave yourself open to get burned twice by the same fire, never give up on the people you love, and *always* do your own hair."

Before Ry or Sugar Anne could comment on my pronouncement, I snatched up my purse and my camera and headed for the door. "That's why I have to go along today. And why I won't take no for an answer."

Chapter 16

"Damn, but I hate dead ends." He steered the Starliner through the wrought-iron gates at the end of the long drive.

The tires kicked up a cloud of dust as he turned back onto the country road that had led us to the artist's secluded cabin earlier in the day.

On our right stood a sculpture designed from old farm implements, scrap iron and garbage-can lids. Don Quixote challenging a windmill. It seemed to mock us and the futility of our mission.

"Well, it wasn't a total waste of a day." I smiled and courted comment from Ry with a sidelong look. "We went for a gorgeous drive in this ingeniously restored old car."

"Thank you." He nodded to accept his role in getting the old convertible running again.

"And we met a truly, um . . . unique fellow. . . ."

"Unique." He shook his head. "Now there's a diplomatic way to describe Jeth Fugate."

"Eccentric?" I suggested. "Flamboyant—in a singularly North-Carolina-Mountain-man way?"

"With the body of a lumberjack, the soul of an artist and the mind of a Fortune 500 businessman," Ry added.

"And just because he couldn't help us preserve the old sign doesn't mean he didn't come up with a few dandy suggestions of his own."

"Don't start."

"Hmmm." I tapped my cheek to overplay it a bit. "Who'd have thought that we'd drive all this way and find a man occasionally in need of a private pilot to fly clients in or take finished art pieces to their new homes?"

"I'm not listening."

"Not to mention a hardcore devotee of the Every Second Saturday Flea Market who knows we could bring in bigger and better bands for the Jamboree if we had access to a plane and a private airstrip?"

"You know I didn't realize it would take this long to get out here." He shifted in the seat. "You sure Granny Missus won't start fretting and send a search party out for us?"

"Are you kidding? Dylan lives for nights when I don't cook. Granny Missus whips that deep-fat fryer out so fast it would set your head spinning. Then she batters every thing she can get her hands on and in it goes. Nothing touches their lips that isn't coated with golden fried cornmeal and dripping with grease."

"Mmmm. Think there'll be any left when we get home?"

I laughed. "Probably. No one in my family ever learned the art of cooking in small quantities."

"So, Jolie?"

I closed my eyes, my head still resting on the back of the seat. "Yes?"

"You okay?"

"Fine. Why do you ask?"

"Well, for one thing Jeth just told us he wasn't going to be able to help us in salvaging Esther."

" 'An interesting concept but not commercially viable for me at this time.' " I repeated the man's succinct summation.

"I wish you hadn't been along to hear that."

"No, that's okay. That was good." I rolled my head to one side and my hair did not blow in the wind as it had the first night in the car. "I needed to hear it, Ry. That was the whole reason I had to come today. I *had* to help make a case for saving the sign and hear the reply for myself."

"So, you're not upset?"

"Of course I'm upset. I'm livid! Can't you see I'm practically vibrating with agony and rage?" I opened my eyes and stretched like a cat after a nap in the sun.

"We really shouldn't have come on this trip together, Jolie."

"Stop worrying. I said I was okay with it. Honestly. I feel . . . I feel a real sense of peace about it all now."

"No, I meant we shouldn't have . . ."

"It's . . . it's like that snow globe, Ry." I shaped my hands to indicate the small, domed souvenir. "The one you gave me this morning, you know what I mean?"

"Yes." He tried to keep his eyes on the road and his focus on me. "And no."

"Well, that snow globe has this pleasant little scene, right?"

"A lady sitting under a palm tree. Pretty strange choice to advertise a twelve-unit Trav' O' Tel nestled along a highway in the Blue Ridge Mountains."

"Howdy got them dirt cheap from a hotel gift shop in Florida that went out of business."

He laughed. "Of course. There had to be an angle that made sense of it all."

"But the nature of the scene or how those snow globes came to be at the South Winds aren't the point, Ry. The point is that the scene inside the globe is a constant. Something that never changes."

"Not unlike my grandfather's petty penny-pinching."

"Yes, but unlike poor, lonely old Howdy, the scene has its own kind of quiet perfection. It's sealed up and nothing can be added or taken away."

"And?"

"And from time to time someone comes along and shakes the dickens out of it and releases a flurry of snowflakes and confusion. Then it all drifts down, settles and everything is just like it was—perfect again."

"Jolie, are you saying Jeth not having any solutions for us is just a brief storm and you expect Esther and the sign to still be standing when the skies clear?"

"No." I looked down and then up again, putting my hand on his arm. "No, Ry. I expect the sign to come down, just like the South Winds and the Buffet will. But now that I know that's what's got to happen I can take solace that after this little shake-up Verbena will still be there."

"Oh. Verbena will still be there, just without Esther or the South Winds. Or me."

I gave his arm a squeeze.

"So, Miss Jolene, is this your way of saying that deep down, you're looking forward to my leaving and getting your life back to normal?"

I didn't answer. Just sat back in the seat and looked at the sky.

Around us the leaves rustled and the tires hummed over the old patched concrete road. Fall would come—winter, too, and in the spring most of Verbena would have forgotten Ry O'Malley had ever been there except when they passed the vacant lot where the Trav' O' Tel had once stood.

"I really wish he would have wanted to use Esther in one of his projects, Jolie."

"Me too. But then there's no accounting for taste, huh?"

"He must have some taste. He thought your photographs showed real talent."

I nudged my purse—with the photo packet in it—farther under the seat.

I crossed my legs. My jeans rasped as my thighs pressed together and one calf brushed over the other.

"Dead ends and demanding relationships, it's like I'm destined for one or the other," he muttered.

"It was *not* a dead end. It was what it was, and that's okay." I put my hand behind my neck and lifted my hair to expose the damp skin to the cool air. "It did rile me some when he called your wonderful old postcards tacky, though."

"I took it as a sign he wasn't going to help us."

"*You* took it as a *sign*?" I traced my fingertips down from my neck to the exposed skin above the top of my sweater. "There's a saying around here: As the whale said to Jonah, I ain't a-swallowin' that."

"Swallowing?" He cleared his throat to shoo away the

lingering huskiness. "Do you . . . Do you want to keep those postcards?"

"No, you should keep them. I must have a thousand photos of that sign and of the South Winds too. But what do you have?"

"Don't worry about me. Just say you'll take the postcards, damn it."

I scowled at his terse reply. "What is up with you all of a sudden?"

He gripped the wheel. "You do not want to know what is up with me, Jolie."

"I just asked a simple question. You don't have to get all crotchety."

He raised his eyebrows. "Crotchety?"

"It's a word," I snapped. "Why have you gotten so tense all of a sudden? And don't try to deny it, you are tense."

"I wouldn't dream of denying it. In fact I'd say I'm downright stiff."

"Yes . . . oh! O-o-o-o-h." I winced—if you can wince and grin at the same time.

"Just let it go, okay? My only goal now is to get us back to town without this old car breaking down."

"It's not going to—"

"Don't start that again. The last thing I want to hear right now is how safe you feel with me."

"Ry?"

"You really shouldn't have come along today."

"You said that before and I don't know why."

"How could you not know why, Jolie? How many times have we admitted to each other that the worst thing we could do is be alone together?"

"I wouldn't have pushed you to let me tag along if I hadn't thought it was the right thing to do, Ry. I'm a grown woman, you know."

"You don't have to tell me." He flipped on the car's headlights.

"Yeah, well, maybe I do have to tell you that when I mentioned the snow globe I wasn't just talking about the town."

He shook his head. "I—"

"I can weather a little storm myself, and after things settle I will be all right again." I reached over and stroked his thigh.

Ry jerked at the unexpected contact. His foot went down heavy on the gas, then instinctively he slammed on the brake.

I gasped.

The old car shuddered, sputtered, then died on the spot.

"Shit." He pumped the gas and turned the key, to no avail.

"Ry?"

"It's okay. It's probably just flooded and will need to sit for a few minutes." He worked to keep the car on the road. It coasted down a slight slope where Ry turned the wheel and brought it to a stop just off the road, under the low-hanging branches of an old tree.

He turned in his seat. "So, Jolie, do you *really* believe in signs?"

"You know I do."

"I wish I had your faith." The car jerked as he rammed it into park and set the brake. "Because I could sure use a few unambiguous guideposts to point me in the right direction about now."

I reached under the seat. The small bag from the Sun-shine Market crackled. "You don't want a sign, then, Ry."

"I don't?"

I shook my head and pulled something from the bag without letting him see what it was. "Signs are hardly ever unambiguous."

"That so?"

"No, sir. They are not." I scooted over in the seat. "What you want is a *signal*."

I ran my hand over his chest, placed my thigh on top of his and kissed the side of his neck.

He groaned.

I pressed a small foil packet into his palm.

"Unambiguous enough for you?" I nuzzled his ear.

He let his breath out in a low whistle.

"While you paid for my pictures and those few beauty essentials . . ."

"*Few* beauty essentials? Breath mints, aspirin, sunscreen, hair spray . . ."

"Just the basics for any short road trip." I slid my hand inside his shirt collar and placed the tiniest of kisses on his cheek right where his dimple would be if he could have managed a grin just then. "But while you bought those for me at the market, I went around to the backside of the DB Saloon and, um, picked up a few of these other essentials."

"You were that sure?" He held my face in his hand and searched my eyes.

"That this would happen?" My shoulders rose, then eased down. I wasn't sure about anything but that Ry would be gone soon and my one chance to throw myself off of this particular high dive would go with him. And I would spend the next twenty years wondering "What if. . . ." If I really hoped to find peace in the aftermath of this monumental change, then I knew what I had to do.

I pushed my hair back and wet my lips. "I wanted it to happen and I wanted to be prepared if it did."

"Can you promise me—no regrets?"

"None."

I inhaled deeply to draw the warm scent of him into my lungs. The soft fabric of his shirt crushed into my fist and I kissed him lightly on the lips. "I feel like a couple of kids who've snuck off to be together, writhing naked in the moonlight in the backseat of the car."

"Except the moon isn't quite out yet." He kissed me gently.

"It will be." I flicked the tip of my tongue against his earlobe.

"And we're not writhing . . . or naked."

"We will be."

"And we are definitely in the front seat."

"Not for long." I stretched over him and opened his car door.

He took my hand, and helped me out, then twirled me around and pinned my back against the passenger door, his body pressed hard to mine. His fingers spread and wove through my hair. He supported my head while he kissed me long and deep.

Perhaps I hoped for too much to think this encounter would leave me with any sense of serenity. Satisfaction, maybe, but not the great, calming peace I thought was my due for weathering the storm. And I didn't care. If I never had another moment's peace about the changes that would come to Verbena at least I'd have this one sacred memory.

And that was okay. I would take this plunge willingly and live with the consequences without regrets.

He broke away long enough to open the car door and ease me backward, lowering me gently.

The next moment the car bounced under our combined weight tumbling into the expansive backseat.

I buried my face alongside his neck and muffled a laugh of pure joy.

No more overthinking this.

I would not weigh the consequences. I wanted what I wanted—what I had always wanted—Ry O'Malley.

The car door slammed.

He trailed kisses down my neck.

My pulse raced so fast it left me light-headed. Lost in the sensation, I closed my eyes to keep anything but the wonder of Ry's touch from intruding.

His fingers slid down the small of my back and just inside the top of my jeans.

I flattened my hands to the flexed muscles of his broad back.

His weight pressed down on top of me.

I gasped for air.

He put his elbow in my ear.

My knee jabbed him in the armpit.

"Ow! Ow! Ow! My hair!" I thrashed about and pushed his shoulder off my smashed nose. "You're on my hair. You're pulling my hair!"

"Sorry . . . I . . ." He lurched to one side.

He must have misjudged the width of the seat. He pitched down and forward, banging face first into the window crank of the passenger door. "Ouch! Damn it. Ouch!"

I rubbed my smarting scalp.

Ry sank down to sit on the floorboard. "Why the hell are we trying to do this here?"

I looked at him there, with the heel of his hand pressed to the red mark in the middle of his forehead, and I had to laugh. "Asks the man who owns literally more than a dozen beds in his very own private motel."

"That would be the least private place on the whole entire face of the earth for the two of us to go." He kissed my lips lightly, then pushed himself up to sit on the seat beside me. "You okay?"

"Nothing a little hair spray won't fix."

"Too bad they don't make extra-hold dignity in an aerosol can. This debacle could use a shot of that for sure."

"Dignity?"

He'd said it like a man defeated.

This was my one shot. My big leap. I'd be damned if I'd let bad timing and lack of space cheat me out of it. I pushed Ry back against the seat with one hand, lowered my chin and raised my gaze to meet his. "Did you say dignity?"

His lips crooked up on one side and just the hint of a dimple broke through. "Yeah, I did."

"Oh, Mr. O'Malley, I have just one thing to say to that." I had put aside every precept, every tenet, every principle I had lived my life by in order to get into that backseat with him tonight. I was not going to let something like looking a little foolish stand in my way now. "Screw dignity."

"Jolene!" He feigned surprise but couldn't hide the deep, appreciative chuckle rumbling in his chest.

"If people waited for every sexual encounter to be digni-fied"—I threw my leg over his lap and straddled him—"then the world would be filled with nothing but up-tight, highfalutin, hoity-toity *horny* people."

"You mean it *isn't*?"

"Can't speak for everyone, but I swear if it's humanly possible there'll be two less of that type after tonight." I pulled him toward me by his shirtfront.

"Could be awkward." He met my gaze, his face so close to mine that I could actually see his pupils dilate.

"I think the two of us can work this out." I bent forward as if to kiss him, but at the last moment pulled back and only dipped my tongue between his waiting lips. I wound my fingers in the thick waves of his coarse hair, darting my tongue in and out of his mouth.

In and out.

He pulled away, his chest rising and falling in heavy, erratic breathing.

"Desperate, determined teenagers have been negotiating sex in backseats since cars were invented." I grabbed my sweater by the hem and pulled it upward, peeling it off and tossing it aside.

He groaned.

"It just takes a little good old American ingenuity." I put my hand to the clasp of my bra, then hesitated. "So, what do you say?"

"I say, God bless the USA," he muttered.

I tipped my head back and the ends of my hair tickled my exposed shoulders.

Ry placed his hands on either side of my neck, then made featherlike strokes downward until his work-roughened palms all but covered my white lace cups.

I undid my bra. I arched my back.

"Magnificent."

I smiled and cupped the full weight of my breasts in each hand.

I felt so free, so wicked, and I ached for Ry to join me in the phenomenon.

"Take your clothes off," I demanded.

He undid the buttons of his flannel shirt and tore it roughly away to reveal his bare chest.

I dragged my nails across his skin. The tight coils of his dark and silver hair caressed my knuckles as I did.

"Jolie, we really should—"

"Naked," I commanded. I would not let him talk me into acting reasonable, not with what we both needed so badly so close at hand. "Now."

"Yes, ma'am." He popped the top snap of his jeans.

I slid back along his thighs, tugging at the denim as I did.

He raised his hips to allow me to free him from his clothing.

I whisked the jeans away in a no-nonsense jerk but took my time with his boxers, slipping them down his body centimeter by centimeter.

He hooked his thumbs under the elastic waistband, rose up, then yanked his shorts away so fast the fabric tore. "As my favorite philosopher once said, Screw dignity."

"To hell with dignity. Screw *me!*"

I threw myself with complete abandon into the moment, letting go of the comfort of the past, not fearing the insecurity of the future.

Free.

And strong enough, I thought, to handle whatever consequences might come.

Chapter 17

"Combing your hair while riding in an open convertible might not be the best use of your time, you know." Ry glanced my way without fully taking his attention from the drive down the narrow road in the middle of the night.

"I have to try." I poked the tip of my tongue out and went after a particularly stubborn bump in my otherwise flat bangs.

"Why?"

"Because talk about us going off together will occupy folks in town for a day or so."

"Only a day? Gee I'd have thought we rated at least a week."

"Let me finish," I chided, my teeth gritted as I went after the uncooperative strand unmercifully. "The winking, the nudging, the snickering behind newspapers and the knowing nods passed from one church lady to the next about our being 'delayed' by car trouble—I give those 'til Christmas to lose their luster."

"Surely someone will have the common decency to pull something scandalous by then and take the onus off our sorry tale."

"Excuse me?" I batted my eyes. "Can we not use the terms 'sorry' or 'tail' when talking about tonight's . . . interlude?"

He grinned at my sudden prudishness. "You were explaining this compulsion to struggle against the laws of aerodynamics for the sake of salvaging your hairdo?"

"Well, think about it, won't you?"

Ry scowled.

I supposed he thought he was being clever, hoping to convey the image of a man deep in thought about such matters. He only managed to look adorable to me. Adorable and sexy. And just a tad annoying.

"Really, Ry! Use your head." I clucked my tongue. "Questionable departures and delays are one thing. But if I come dragging back into town with you armed with an old chestnut of a story about the car breaking down *and* my hair is a wreck?"

"Heaven forbid," he muttered.

I shook my head not out of irritation but in a vain effort to get my teased and reteased hair to fall into place again.

"They'd never let me live it down," I said, finally resorting to shaping my hair with my hands.

He scoffed. "Do you know this town or what?"

"I *do* know it. And it knows me. No one will drag my name through the mud over this as long as I'm—"

"I know, not *obvious*."

"Right."

"Jolie, I confess I have no idea how I can accomplish that."

"Why not?"

"Because I fully expect that every time I see you from this moment on everyone will know exactly what is on my mind."

"Will your eyes betray you?" I teased, feeling full of a womanly power and pride I had never known before.

He shifted in his seat. "If not my eyes, then something a little lower on my body will."

He stole a glance my way and my heart all but stopped.

"Well, you'll just have to . . . we'll have to . . ." What the hell does one say to a man who has just pledged not his undying love but an everlasting hard-on to you? I guess I should have been insulted, but I wasn't. I felt . . . exhilarated.

I wet my lips and cleared my throat. "Anyway, as long as no one in my family ever suspects that we have shared anything but animosity, everything will work out fine. My family must never know."

"Jolie, it's nobody's business but our own." He reached out and snagged my hand, comb and all, without taking his eyes from the road. He brought my fingers to his lips and kissed them. "What went on tonight is ours. Not for anyone else to share in, much less judge us over it. Just for us."

"Thank you." I brushed my knuckles along his cheek, then withdrew my hand and returned to frantically arranging my red curls just so.

"Thank me? For what? For protecting your honor? For keeping this small, secret part of our lives private? Hell, I'd have done that even if I had wanted just the opposite."

"I never thought you were the type to kiss and tell."

"Don't make light of this, Jolie. This was a once-in-a-lifetime night and you know it. Somehow, that makes it almost . . . I don't know . . . sacred."

Damn him. When he had reduced it to the simple issues of horniness and hearsay I could deal with it. I could pretend that nothing had really changed. That it had all been a brief, meaningless—and all too wonderful—interlude from my real life.

But when he said the very word I had thought to describe it myself . . . *sacred*! If this were about anything else on earth but sex, I'd have decreed it a sign on the spot.

I tried to catch my breath. I tried to shut it all out, but I simply wasn't strong enough—not after tonight.

Sometime shortly after our third bout of heavy lovemaking we had had to face the facts. We could not simply stay out all night naked in a Starliner by the side of the road and pretend the rest of the world didn't exist—which had been Ry's suggestion.

I vetoed it, having become—through the machinations of signs, wonders and totally undignified, throbbing, naked, wanton sex acts—a woman wise beyond her years. I said we had to get dressed and go.

The old, reliable, unreliable car purred to life with nary a gasp or sputter.

I did not proclaim that a sign. I simply said, "I guess it's time to go home, then."

Now, with Verbena only a few minutes away down good old Highway 612, Ry broke the silence that had settled between us. "Let me get things straight, about this not being 'obvious'?"

"Mmm?" I had my comb in my teeth and my hand submerged in my purse, rummaging around.

"Guess that means I can't send you flowers in the morning."

I dropped my comb into my open purse. "Not unless you want to be picking flowers out of your ass all afternoon."

He half laughed, half winced. "Uh, okay. And calling you? That's also out?"

I produced a pint-sized spray can and popped off the white plastic top. "Why would you need to call me?"

"Why?" He snorted. "Because . . ."

I shrouded myself in a mist of hair spray. Like that snow globe I'd talked about, I was trying to make everything go back to the perfect stillness I had known before the fleeting hours of earth-shaking sex. I needed to shield myself.

Ry must have understood, because he dropped the subject and just drove on. At least for a few minutes.

"So tomorrow we act as if tonight never happened?" he finally asked, quietly.

"Yes. Tomorrow—when the demolition crew shows up—we pretend like tonight never happened."

"The crew. I'd forgotten they had planned to come tomorrow." He looked at his lighted wristwatch. "Today, actually, in only a few hours."

A few hours until the beginning of the end. It should have pained me more, but somehow, with this one incredible night to draw strength and solace from, I wasn't afraid of the future. Just . . . resigned.

"Tomorrow." I sighed. "And the tomorrow after that and the tomorrow after that and all the tomorrows after the South Winds is gone and you've left Verbena forever, I'll go on pretending that tonight was just a dream. That you and I were only—I don't know . . ." I drew my shoulders up, folded my arms tightly and shook my head. "A couple of dreamers?"

"I . . ."

"Let's don't talk this to death, Ry." I smiled, but even in the darkness I think he could see I had to force my casual expression. "We're almost to town. If you turn your lights out now and drive slow, we won't accidentally wake anyone up as we go down the hill."

"I am not driving on a highway with my lights off."

"For a few hundred yards. Just until we're past my grandmother's house?"

He started to argue again, then looked at me and nodded. "Just while we drive by the old gal's place."

"Thanks." I bowed my head and began pawing around in my purse again.

"What are you looking for now? Hair accessories? More personal protective gear? You got a tiara and a Hazmat suit in your magical bag?"

"I need my keys, silly. I have to have them ready so I don't waste any time getting inside. Every minute this takes risks us waking someone up."

He muttered his opinion about that and jammed in the button to turn off the headlights. The convertible eased up the hill on the east side of 612 at a snail's pace. "Jolie, honey, you sure everyone will be asleep in town right now?"

"Of course I'm sure." Head down, I gave my purse a jiggle and kept right on fishing around in it. "It's three A.M. in Verbena. It's quiet as a tomb."

"What tomb? The tomb of the undead?" We topped the hill. "Because every last light in the Trav' O' Tel looks to be lit up brighter than Christmas."

My head snapped up.

He stopped the car, careful to leave it quietly idling.

I dropped my keys back into my purse. They *thunked* and jangled just enough to cover the succinct curse word that I chose to sum up the situation.

"No kidding." Ry agreed wholeheartedly with my assessment.

"Do you think they're waiting up for us?"

"I don't think they're having an all-night quilting bee."

I clutched at his shirtsleeve. "Go back."

"What? What do you mean?"

"Go back. Go back. Reverse. They can't have seen us yet. Go back down the hill, now!"

"And do what?"

"We'll ditch the car in the woods a ways back, rough up our clothes and hair and walk on in."

"Jolene Hadley Corbett! I don't know what shocks me more—that you want us to go down there and lie to our loved ones or that you'd mess your hair up to do it."

"It's not a lie. We'll say we had car trouble. That's not a lie."

"Jolie, trust me on this, you don't want to start compromising the truth to appease other people. Not even for your family. Because once you start down that road you can't go back."

"I don't care about that road, I care about *this* road, about Highway 612. We can still go back on this highway, Ry."

"Maybe you can, but you'll go it alone." The light from the South Winds sign reflected in his dark eyes. "Tonight you make up a lie to mollify your grandmother. Then all those tomorrows you talked about you'll have to live out that lie—that this night never happened, that our time to-gether did not mean a thing—for the rest of your life. I will not be a party to that, Jolie."

Had the man lost his ever-loving mind? I tried to fathom what he expected me to do.

Every mile that brought us closer to town my heart had beat faster, harder. My throat had seemed to close tighter and tighter. I could not concentrate on anything.

I had hoped that tending to my appearance would help. But it had only served to remind me that whatever face I put on in front of my friends and family, it would be a false-hood. When I had promised Ry I would have no regrets, that I could let all my inhibitions run wild with him for a few hours, then go back to everything just as it was, I had perpetuated the worst falsehood of all. I had lied to myself.

And now he wanted me to tell the truth to everyone? I gripped the side of the passenger door and tried to take a deep, calming breath. "So, you're saying you want us to go cruising into town bigger than life and confess that the two of us have been making love in the back of this car?"

"I don't think a confession is necessary, do you, really?"

"No. Of course not." I feigned a laugh that came out sounding like a child's nervous imitation of a pony neigh-ing. "Why would we have to confess, when everyone will know just by looking at me that I've just spent hours bare-breasted in public, bouncing naked on the lap of a man des-tined to walk out of my life in a few days."

"Jolie, that's not—"

"Mercy, Ry. What if my minister notices some intangible aura of sexual satisfaction about me? What if he takes one look at my face and points out from the pulpit that only a woman who has sinned mightily—recently and repeatedly—could have skin so luminous?"

"Jolie, don't you think you're exaggerating just a little?"

"Am I?" I wet my dry lips and put my hand to my throat. "It might surprise you to learn, Ry, that I have always been virtuous to the point of being a regular tight-ass in some people's point of view."

"They clearly don't know you as I do."

"No, they don't. They know me better." I'd been naïve to think no one would pick up any subtle changes in me, hadn't I?

"No one is going to know. Trust me, there is nothing re-markable about you for them to pick up on."

"Right. Thank you so much, those are exactly the words a woman wants to hear from the man she just let boink her brains out."

"Naw, you still have all your brains, honey, I just boinked a little of the curl out of your hair." He reached out and stroked my cheek. "And you've done such an amazing re-construction job on your hairdo that no one will ever sus-pect a thing. And what if they do?"

"What if they do?" I shook my head and piled the sar-casm on extra deep. "You mean what if the women whose hair I style to look good for the men at the VFW and DB Sa-loon detect some new vibe from me and suddenly welcome me into their sisterhood? Will the high-school home eco-nomics teacher volunteer to use her computerized sewing machine to embroider a great big scarlet *A* on my work smock?"

"Then that would be her bad because technically we didn't commit adultery." He grinned at me with those double-barreled dimples and eyes blazing with self-satisfied mischief. "I believed the term you're thinking of is fornication."

I shut my eyes to try to stop the pointless ramblings of my panicked mind but all I could see was myself, greeting customers at the Combin' Holiday with a big ol' *F* emblazoned on my bosom.

I drew a shuddering breath and made myself look at him without giving in to my anxieties. "I don't want anyone to know the details of what we shared tonight, Ry."

"And neither do I. I told you, Jolie, that's our business." This time when he reached for me, not even the hint of kidding shone in his clear, potent gaze. "That's our special memory."

"You said to tell the truth."

"Yes, because I won't cheapen what has passed between us tonight with some stupid story that no one will believe anyway."

"So . . . so what *are* you saying? That we should just drive down into the heart of . . ." I leaned forward in my seat and squinted. "Of whatever the hell is going on down there? And say what?"

"How about, 'What the hell is going on down here?'" He laughed. "Jolie, they knew we were going on this trip and that we expected to be gone awhile, right?"

"Well, yes, I made sure everyone knew I'd stay as long as it took to plead Esther's case."

"They also knew we took this car, and that it's not the most reliable choice of transportation."

"Granny Missus did tell me we were danged fools not to take your SUV."

"See? There." He took a deep breath and reached down to turn on the lights. "We are not the ones on the explaining end of this particular situation."

I looked at the scene down the hill. I couldn't see any people there, just lots of lights. But then the trees that still hid us from sight also blocked my vision. "So we're just going to go down there, blowing back into town a few hours before dawn like we're totally in the rights and demand to know what's going on?"

"Yep." He yanked the knob.

The headlights came on.

I stared straight ahead, trying to decide if I would go along with his idea or get out of the car and try to come up with something better on my own. I curled my fingers around the door handle when suddenly, there above the treetops, I saw the flickering tips of Esther's upraised hands.

Tonight I had jumped off the high dive, knowing full well what awaited me. I could not go back now. Ry was right, we did not have to tell anyone anything. But to make up a lie from the get-go, that was just plain silly. I made a quick check in the side mirror, pressed my lips together, then tipped up my chin. "Okay then, no preposterous stories about walking back to town. No confessions, no admissions, no regrets."

"Tell the truth and move on?"

I nodded my agreement.

He reached across the seat, gave my hand a squeeze and gunned the motor. "Hang on to that pretty hairdo of yours, then, because here we go."

Chapter 18

🌀 "Handcuffs? Good lord, Sugar Anne, where on earth did you get handcuffs?" Ry strode toward the scene that awaited us, barely avoiding knocking over the handprinted SAVE THE SOUTH WINDS! poster leaning against the swimming pool fence.

"I know a lot of people who own handcuffs, Dad."

"That's not an answer, young lady."

At least not the answer that the father of a seventeen-year-old girl—a girl living right on the razor-edged divide between teenage rebellion and responsible adulthood—wanted to hear, I guess.

He clenched his jaw.

Sugar Anne raised her chin.

I supposed she would have crossed her arms and turned her back on him, too, if she hadn't been shackled to the fence. Still, with them having to look each other in the eye with no place to retreat, it did seem that they might finally talk to each other. Imagine that: two family members who obviously cared for each other but did not agree on some very basic principles of conduct regarding how to *talk* to each other. And all it took was shackles and sealing off all means of escape.

"Where the hell did you get this ridiculous idea?" Ry demanded of his daughter. "And don't tell me lots of people you know have ridiculous ideas."

"Whoo-hoo! Look who decided to come on back and join the party." Emma strode toward us with a thermos in one hand, a cell phone in the other and the Logie County Yellow Pages under her arm.

"This was your doing." Ry pointed to the dark-haired woman in skintight leather pants.

"No, Yummy-muffins, *this* was my doing." She held up the thermos and handed it to me. "Hot chocolate for our favorite mane-mutilated militant."

I took the drink and lifted the lid, letting the sweet-smelling steam swirl up into my flushed face. It was a cheap stalling tactic to be sure, but I tried to milk it for every minute of calm and comfort I could.

"Don't blame Emma, Daddy. If anyone helped me decide to finally take some action, it was Jolie."

Can you gag on hot-chocolate steam? Because I swear I gagged on hot-chocolate steam. That and Sugar Anne's scalding accusation, which shot any hope for calm and comfort all to hell.

"Me? But I was ready to surrender on saving the South Winds," I protested. Diving into a mess of your own making was one thing, but I had no intention of letting this hair-impaired child push me into the deep end. "I just wanted to preserve the top part of the sign, if at all possible. I never advocated anything involving handcuffs!"

"Then you don't know what you've missed in life,

Sweetcakes," Emma muttered into my ear with her shoulder to my back. "Though something tells me you've been making up for some lost time this evening."

"Shut up, Emma." I simply could not handle an attack from all sides right now. I had dared to step one toe—one lousy toe—over the line tonight and couldn't help thinking that fate had turned around to kick me in the butt for it. "Sugar Anne, when did I ever say anything about you doing anything this crazy?"

" 'Always do your own hair,' " she repeated my parting words with more passion than anything I've ever uttered deserved. "It was a metaphor, right?"

Oh, great! All my life I've gone around spouting metaphors and this is the one time somebody actually *gets* one and follows through on it!

"You were telling me that if something matters enough to you, you should take care of it yourself. Don't leave it up to others to see it through." She rattled her handcuffs with a level of righteous smugness one rarely sees outside of small-town minister selection committees and Atlantic Coast Conference college sorority Rush Week. *"Always do your own hair.* That's what I'm doing."

I groaned.

Ry grumbled. "You should never have used that phrase with someone who has already demonstrated a willingness to do *that* to her own head."

"Cool your jets, O'Malley." Emma pushed past me to defend my honor before I could actually decide if it needed defending or not. "Jolie might have provided the initial inspiration, but the chain-yourself-to-the-chain-link campaign was all your darling daughter's doing."

Emma dropped the phone book onto one of three folding chairs parked in a semicircle beneath the halo of light from the South Winds sign. "Lauren and I didn't think it was right to leave her out here like this all on her own, so we've kept her company."

I nabbed Emma by one angular elbow and demanded, "You got the lady minister involved in this too?"

"Sure, she'll be back any minute now. She ran over to the church to get a media list."

"Media?" Ry looked toward Sugar Anne, then to Emma and finally rested his weary gaze fully on me.

I shrugged but felt confident it looked unconvincing.

"Yes, 'media.'" Emma made invisible quotation marks in the air to show she understood it wasn't an apt description for the resources of Logie County and the surrounding areas. "You know. A list of all the radio, newspaper and TV contacts they can use if they ever need to do a press release."

"Press release?" He laughed, but it didn't sound all that authentic to me. "God save us from Southern women with a cause and a cell phone."

"What 'media'"—I mimicked Emma's quotation marks—"would be the least bit interested in this nonsense?"

"Are you kidding? The *Logie County Sun* for starters."

"Oh, Emma, you wouldn't!" I froze, the plastic thermos top in one hand and the silver-and-green cylinder of hot chocolate in the other.

"Damn straight I did. Had to leave a message on the machine, but they'll get it when they show up in the office in a few hours."

"Why did you do that?" Ry ran his hand back through his hair.

"Why not? It has all the makings of a terrific story: family conflicts, fighting to preserve a piece of local history, and a teenage girl in handcuffs!" She gestured boldly as she spoke, her eyes alight with the pure fun of having had a hand in stirring up so much trouble.

I wanted to pinch her fool head off but in the end couldn't be too irritated with her. After all, she had stepped in to watch over Sugar Anne while the girl's daddy and I were out doing unspeakable and incredible things to each other in the back of a convertible.

So I decided to do what I do best—play it cool, play things down, play anything but hardball.

"With the exception of some old-fashioned dishing-the-dirt value to our local weekly paper, I can't see why anyone else would have the slightest interest in this." I spoke with a casual dismissive tone and finished pouring the steaming liquid into the cup. For the first time, I stepped fully into the light as I handed the cup to Sugar Anne. "What kind of press release did you have in mind?"

"Nothing big, just a little announcement." Emma cocked her head, narrowed her eyes, then approached slowly.

With no advance warning, she swept back the steadfast curls along my neck.

The cool night air blew over the still-tender marks on my skin left by Ry's voracious lovemaking. "Of course, if you two have a little announcement you'd like to make, don't feel you have to hold off for the proper channels."

I jumped back.

Ry stepped forward. "No one is making any announcements of any kind. What the hell's the matter with folks

around here, always wanting to poke around in other people's business?"

"Just human nature, I guess. No harm meant by it."
Emma slipped the thermos out of my hand, then turned on
him. "Haven't you ever had the urge to poke around a little yourself, Ryman?"

"Knock it off, Em." I tugged at my hair, pulling the hard-
managed shape out of it in order to cover up the telltale
marks on my neck.

"If you just came here to keep my daughter company,
then you might as well go home."

"Because we're here to watch over her now," I rushed to
tag on my finishing touch to his already completed thought.

"No." He put his hand on my back, then looked over his
shoulder at Sugar Anne leaning back against the old fence,
her raised arm cuffed to the rusting links. "Because Sugar
Anne's one-girl protest has come to an end. You don't
need to keep her company out here because she is about to
go inside."

"I am not!" Sugar Anne went rigid, daggers in her
squinty-eyed gaze. "I'm staying right here until you rethink
your position about destroying the South Winds, Dad."

"Sugar Anne, I've thought and rethought it every day
since Grandpa Howdy died. Did you honestly believe I arrived at this conclusion carelessly?"

"No, I think you came by it cowardly."

Cowardly. It rang in the night air like a gunshot echoing
in the mountains.

And yet, he did not refute it.

I guess he could see how his taking the South Winds in
lieu of his rightful inheritance, then planning to level the

old place in order to find peace in his family might well seem cowardly to an onlooker. Hell, I honestly believed he understood that it might actually *be* cowardly, the easy way out of a seemingly impossible situation.

"You're not doing this because it's what *you* want, Daddy. When you made me come here against my will, you told me that being a grown-up sometimes means making decisions that had nothing to do with what you want but that are the best choices for others."

"You don't have to remind me," he said softly.

"You told me that you regretted not coming back to see your grandfather again, didn't you? And you did that just to keep peace with Granddad O'Malley and your aunt Renata. How is what you're doing now any different?"

Funny how what he had seen as a bold, decisive step toward walking away from his family's relentless demands was seen by his daughter as just another way of caving in to them all over again.

And not so funny was that I could see her point. But could he?

"If your staying away from here before didn't make them happy, then what makes you think getting rid of the South Winds entirely will?"

He took a deep breath.

"You have no right to tear this place down, Dad. It means too much to too many people." The fence rattled. Sugar Anne gripped the chain link with her free hand and looked past him pleadingly. "Tell him, Jolie."

If we had not just spent the evening making love, things might be different. But I had crossed the line drawn through the middle of Verbena and through the core of my family. That very line had defined who I was and how I was supposed to behave for as far back as I could remember. If I had not resigned myself to the demise of Esther and the South Winds and counted on Ry getting the hell out of town, I would never have given myself so passionately to him.

In fact, if Sugar Anne had pulled this demonstration of hers just one day earlier, I might have chained myself up right alongside the girl.

"As I see it he has every right to tear this place down, Sugar Anne." I took a deep breath and stepped backward, withdrawing partially into the shadow. "And the sooner he does it, the better."

"You've got to be joking!" Emma moved forward.

I cut her off and got her to back down with an upraised hand.

"You can't mean that," Sugar Anne cried.

"I do mean it, honey," I whispered. "You have your whole life ahead of you and the whole wide world to live it in. What do you care about this place? You can travel, go to college, have adventures."

Sugar Anne cast her gaze to the ground. "And when I'm tired or overwhelmed, or lonely from doing those things, where will I have to come home to?"

Home. She had every luxury and any place she could imagine available to her, yet she wanted to call this grungy little building in a grubby little town in the sweetest spot in North Carolina *home.*

"This is a motel, Sugar Anne." The flatness of Ry's tone echoed the absence of emotion in his eyes. "It's not your home."

"But it could be. I've only been here a week and it feels like home already."

"What about your mom's house in Straffer?" he asked.

"That's my home with *her*. I want a home with *you*, Daddy."

"I can give you that, Sugar Anne."

"Where?" she demanded.

I knew he had sublet his apartment in Atlanta for the next year, thinking that after traveling with his daughter he'd spend some time on his own, doing who knows what. But he could find another place to live, to provide them both with a home base. He had the world at his disposal and could choose any place in it to live.

"You know that you'll always have a home with me, wherever I am," he said, undertones of compassion and surrender in his quiet, powerful voice.

"Then why not make a home—"

"Just not in Verbena," he finished.

Any place but here.

"Why not?" Her earnest eyes honed in on him.

He clenched his jaw.

"It's about all this inheritance crap, isn't it?"

He kicked at a rock near the base of the South Winds sign. "Don't say *crap*."

"I know it is. In fact, when you took so long getting back tonight I had a lot of time to think."

"And *this* is the best you could come up with?" He pointed toward the handcuffs and gave a passing-fair attempt at a laugh. "Your time would have been better spent watching TV."

"I needed some way to get your attention."

"Attention? I thought that's why you cut your hair. To get my attention."

"You . . . you noticed that's all I wanted?"

"He noticed." I had no right to speak for him, but better me rushing in than him acting like a . . . a . . . a *man* and volunteering that I'd had to point out the obvious to him. "And he was willing to give you his full attention. Willing to put a hold on his life these next few months just to help you get your own life off to a better start."

The girl did have the presence of mind to look the tiniest bit ashamed.

"This, Sugar Anne, this is no simple plea for attention and you need to admit it. You're trying to push me with this crazy stunt, trying to force my hand, trying . . ."

"Trying to test her boundaries," I murmured.

He turned around and with a single foiled and frustrated male look asked me to stop butting in.

"Not that any of this is any of my business, of course."

The lady minister's car pulled into the drive a few feet away.

I retreated another step into a dim spot in the otherwise brightly lit parking lot.

"Just what I need," he muttered, rubbing both hands through his thick, silver-tinged hair. "One more woman on the scene ready and rarin' to give me advice."

"Might as well know," Emma chimed in before Lauren could even climb out of her shiny, new economy car. "Mr. Wyatt is with her. Sorrell volunteered him to cook breakfast for your girl. I wanted to set up a stand and sell coffee and biscuits to well-wishers, onlookers and the demolition crew, but we were afraid there might be some kind of regulation against it."

"Hey, ya'll!" Lauren called out. "I brought that set of

handcuffs we've had in the lost and found for the last two years in case anyone else feels led to join the cause."

Silver metal flashed in the neon light.

Mr. Wyatt climbed out of the passenger side of the car.

Even from where I stood, I could hear the old man's deep, raspy chuckle.

"Damn it all to hell, who else have y'all dragged into this mess?" Ry glared at his daughter, then at my cohort. "Y'all got a town drunkard or a toothless mountain man you want to haul in for comic relief?"

Emma had the consideration to look apologetic, bowing her head a bit and pretending a sudden fascination with her cell phone but Sugar Anne cleared her throat.

Ry stiffened.

"Daddy, I, uh, I guess you deserve to know. I called Granddad."

He turned slowly to face his child. "You called *your* granddad?"

"Well, I couldn't very well call yours." Her weak smile and playful comeback did not charm him as I suspected it often had before.

He grew intensely quiet. "Why in the name of all that is holy did you do that?"

"I thought if I could explain to them how much I liked this place and make them see how it didn't serve anybody to destroy it they might back off a little."

"Back off? My father? When there's a buck to be made?"

"I'd say when hell freezes over, but if there was a nickel to be got I'd say them O'Malleys would fashion ice skates out of demon's ears and keep right on at their money-grubbing ways."

Ry did not have to turn around to know who had barked out her long-held opinion of his family, but when I gasped, he could not keep his eyes away.

"Granny Missus, you weren't waiting up for me, were you?"

"No, I went to bed my reg'lar time. Why?" She leaned in to peer at me. "Did you come in particularly late?"

"Granny Missus." Ry reached the old gal's side in two swift strides and placed himself between the two of us. His arm fit around the sloped-with-age shoulders padded by a wool coat, a knitted shawl, a quilted bathrobe and what looked like men's pajamas underneath it all. "Let me help you sit down. A woman your age really oughtn't be out in this cool night air, you know."

"I know no such thing." She batted her gnarled hand at his offer to assist her.

He did not let her reluctance deter him. "Wouldn't you be more comfortable in your own home?"

"Now what kind of a stupid question is that?" She nodded to Norris Wyatt and to the lady preacher as they came up to join the group. "*Of course* I'd be more comfortable in my home. But I got up a few minutes ago and saw all this commotion going on over here and had to come see with my own eyes what it was all about."

"You got up?" I pushed past him to take his place beside my grandmother. "Are you okay?"

"Of course I'm okay. I'm over eighty, child. At my age you either get up at night or start wearing them big old adult diapers." She kept on walking toward the fence, despite Ry trying to guide her to a folding chair. "What I want to know is, what kind of O'Malley tomfoolery is going on here?"

"You know what, Granny Missus? It *is* O'Malley tom-foolery. And it's for us O'Malleys to tend to. By ourselves. So, if everyone will just go on home . . ."

" 'Save the South Winds'?" Granny Missus scowled as she read from Sugar Anne's homemade sign. Then she set her jowly jaw and scrunched the soft folds of her round face up at Sugar Anne. "You mean to tell me, Miss Hatchet Hair, that *you* would do this? That you would go against your very kin right out in the open for everyone to know and talk about?"

"I . . ." Sugar Anne stole the briefest of all looks in her father's direction, then squared her shoulders as much as her confinements allowed. "Yes. I would. To do what I think is right, I would go against my family's wishes."

Granny Missus shook her head and clucked her tongue. "You O'Malleys."

"That's right." I moved into the light, my back to my grandmother and my eyes locked in Ry's gaze.

"That's right, Granny Missus." I swallowed hard, my expression pleading with him to understand my motives. I wanted my life back. I wanted my calm, my serenity after the storm.

I wanted this over with before I had a chance to confront the enormity of it all. Before I had to totally rethink my life and choices forever.

I wanted Ry O'Malley out of my sight, out of my thoughts and out of my hair once and for all.

"You know how these O'Malleys are, they'd sell each other down the river if they had a mind it might gain them something."

The unnatural glow of the electricity humming through the sign above gave the scene a surrealistic quality.

"You wouldn't catch a Hadley up to this kind of non-sense." I faced the others, my head held high. "Because the Hadleys are all for this nasty old eyesore coming down. It's long past time the O'Malley family got out of Verbena."

"No. You wouldn't catch a Hadley doing this kind of thing." Emma directed my attention to the old fence.

Norris broke into a full belly laugh.

"Granny Missus!" I thrust both my hands in my hair.

"Did somebody say they had a second pair of them hand-cuffs? 'Cause if you don't I got a pair in my garage. One of you young ones will have to go and fetch them back to me."

"Are you joining my fight to save the South Winds?" Sugar Anne's smile grew bigger than daylight.

"I am," Granny Missus confirmed, her own smile not so big. But only because she clearly had not put in her partial dental plate and the big gap showed through her wide lips. Her eyes sparkled.

Lauren stepped up to volunteer her services by latching the elderly woman to the metal fence with the cuffs she had brought along.

"Oh, yeah, Dad. Grandpa said that if he doesn't hear from you by tomorrow evening telling him everything is on track, he's sending Grandma and Aunt Renata to Verbena to look into matters themselves."

Norris strolled up to Ry's side. Planting his feet wide, he shook his head, folded his arms and laughed again. "Looks like you got woman trouble from all sides, son."

"Not anymore." Ry pulled up his shoulders. "The demo-lition crew will be here at 7 A.M. I expect you to uncuff your-selves by then, or I will personally borrow a wire cutter and do it for you."

"But Daddy . . ."

"No 'but Daddy.' No getting around it." He reached into his jeans pocket to retrieve the keys to the Starliner and found with them the quarter I had told him was his sign.

He gripped the coin for only a second before taking it, along with the keys, and pressing them into my hand. "I wish things could have turned out differently."

"I've wished that for a long time myself." I closed my fingers around the keys and coin.

"Enjoy your little protest while you can, y'all. Tomorrow the South Winds is coming down."

He walked toward the lobby door without a single backward glance.

So that was it. That was my reward for rushing headlong into things and thinking I could keep a level head, maintain control of something so clearly beyond my capabilities.

I dragged my fingers through my hair and when I took my hand away couldn't help but notice that a few thin strands clung to my trembling knuckles.

I'd lost my focus.

I'd lost my dignity.

I had lost the tenuous sense of security I had always struggled to hold on to in my life and for my home in Verbena.

I also suspected I had most assuredly lost a good measure of my mind over these last few days.

And now I was losing my hair.

I no longer wanted to be like Esther Williams, movie star or motel icon. I just wanted my life back.

Chapter 19

"Say 'keys'!" With the first rays of morning warming the eastern sky, I fond my subjects framed in perfect light, if not in perfect form. I raised my camera and held my breath to steady it.

Granny Missus and Sugar Anne stretched their lips into cheesy grins but they could not dispel the shadows of weariness under their eyes. Still, ever game, black thatches of hair brushed against gauzy poofs of white curls as they pressed their cheeks together. Each extended her arms—as much as the circumstances allowed—and showed their hands still cuffed to the dull steel fence. "Ke-ee-ee-zzz."

Despite one totally sleepless night, too many issues weighing down upon me and the pressure of knowing I had three minutes to get this photo before Ry showed up to chafe at my already raw-edged nerves, I had to laugh at the pair. They hadn't backed down an inch under Ry's tirade, but then, how could they? No one seemed to have any way to free them from handcuffs they'd slapped on so cavalierly.

I had searched all night for a means to undo the simple latches. I hadn't even gone home long enough to do anything but get Dylan ready for school.

As soon as I'd put him on the bus a few minutes ago, I'd grabbed my camera and headed over to record this event for my memory books. I had not even run a comb through my hair or gulped down a cup of coffee. I looked a total wreck, for sure, but hardly had the time or energy to worry about it now.

"You going to take that picture before our faces break in two? You are not looking at a couple of natural-born supermodels, you know." Granny Missus twitched her cheek and made a sound like she had just sucked a kernel of corn from under her dentures.

"Yeah, hurry up, Jolie. I haven't smiled this long since I was four and Mama entered me in the Miss Pretty Petite pageant."

"Oh, that ain't nothing," Granny groused. "I ain't smiled this much since 1962, when I had all my real teeth."

Sugar Anne laughed and a light came over her whole face.

Whatever this experience had cost me in beauty sleep and personal comfort, seeing that brief, genuine smile went a long way toward making it all worthwhile.

"You both should smile now." I snapped the picture, then another, the flash made more brilliant by the subdued morning light. "I swear I don't know what either of you has to act so sour about all the time. My mama always told me that an affable appearance is a girl's best offense."

"Must be true. I sure find that statement offensive enough." Talking from the corner of her mouth, my grandmother spoke up loud and clear, adding, "Gets that pretti-fied crap from my mother's people, you know."

"I don't know where she *gets* it," Sugar Anne snarled. Well, not so much snarled as slurred with a superior atti-tude, yet lacking real animosity. "But from what I've seen and what you've told me, Granny Missus? I'd say Jolie's best offense is Dippity-Do and denial."

"You taught her that!" I pointed at Granny Missus. "She's way too young to even know what Dippity-Do is on her own."

"Truth is truth." Granny scooted her lawn chair over. The metal frame scraped and screeched against the chain-link fence. "Right, Sugar Anne?"

The young woman did not say a word. Just looked at me with big, searching eyes.

Of course, right. She didn't have to say it to send me the message. The girl had pegged me from the start. Sheer will and no small amount of longtime stylist's trickery were all I had to safeguard my sheltered, shaky existence.

I gripped my camera until my fingers ached and told my-self not to dwell on it now. I was just here to get a few pho-tos before the demolition crew arrived, not to analyze myself or to reach out to Ry O'Malley's daughter.

After the dust of the next few days settled, there would be plenty of time for soul-searching. Long, lonely nights when I would remember every intimate detail of the first boy who ever touched my breasts and the last man who would ever . . .

"Fire up your engines, darling, and shift your fanny into high gear." Granny Missus rattled her cuffs and whistled through the gap in her teeth to draw my attention.

"What?" I blinked.

"Either take another picture or come over here and un-leash us."

"Unleash you?" I took one more photo for good measure. "I don't know if the world's ready for that."

Granny Missus squinted and made her opinion almost known by sneezing to cover a mild but interesting curse word.

Sugar Anne pressed her eyes shut and leaned back against the fence. It clanked and moaned even under her sleight weight. "You going to give those pictures to the local newspaper?"

"No, just taking one last personal memento before I un-lock the Trav' O' Tel Two."

"You've the keys then?" Ry's voice caught me completely off guard.

For an instant I thought of the keys and the quarter he had thrust into my hand last night and I tensed up. Though Granny Missus had demanded I return the car keys—like I was a kid being grounded—I had tucked the grudge money into my jeans pocket. It remained there as a reminder of everything that had gone on since Ry's arrival and of all that would go with him when he departed.

"Jolie?" He touched my back lightly, then pulled his hand away, as if my body burned his fingertips. "Did you find the handcuff keys?"

"The handcuff . . . oh. Oh, yeah." I shifted my feet so that I could face him but kept my gaze aimed just over his left shoulder. "We had to turn the A. E. Auto Garage and Mu-seum inside out to do it, but we finally dug up a key."

"*A* key? It fits both sets? How can that be?"

"It's simple, really." I hung the camera around my neck by its long, black strap. Then I plunged my hand into the pocket of my father's old high-school letterman's jacket, which I'd found in one of my grandmother's closets. "Half the people in town have a set of these very same cuffs, but practically no one has the keys that go with them."

"I'm beginning to think there's a lot about this town that I don't know."

"And why would you?" It came out sounding sad to me, but I could see by the look in his eyes that he took it as an accusation. Well, let him think whatever he wanted. It no longer concerned me, after all. I withdrew the small metal key and showed it to him. "Those handcuffs are a big-selling novelty item at the Flea Market. Practically every place in town with a lost and found box has a set of them, along with bamboo backscratchers, little girls' ribbon wreaths and plastic blow-up wiener dogs."

"Handcuffs, backscratchers, ribbons and wiener dogs—they say you learn as much about a society from their cast-offs as from their culture. What do you suppose all that says about Verbena?" He took the key, his fingers brushing mine.

I tucked my hand into my jacket pocket. "Maybe it says we honor justice, self-sufficiency, beauty and do not lack for a sense of whimsy."

"Doesn't sound like such a bad place, does it?" He narrowed his eyes toward the highway and the town beyond it.

"And I didn't even mention the occasional pair of panties or boxers that folks find in their parking lots the morning after the Jamboree." Why the hell did I have to tack that on?

I felt my face turning beet red. I wanted to say more, but I didn't dare open my mouth.

Ry let me off the hook by chuckling and saying, "Probably lost by travelers in a rush to get to church services and forced to change in their cars."

"Yes, I'm *sure* that's what it is." I laughed, but joining in on the joke did nothing to dispel the warmth from the blush on my neck and face.

But then, how could I not feel it? Daylight accentuated the gruffness of Ry's beard. The silver in his otherwise dark and tousled hair, and the rumples in the clothes he had worn—and for a few hours, *not worn*—last night generated a heat all their own.

"Because no one in quaint old Verbena would ever—"

"Oh, no, of course not!" I gathered the camera strap in one hand over my chest. "Never!"

"If I didn't know better, I'd swear you guys are flirting with each other," Sugar Anne called out.

"I don't know about that." Granny Missus gave her most indignant snort. "But they are surefire flirting with disaster if somebody doesn't come over here and get these handcuffs off of me."

"Why do I feel like that's not the first time you've had to shout that, ornery old woman?" Ry gave me a wink, then another fleeting touch to my arm as he headed up to the fence.

Granny Missus scoffed and sputtered, but she clearly had gotten a kick out of Ry's slightly ribald ribbing.

"Let me do the honors." He grasped the cuff around the old, pale wrist. "What's the saying? Age before beauty?"

"I prefer the warning 'Close cover before striking.' "

Granny gave him a little backhanded swat. "If you so much as nip the skin taking these things off I'll bat your ears, boy."

"You are a mean and spiteful old woman." He turned the key in the lock.

Her hand slid free.

"And I am truly going to miss you. . . ." He bent down and kissed Granny Missus once lightly on her full, soft cheek. "Hannah Rose."

I gasped, but to my amazement Granny Missus did not explode at his impertinence or try to cover up how much his sweet gesture had touched her. She just sniffled, withdrew a hanky from somewhere in the folds of all the layers of nightclothes and outerwear and dabbed her eyes.

"You have a fine daughter, Ryman. She's smart. She's honest and she's got the grit to go after what she wants. Be proud of her."

He nodded.

She reached up to Ry and he bent to meet her halfway.

She grabbed his ear and gave it one firm, no-nonsense twist. "So learn something from the child, why don't you?"

Mouth open, Ry rubbed his ear but didn't say a thing.

In the same kind of stunned silence, we all watched the old woman waddle over to the glistening red Starliner.

She got in, started it up and drove it like a Sherman tank over every pothole and bump in the parking lot. Then on she went, across Highway 612 without so much as a cautionary look. She took it around to the backside of the museum, out of sight at last and in its usual resting spot.

"She is two fistfuls of ornery, Jolie, I'm telling you," Ry muttered.

"What about me?" Sugar Anne demanded.

He turned to his daughter. "You're only a handful of irritable right now, but you are working on it."

"Ry, Sugar Anne is just young and impulsive. . . ."

"Kindly stay out of this, Jolie," he said without looking my way.

Even though he was within his rights to remind me that I had no place in his family squabbles, it stung to hear him shut me off so definitively. I took a step backward and the heel of my shoe scraped the concrete base of the South Winds' giant sign.

"And you, young lady. I'm half-tempted to leave you here until I call your grandparents and ask them to meet me between here and Straffer to pick you up."

Even from this vantage point, I could see the surprise and disappointment in the young woman's eyes. I empathized with that emotion completely at the moment.

Sugar Anne squirmed at her restraints. "You're still sending me back?"

"I'm not backing away from my decision, Sugar Anne. All your life you've looked for ways to whine and whimper and wheedle your way around the rules and expectations I set down for you. Your grandparents and Mom let you get away with that too much, and so have I. That stops now."

"Last night you said you're doing this to prove that I can trust you to keep your word."

"Exactly."

"But you don't trust me?"

"Trust is earned." He put the key in the lock but did not look his daughter in the eye. "I am doing all I can to deserve your trust. I don't know what else to tell you."

It touched me to watch Ry hold back his own hurt over his daughter's actions. He never said to his child's face, "I don't trust you," and that was wise, since her pranks did not merit that level of tough love. He was fair and even-handed, though I knew how much it hurt to look at a child you adore and receive anger and defiance in return. Yet he did not shy from letting Sugar Anne know what he expected—for her to be trustworthy. Just like her father.

I took a deep breath. Ry was many things, but most of all he was a man to be trusted, trusted with your very heart if it came to that.

He turned the key in the second lock and the cuffs fell free with a dull clank. "I'm just not sure what to do with you until I have the free time to drive you halfway home."

"Let her stay with me."

"With you?" Ry froze halfway down to picking up the handcuffs.

Snap decisions and blurting out spontaneous solutions to other people's problems were not my style. And yet here I was again, throwing myself into the middle of a situation where I did not belong because . . . because it was Ry and his daughter and I wanted to help if I could. "That is, I could use her around the salon until you can make arrangements."

"That's okay by me." Sugar Anne rubbed her wrist. "I can help Jolie and finish paying her back before I leave. I want to do that."

"I'm not interested in what you want, young lady. I'm interested in what's best." He took his daughter's arm, then stretched it out into the sunlight and examined it for injury. "What could she do for you today, Jolie? You have a big client load?"

Wednesdays? I never had a lot of clients on Wednesdays. I considered lying and saying that I did, but the truth-telling bug must have taken a bit out of me. "No. I don't have a single appointment. That doesn't mean I can't keep her occupied."

"Why would you volunteer to do that?"

The girl needed to know that someone trusted her. *I* trusted her. I shared the same respect for the young woman that Granny Missus had expressed. The Dippity-Do and de-nial remark not withstanding.

Dippity-Do and . . . Suddenly I knew the one perfect thing to show Sugar Anne that I had complete and utter faith in her. "What can she do? Well, look at me. I'm a mess."

"Oh, yeah, you're a regular train wreck." His dimples flashed and his eyes glittered.

The roar of the heavy trucks grinding their way up the hill filled my ears. My heart thudded a little harder. I wanted to blame the approaching machinery, but I couldn't. Just stand-ing here, my gaze fixed on Ry's, did things to me I could not describe and dared not dream about, not anymore.

"I . . . I could stand to have my hair washed and maybe a good conditioning treatment." I moved my attention to the girl. "If you think you can do it."

"Sure. Emma said I did a really good job shampooing the other day. It's not brain surgery."

"You're going to let someone who has done *this*"—Ry stood behind his daughter, his hands open—"to her head get her hands on *your* hair?"

I inched backward only to find my jeans scraped by rough brick. My knees bent. I wobbled, then plunked down on the edge of the big sign's foundation.

I caught my breath and looked up. By this evening Sugar Anne would be gone and the South Winds would be battered beyond redemption. Now was the time to dive in without reservation.

I swallowed hard and lifted my chin. "Yes, I am."

"Well, if you're willing to take that risk . . ."

I stood and patted the metal base of the sign. "I've taken risks before."

Ry shifted his boots in the gravel until he faced the oncoming caravan of trucks and demolition equipment. "Not with the things that count . . ."

Last night didn't count?

He hadn't said it outright, but that's what I heard.

I had taken the greatest risk I could muster for this man and he had the nerve to say it didn't count? I gritted my teeth and edged toward him, whispering, "What the hell are you trying to say, O'Malley?"

"What the hell are either of you trying to say?" Sugar Anne extended her arms.

"Don't say *hell*," Ry barked, his eyes on me, not his child.

"I don't know why I bother to say anything at all." Sugar Anne rolled her eyes. "You both think you're so different from each other when anybody with half a brain and two good eyes can see that you're really just alike. You have your minds made up about everything and won't listen— not even to each other."

Before I could take the girl's complaint in and formulate a response, a white pickup truck pulled into the drive, followed by a lumbering dump truck. Then, slowly, a faded yellow dinosaur-looking contraption with huge, rusted teeth and THE EXCAVATOR painted in black on its side came into view. That monster—not the happy little red steam shovel of children's books I'd expected—could gobble whole sections of the small motel up in seconds.

I dug my fingers into the soft fabric of my daddy's old jacket and whispered, "Oh my word, it's really going to happen."

Ry drew a deep breath and pushed past his daughter, muttering as he went, "Go on with Jolie, Sugar Anne. I've got a lot to deal with right now. I'll be over later."

I could only nod as he moved on by me.

Sugar Anne came to stand at my side. "You're just going to let him go ahead with this, aren't you?"

"I couldn't change his mind even if I wanted to—which I don't."

"You want him to destroy this place and leave?"

"It isn't about what I want."

"Oh, yeah, right, because you're being mature and grown up, right?"

"Yes. Your father has his reasons for tearing this place down, and I have my reasons for wanting it done and him gone from here as soon as possible."

"And when it's over, what do you both have?"

I pressed my lips together. I glanced over my shoulder to watch Ry.

He stood firm, hands on his lips as he spoke to a stocky man with a hard hat tucked under his arm. The man gestured toward the old building with the clipboard in his hand, then made a slashing motion in the air.

"I'm afraid Dad is not going to realize what a mistake he's making until he sees this great old place turned into a pile of rubble. Not unless something drastic happens to wake him up before it's too late."

A pile of rubble. Just like my every effort to be bold, to be daring, to be the woman I had once hoped I could be had turned out. I tipped my head back to study the figure on the top of the old, doomed sign.

Rubble.

And the only thing to do with rubble was to sweep it away and forget about it.

"C'mon, Sugar Anne. Let's go over to the salon."

"Are you still going to let me do your hair?"

"*Wash* my hair," I corrected. I met the girl's hope-filled gaze.

Sugar Anne shook her head and made a deep guttural sound from the back of her throat. "If you are so obsessive about your hair, why even let me touch it at all?"

"Because I . . ." I glanced at Ry, then at the old motel and already felt the ache of both their absences. "Let's just say I'm trying to give you a sign."

"A sign?"

"A guidepost. There are signs all around us that point the way if you open yourself to them, consider them carefully in order to fully understand them and have faith."

"What about taking action?"

"What?"

"Well, if you see a sign and it points the way, then you can't just sit there, you have to take some kind of action, right?"

"Well . . . yes . . . uh . . . after a lot of thoughtful study and . . . um . . . effort to interpret them properly and . . ."

"Interpret them?" Sugar Anne laughed and massaged her wrist again, her head down as she said, "Sounds to me like no matter what kind of sign *you* see, you automatically take it for a 'Stop,' 'Do Not Enter' or one of those big, red circles with a line across it."

Did I do that? Watching Ry discuss the demise of the South Winds across the way left me ill-prepared to argue that I didn't. Caution had become my beacon and my watchword. So much that I suddenly wondered how many times I had mentally manipulated situations so that the "signs" pointed me toward my preconceived notions. Whenever I had acted rashly this past week and a half, I had told myself I was acting without a sign.

The Excavator growled and rumbled and shook the ground as it pulled into the parking lot.

I found myself without solid footing in more ways than one and it scared me like nothing ever had before.

"Jolie? Are you still going to let me wash your hair?"

"Um, yes, I suppose so."

Sugar Anne threw her thin arm around my shoulders. "Well, that's a good *sign,* isn't it?"

"I . . . uh . . . I don't know."

"Great! I think everyone could use some inspiration from on high right about now, don't you?" She beamed, then her eyes shifted like she was stealing a peek in her father's direction. "Say, Jolie, since you're being so bold and letting me wash your hair, why not go crazy and let me use my own shampoo?"

"I've always used the same shampoo, Sugar Anne. I have it specially mixed for my hair's texture and . . ."

Sugar Anne's expression fell somewhere between disgust and disbelief at my unwillingness to even try something new, just once.

Stop. Do Not Enter. Caution. I looked up, then over at Ry, then at the girl waiting for some kind of answer.

For a person trying to show how much I trusted and re-spected the girl, I was acting like a controlling bitch. I did not need a divine road map to tell me what path to take in this instance. "Fine, you go get your shampoo and meet me over at the salon in fifteen minutes."

Chapter 20

⑥ "No. You cannot be telling me that even by tearing this place down I stand to cash in on this much money." Ry stared at the paper the man had handed him.

"Hey, Red!" I raised my hand in hello to the owner of Rose Demolition and Salvage. We'd gone to high school together and I was the only person in town who knew that he used one of those over-the-counter men's hair dyes to keep his mustache and temples as bright red as the rest of his hair.

Ry looked up from the paper in his hand and scratched his head. "Look, I only had you look into selling off the fixtures and things in order to offset the cost of taking the South Winds down. I thought they'd pretty much cancel each other out."

"It's just an estimate. I could be off by a few grand either way." Red scratched his sunburned nose and took the clipboard back from Ry. "I know to an O'Malley it might look like chump change, but—"

"Are you kidding? My grandfather ticked off his vending distributor so badly he never got a discount again and all over a few free sodas. To the O'Malleys there is no such thing as chump change." He looked at the total again. "I just don't see where you get this number."

"You got resale on the furniture and TV sets, then you add in what you get for all recyclable material—you did want to recycle whatever you can, didn't you?"

"Yes. But I didn't realize I'd turn a profit by being such a conscientious citizen, damn it."

"Then there's the routine salvage materials," Red went on without missing a beat. "You could lump a lot of stuff into that, but frankly only a total dumb-ass would do that, especially with the retro market still really hot right now."

"Retro market?"

"Oh, yeah. This is where it really pays off that your grandfather was such a conniving, angry old cheap-ass bastard—no offense intended."

"None taken."

I could see that Ry meant that from the bottom of his heart and suspected that was because he was thinking far worse things about the cheap old bastard himself.

"You've got a few original fixtures in here that date back to the 1930s. Not to mention updates representing every decade since, all kept in prime condition."

"I hadn't even bothered to check the rooms to see what shape they were in."

"Kind of like the farm kids who don't make pets out of animals they later have to sell off to become someone's supper?" I asked, trying only to be helpful, of course.

He narrowed his eyes at me but did not argue.

"The old man hated to have to replace anything." An admiring hush infused Red's words. "So he made sure that his guests understood he'd charge them double for damage."

"And the old buzzard did it, too," I added, again only adding my thoughts in to better illuminate the situation. I did not revel in making Ry feel rotten. I wanted this as much as he did. Didn't I?

"On top of that, every mirror and faucet, every doorknob and picture frame was pampered and protected. Yes sir, he treated this place like it was his baby."

"I can picture his grandfather polishing every doorknob." Ry rubbed his eyes.

"And we haven't even talked about the restaurant—all that equipment, the dishes, the gift-shop junk. Hell, even the booths would bring something."

Ry nodded. "I can see that. If I had a home—you know, instead of an apartment—I wouldn't mind having an All Day Breakfast Buffet booth in my own kitchen."

"Your grandfather didn't connect himself to much in this life that didn't make a buck both coming and going."

Ry took a deep breath and surveyed the façade of the old motel. "Yeah. I suspect if he knew he could make some cash by selling off his life's work bit by bit he'd have done that, too."

"I don't think so. He loved every nook and cranny of this fleapit and greasy spoon." A note of reverence permeated Red's superficially insulting description. "He said the South Winds was like a great old broad."

"He compared the Trav' O' Tel to a woman?"

"Said she'd weathered the best and the worst of times and still had everything a man longed for when he was ready to climb into the sack." He chuckled, then shook his head. "A lot of folks agreed with him. That's why you got to factor in the sentimental crowd."

"The what?"

"Man, every family in Logie County, all their friends and kin in outlying areas, countless thousands of tourists dating back to when this was a shiny, new motor court, have spent a night, a vacation, a honeymoon, a weekend—hell's bells—even a few stolen hours at the South Winds. It *means* something to them."

"And that would bring more money *how*?" he asked.

"Can't put a price on a memory. But oh, say, figurin' five dollars a hit for a chunk of this old place along with a certificate of authenticity and a reproduction of an old postcard sold at the monthly Flea Market, I'd say . . ." he scribbled a number on the pad.

Ry studied the amount. "My head hurts."

"If you don't believe him, just go around and read what people wrote on the back of the building last weekend." I flashed my open hand to Sugar Anne when she appeared in the doorway to ask her to give me five minutes, then pointed to the shop across the street.

She waved the plastic grocery bag in her hand, grinned and headed to the salon.

I looked to Ry again. "Or have you gone back to read the messages already?"

"I haven't had the time . . . or the heart . . . to go back there yet."

"You should. Before . . ." I turned to study the dump truck and excavator parked like sleeping giants in the lot. "Before it's gone."

"You could give me the guided tour." He reached out, almost touching my arm, then let his hand fall back by his side.

"I think you can find it by yourself," I said. "I promised Sugar Anne I'd meet her in the salon in a few minutes."

He smiled, just a bit, as he shook his head. "That works out just fine, because I need a few minutes to let this new information soak in. I wouldn't mind spending them in good company."

I spoke to Red instead of Ry. "Can you tell me about when you'll start work here?"

"Depends." Red threaded his pencil behind his ear.

"On?"

"If you don't mind my saying, Jolie, that's not your question to ask. Aren't you kind of on the wrong side of 612? I always heard a Hadley wouldn't cross that highway even if their hair was on fire and the only water for miles to put it out was in the South Winds pool."

"Hey, now don't drag hair issues into this, Red, or you might regret it." It was a threat I could back up like nobody's business, and the way he stroked his mustache told me he knew it.

"Not trying to be difficult, Jolie. Maybe I should have said that if the South Winds was on fire the Hadleys wouldn't cross the street to spit on it."

"Piss on it," I muttered.

"I beg your pardon?" Ry cocked his head.

"The Hadleys wouldn't cross the street to *piss* on the South Winds. If you're going to say it, get it right." I pointlessly primped my limp, tangled hair. "Spitting is so unladylike."

Ry laughed outright then and leaned in to whisper for my ears only: "Damn, but you are one fabulous woman, Jolie Hadley Corbett. Like Grandpa Howdy said about the South Winds, everything a man longs for when he climbs into the sack. Or gets up from it. Or walks into the kitchen, or out into the coldness of the world. Jolie, you are the kind of woman a man wants all the time and everywhere, not just to make love to, but to live his life alongside."

He took my breath away. A thousand thoughts flashed in my mind all at once. My skin tingled. And yet I found the outer reserve to whisper. "Are you comparing me to an old if well-preserved Trav' O' Tel, Ryman O'Malley?"

"No."

His breath tickled my ear.

"If I were to describe you, Jolie, it would not be as the South Winds personified but as something even more wonderful, something higher." He looked up to the top of the sign.

My pulse thumped hard in my temples, but I followed suit and looked up, too. Esther towered above us, bold and perfect and teetering on the very edge of oblivion.

"Pardon my saying so, but as far as I can see, nothing around here is on fire, Jolie. It just seems out of place to find a Hadley at the South Winds," repeated Red.

"I'm sure. But there's a simple reason for my visit. I've come . . ." I made a sweeping glance from the pool to the buffet building. My eyes clouded, but the tears did not fall. I sniffled, tipped my head up and slid my arm into Ry's. "I've come to take Mr. O'Malley behind the motel to literally read the writing on the wall."

"Can you excuse us, Mr. Rose? I really need a few minutes to reflect on all the new information you gave me today."

"Sure. We bill by the hour, whether we work or wait."

"Okay." Ry took my hand and started toward the back of the building. "Feel free to go inside. Through the lobby and down the hallway in the kitchen of my living quarters you'll find a coffee pot and all the makings if you want to help yourself."

"Living quarters? Coffee?" Red tossed his trusty clipboard into the open cab of his dusty truck. "You mean to tell me you don't have the gas, electric and water shut off already?"

Ry swore between his teeth.

"Go see about this, Ry." I stepped away. I didn't have any business spending time alone with the man now anyway. "Come to think of it there really is no reason for the two of us to go there together, is there?"

"I want to go, Jolie, and I want you to take me."

I shook my head.

"You don't want to take the chance of being seen ducking off with me? To risk scandalizing the whole town?"

"That must be it. Since I never take chances with anything that counts." There I was again, being an ass, throwing the man's own words in his face. Then again, maybe it wasn't me who was the ass in this situation.

"I never did get to explain that, I—"

"Don't try." I held my hand up. "I don't really have much time myself. It's good all this came up, maybe it's . . ."

"It's not a sign that we shouldn't go back there." He gave my hand a squeeze.

"Of course not." I knew that now. "Don't you know, Ry?"

"Know what?"

"Signs are just a silly superstition that some people use as a crutch in a world filled with so much they can't control."

"Who told you that?"

"Told me?" I shook my head and laughed just a little. "It's not like some bratty kid broke the news about Santa Claus, Ry."

"What news about Santa Claus?" He lifted my chin with one finger. "Did the elves go on strike? Did he get a bad case of mistletoe?"

"Don't try to cheer me up." I pulled my face away from his touch, cast my gaze down and ran my hand along his arm. "I'm just saying that everything that's happened since you've come back has made me stop and think and, maybe, question to some degree things that . . . well, that once seemed rock solid and dependable in my life."

"Go make coffee," he told Red. "I'll be back to sort this out shortly."

Red shouted out some rough-voiced, indistinguishable orders to his crew.

I did not look to see if they went into the lobby or just gathered around to grumble. I did not care what they did at this point. My whole focus stayed on Ry.

"I can't go back there with you, Ry."

"You have to."

"Why?"

"Because you have to prove me wrong."

"How?"

"Take a risk on something that counts big time, Jolie."

Heaven help me, I wanted to do just that, but how could I? "What are you asking of me, Ry?"

"To trust me, Jolie."

"Is that all?" I whispered, barely able to breathe. I ran my fingers through my hair and nodded. Without another word, I led the way around the corner of the building.

"Now remember, I can't stay long." I ducked under a low-hanging tree branch and lost sight of him for a moment.

He appeared again and found me standing behind the building, one hand on the cool wall. The well-shaded area behind the South Winds smelled of old leaves and perpetually damp earth.

He paused a moment to let his eyes adjust, then drew in the moist, pungent air. He turned to face the wall.

"Well?" I held my hand out.

"Wow."

He said it so softly I didn't know how to read his reaction.

"I had imagined the graffiti back here, but . . ."

Someone had suggested the concept at the opening of the Flea Market and word spread. All weekend long, people had wandered back here. More than once I'd seen Ry shake hands with an old friend of Howdy's only to draw back a palm covered in chalk dust. So I knew Ry understood that a lot of folks felt compelled to find a way to say goodbye to this place.

"Nothing prepared me for this."

I followed his line of vision as it swept over tribute after tribute, scribbled, scrawled and even sketched over every inch of that gray back wall.

"I got my first kiss here," I said softly.

His brow pressed down, and he cocked his head. "You did?"

"Not me. Look here." I pointed to a tiny squiggle of writing under an oversized drawing of an arrow.

"Oh yeah. Yeah." He pretended to read the words. "Somehow I can't quite grasp the enormity of every individual homage."

"That's because you're a big-picture kind of guy."

"Yeah." He touched the wall. "Deal with the big picture and let the details sort themselves out. I did that raising Sugar Anne. And with my family. I looked to the end result and wished for all the pieces to fit together."

"And have they?"

He drew in a deep breath and let it out. "I chose supposed family harmony over my grandfather's feelings, over my own wishes when I stopped coming to Verbena. And now I'm ready to destroy the South Winds in order to achieve that same goal—but I never thought of the hundreds of shockwaves my decision would send out, affecting so many lives."

"Kind of a different *big picture* then, huh?"

"And the smaller picture. How it affects you. How too many of my actions since I got here have taken their toll on you, Jolie . . ."

"We said no regrets. Maybe we should have also said no returns. Let's leave it as it is."

"I can't."

"Then I'll make it easy for you and go." Leaves crunched and swished under the swift pace of my feet.

"Don't . . . please?"

I paused, my heart pounding.

"Damn, but I wished I had your knack for seeing the otherworldly in the everyday, Jolie. I could sure use some kind of divine direction about now."

"I have to go," I whispered and started to walk away.

"At least . . ." He took a deep breath. "At least tell me where I can find your message."

"Oh. It's . . ." I gave a wave toward the other end of the wall. "It's there. You'll know it if you see it. I have to go now."

"Jolie, I can't stand the idea of you not believing in signs anymore, especially if I had anything to do with it."

"A faith untested is not real faith at all, Ry. I still believe in the one who sends the signs, but I can't stand here and tell you that I will ever put the same kind of reliance on what I once thought of as heavenly guideposts."

"Are you sure you're okay with that?"

"I swear on the very last hair on my . . ." I put my hand on my head. "Have mercy, my hair is an abomination! I have to go."

I got away without ever actually telling him that I was okay. Maybe that was because I could not stand there and lie to a man who had placed such a high value on me, and on always telling the truth.

Chapter 21

"I'll be all right." I wasn't just talking about the chance I was taking by letting Ry's daughter use who knew what on my hair. I clutched the protective plastic cape fastened under my chin. "*Everything* will be all right."

I needed desperately to believe my own words.

But I didn't believe them. And with good reason.

I had wanted to spare the South Winds. That came to nothing.

I had wanted to rescue the icon that had come to embody all the things I had hoped for, for myself and for my hometown. And I had failed.

Esther would never again soar high into the night sky. She would never make another awe-inspiring dive to the pool below.

I had allowed myself one night of abandon with the man I'd lusted after for two decades. One night. A few hours, really, telling myself that a few hours would not change anything. But, damn it, it changed everything in the most fundamental of ways. It changed the way I looked at Verbena, at my family and most of all, it changed something inside of me.

"Pour it on, Sugar Anne." I laid my head back in the shampoo sink and shut my eyes. "In fact double the amount if you want."

"You don't need more, but you can certainly let this set awhile."

Two minutes. Mama always said to never let a new hair treatment rest on your hair longer than two minutes.

Would you shut up about your hair for one minute? You're a hairdresser by practical design, not by divine providence. Emma had tried to make me reexamine my priorities in this very room the day I decided to go to Howdy's funeral. The day I first took the step that got me inextricably entwined with the plight of the South Winds, of Esther and with Ry and his daughter.

You don't just look nice, Jolie. You look . . . untouchable. Sugar Anne had summed it up more bluntly.

You never take a chance with anything that matters. And Ry had driven the point home with neither malice nor mercy.

You never take a chance with anything that matters.

"We'll leave it on as long as you think it needs." It wasn't a big leap of faith, but it was what I could do for now.

"Good." Sugar Anne wrapped a soft white towel around my head.

"Mmmm. I sure do like the smell of this stuff. It's so . . . familiar." I took a deep breath, trying to relax while Ry's daughter tucked every strand of wet hair under the covering. "For some reason it puts me in a mind of summers as a kid, Popsicles and peanut butter and jelly, only without the peanut butter."

"Well, isn't that something?" Sugar Anne poked and fiddled with my hair, then took a damp rag and wiped the skin along the hairline as gentle as a pro. "You comfortable?"

I shifted my shoulders to fit my neck better into the dip in the ceramic hair-washing basin. "As comfortable as I can get, I suppose."

"Good, because you promised to stay there letting this stuff do its magic."

"I promise." I drew an X over my heart with one finger.

Where would I go, anyway? I'm a girl who always wants a safe harbor. Where could I find that now? Where could I go to escape the reality of my own shortcomings and failures? Where thoughts of Ryman O'Malley and all the stupid, silly, senseless things I'd done since he'd arrived in town could not intrude?

"While you're doing that, do you mind if I go out on the porch to check and see if they've made any progress across the street?"

"Progress?" I scoffed, my eyes shut tight against the images of just what kind of "progress" the next few days would bring. "That's a funny word for it."

"Mighty sarcastic from a woman who wouldn't even take up the good fight." Sugar Anne's voice carried to me over the sound of her walking away.

"The good fight." I had to smile at that. "You got that from Granny Missus, didn't you?"

"Um, yeah." The door creaked open. "I did, actually."

I debated telling the girl that's what my grandmother had always called maintaining the feud with the O'Malleys. Whenever I would tease her about her tall tales of wrongs done in the past or scold her over things like the grudge-money quarters, my old granny would grin and say, "just keeping up the good fight."

A thread of air from the open door reached me and I took a deep breath. It smelled of leaves and motor oil from the highway. Not a trace of dust from a collapsing building. I released my death grip on my plastic covering at last and crossed my ankles.

"You know, Sugar Anne, I hope you understand that the acrimony between our families is over now. And that's not just because the O'Malleys are leaving Verbena forever."

Forever. I still couldn't get the concept to take root in my mind. No more feud. No more South Winds. No more . . .

"Shit fire and save the matches! Lock the door behind me and turn out all the lights. Maybe he won't follow me in."

"Granny Missus!" I sat up, and then realized Sugar Anne had left the salon and Granny was talking to me alone. The weight of the damp towel made my head wobble, which seemed only fitting as my head was practically spinning from trying to make sense of my grandmother's indelicate outburst. Not that I expected anything less from the old girl. "What are you carrying on about?"

She flicked the light switch off and flipped the front sign over so it read: SORRY, WE'RE CLOSED! COME AGAIN. Then she fell backward against the door and let loose a groaning sigh.

"Granny, what's wrong? Is there some kind of trouble?"

"Damned mayor's son. Damned newspaper." She let her hands fall to her sides. A pair of handcuffs clunked to the floor, took a bounce, then slid to the middle of the room. "Who was it called them anyway?"

"Emma, I think. Or the lady preacher, maybe. Why?"

"Showed up at my door not five minutes ago. Wanted to get the story and would I please handcuff myself to the fence again so they could get a good picture? Damned fools."

"You chained yourself up to that fence only a few hours ago."

"That was for principle, not for publicity."

"Thought you enjoyed fueling all that feud crap."

"Hell, no!" She made a quick check out the door before shuffling the few steps to look at herself in the salon's mirrored wall. She fussed with her hair and pressed her lips together to even out her lipstick. "Drawing attention to all those years of ill will and anger just seems childish and counterproductive."

"Since when have you considered childishness or any chance to counter an O'Malley's productivity a bad trait?"

She patted her hands down her coveralls, then pinched her naked earlobes. "Ran out the door so fast I didn't have time to get properly dressed."

"You look fine."

She snorted and began searching her pockets.

"Granny Missus, you didn't answer my question. Since when have you not jumped at the chance to dredge up all those old animosities and antagonisms?"

Finally she fished a lilac-trimmed hankie from the depths of her side pocket. She folded it over once, then again. Her shoulders rose and fell and with her eyes on the delicate cloth in her hand she whispered hoarsely, "Since Howdy died."

My breath went still at her confession. I'd gotten so wrapped up in myself I hadn't stopped to think how Howard O'Malley's passing might have affected my grandmother. They had been combatants and compatriots for at least sixty years. She would have felt the loss of him more than anyone in Verbena. Yet pointless pride and tired tradition kept her from outwardly mourning him.

"Just don't see much point in it all anymore without that mean, rotten, ornery old goat to bedevil anymore," she murmured, wiping the hankie over her eyes.

"Oh, Granny." I eased up from the chair and, careful not to knock the towel from my head, went to her and gave her a sideways hug. I laughed softly. Because she would not have accepted anything more emotional from me, I teased her. "You're a mess."

"I'm a mess?" She sniffled and squared her rounded shoulders. "You taken a long hard look at yourself, young lady? And I don't mean your hair and make up and clothes and—"

"I know what you mean." I hugged her again, kissed her cheek and straightened away. "Believe me, I *know*. Nobody knows what a bigger mess I've made of myself than me."

We both stood there a minute in the empty salon, the only light around us coming from the door and window. We did not look into the mirror, or at each other or at anything in particular. Just stood.

Finally Granny Missus blew her nose, then tucked her hankie away. She lifted her head, scowled and folded her arms as she turned to face me at last. "Do you love him?"

"Who?"

"You know who."

I knew who, but I had no idea *she* knew who! My stomach knotted. I wanted to say something glib, like I would with Emma, but nothing came to mind. So I tried an entirely new approach, one not often used with my family. I simply spoke the truth.

"Doesn't matter if I did love him, Granny Missus. There's too much gone between us now." I tightened the folds of my towel turban and sighed. "Hell, there was too much bad blood between us, between our families, since long before either one of us was born. What chance did we have?"

"What chance did you give yourselves?"

Man, she wasn't letting up. "He's leaving."

"Has he left yet?"

"Granny Missus, why are you talking to me like this? I'd have thought you'd encourage me to fight my feelings in this matter. You know, to uphold the family honor and . . ."

" 'Family honor,' my baggy white ass!"

"Granny!"

"I wasn't born a Hadley, you know. Neither was your Mama."

"What are you saying?"

"I'm saying you and Dylan are the only born Hadleys left in these hills. Reckon it's up to you two to take up the feud . . . or end it."

"Y'all have manipulated me my whole life and now you say it was my choice all along?" My heart thudded high in my chest. My mind tried to unravel a thousand thoughts at once. "Good Lord, Granny, you make me feel like Dorothy in *The Wizard of Oz*, finding out she could have gone home all the time."

The old woman snorted a laugh. "Manipulated? Now that's a bit harsh."

"You and Mama and Daddy allowed me to shoulder some of the blame for Daddy not getting that bank loan."

"If we did we certainly didn't mean to. . . ."

"Didn't *mean* to? Do you know how many times I've wished I could have done that day over and not jumped in the water and made a mess of myself?" Almost as many times as I'd reveled in the pure joy of the moment when Ry had jumped in after me.

My most thrilling memory and my biggest heartache sprang from that one incident. No wonder I spent the rest of my life paralyzed with fear that I might hurt someone I loved by one rash action.

No wonder I second-guessed my every choice. Second-guessed. Third-guessed.

And drove everyone around me crazy.

"Well, shit fire indeed, Granny." I plunked into a stylist chair. I looked up at the sign over my door and groaned.

A KNIGHT HAS HIS ARMOR, A GENERAL HAS HIS TROOPS
BUT NOTHING PREPARES A WOMAN FOR HER DAILY BATTLES
LIKE THE PERFECT HAIRDO.

I had longed all my life to become my own living, breathing, diving girl. Fearless, bold, wonderful. Instead I'd turned myself into . . . into my own damned hairdo. An undentable, immovable, watertight veneer of perfection—over a great, big, protected nest of snarled perceptions and tangled emotions.

Damn. Was that what I wanted for the rest of my life?

I sat up straight and tall in the chair. "Granny Missus, I think it's time I took a little of the air out of my hair. What do you think?"

Granny smiled. "I think the change would do you good."

The change would do me good. I liked that thought. But to really change, to step up and finally become the woman I had only dreamed I could be would take a bigger risk than any alteration to my outward appearance could provide. I had to take action.

"Granny Missus, do you still believe in signs?"

"Yes, I do. But the thing I've learned in my many years on this earth, sweetheart, is that it's not enough to believe in them. You also have to trust in them."

"Trust?" I tried to swallow, but my throat felt all closed up. "What do you mean?"

"I think you know."

"You mean it's not enough to just believe. If you honestly think you've seen a sign that points the way, you still have to follow through. To make that first step. Or leap. Or dive."

The bells on the door jangled.

I sank my fingers into my head wrapping, my eyes still shut, glad that Sugar Anne was back so I could get this over with and . . .

"Granny, will you hand me those handcuffs you brought in? There's something I need to do. I just hope it's not too late."

"It's never too late when you believe, Jolie." Ry's deep voice resonated through my body.

The light switch clicked and flooded the salon with soft illumination.

I opened my eyes and smiled to see him standing there.

"You see that reporter skulking around out there with the mayor's idiot son?" Granny peered out the door as it fell slowly shut.

"Last I saw they were talking to Sugar Anne."

"Damn the daylight out of those dirty sneaks." The old gal could really pick up the pace when she set her mind to it. In a matter of moments she was out the door, her fist raised to the heavens as she shouted, "As God is my witness, there will be no pictures of any Hadleys or O'Malleys in that local rag as long as I still live and draw breath!"

Ry laughed and jerked his thumb over his shoulder as the door fell shut. "What's that about?"

"Change has finally come to Verbena. Haven't you heard?"

"Change?" His foot tapped the handcuffs on the floor and he paused to pick them up.

A trickle of cold liquid snaked down my neck from my hair.

"I thought you were all about fighting against change. Wish I'd known about this new attitude before I sent Mr. Rose and his equipment packing."

My hand trembled as I raised it to my head to steady my turban. I stood, slowly. "Ry, what are you saying?"

"I'm saying . . ." He came to me and with the cuffs dangling from one finger he put his hands on my shoulders. His kind eyes darkened with emotion. He took a breath and I could feel the warmth of his body pressing closer to me. "I'm saying, 'I believe there will always be a South Winds.' "

My knees went weak. "You found what I wrote on the wall."

"Yes."

I laid my hand on his chest. "I didn't mean that I thought the building would go on standing."

"I know."

"I was thinking that some part of it would always exist in Verbena and the people here."

"Of course," he said in a low, almost hypnotic tone.

I wet my lips and pushed myself to go on explaining, fearing that if I did not say it all now I never would. "And that because of that, maybe someday I would find it in myself to embody the traits I always attributed to Esther—to be fearless and wonderful and ready to leap into life, even if I didn't know for sure what awaited me."

He traced the edge of his finger upward, along my throat, under my chin and over my cheek. "You already are all those things and more, Jolie."

"Am I?" My lips remained parted in invitation of what I hoped would come.

"Yes." He sealed his answer with a kiss, delicate at first, then harder and deeper.

I dipped the tip of my tongue into his warm mouth and grabbed the back of his shirt with both hands to draw him to me.

He supported the small of my back with one hand and with the other reached for the back of my neck.

When the towel around my damp hair fell away, I did not care. I only arched my back and pushed my hips upward to press intimately against him. I moaned.

He pulled back, just a little, then kissed me lightly, saying between each brush of his lips, "Jolie?"

"Mmm?"

"Can you tell me why it is—"

I kissed the corner of his mouth, his dimple, his lower lip.

"That you." He kissed my cheekbone, my lips, my cheek again. "Smell—"

He kissed me fully once, hard and hot, then broke away suddenly, his eyes wide. "Like a big grape?"

"Grape?" I sank my fingers into my hair, which had already begun to dry, to my surprise. I took a deep breath.

"Holy shit, Jolie. You might want to take a look at yourself in the mirror."

I pushed away from him, finished tugging the towel off of my head and stood, awestruck at what I saw in every mirror on every wall in the salon.

"Damn, Jolie, your hair is . . . it's . . ." He burst out laughing.

"Purple!" I shoved my hands into my hair and found it stiff in the spots where it was not damp. "My hair is purple!"

"On you it works, though."

"Oh, my word, it's Kool-Aid," I said softly.

"What?"

"Kids use it as a temporary hair dye."

"Will it do any damage?"

I shook my head. "Only to my pride. And it may take a few days to get it all washed out."

"Maybe it's a sign. . . ."

"Maybe it is." I stared in disbelief at the matted clumps already drying on my head. "Or maybe it's a message. Sugar Anne's not-so-subtle way of reminding me to be bigger than my hair."

"Bigger than *your* hair?" He bent down to meet my eyes in the mirror and smiled, murmuring, "Miss Jolene, you'd have to be tall as Esther herself to do that."

I could have smacked him. I'd done it before.

I could have burst into tears and run and hid from the world. I'd done that most of my life.

I could have laid the blame for everything that happened

on someone else's doorstep, as I had when my marriage failed.

I could pitch a fit, pretend to be strong and sure when I was really just being scared and stubborn.

Or I could step up to the edge, hold out my arms and trust.

"Jolie, are you all right?"

"All right?" I took in the image of myself standing there looking for all the world like a drowned rat—drowned in grape Kool-Aid, no less. And did the thing I could not have done ten days ago. I let go.

"All right?" I scrunched my fingers in my hair, had a long overdue laugh at myself, and choked out, "I'm perfect!"

"Yes, you are." He pulled me into his arms and kissed me. "And I love you."

In one instant my whole body felt lighter than air. I kissed his mouth firmly but without letting myself get too carried away.

When I pulled away I had to swipe a drop of purple liquid from his cheek. "But how could you love me?"

"How? How could I love a woman who is sexy and smart, and funny and passionate about the things she values?"

"No, how could you love someone you've only known for ten days?"

"Twenty-two years and ten days," he corrected.

"But still . . ."

"Don't be too cautious this time, Jolie. Don't let your fears overrule your feelings."

I tipped my head back, ignoring the tangled mass brushing my shoulders.

Ry loved me.

We had come full circle from that day when he had jumped in the pool after me.

I touched my hair, remembering how it had been ruined that day too, and looked into the eyes of the man who had tried to save my dignity all those years ago. I couldn't help wondering if some divine intervention had brought him back to Verbena to save me all over again.

"I love you too, Ry, you know that?"

"More than your hair dryer?"

"More than my entire made-to-order hairdressing kit, monogrammed blow dryer and super-hold Aqua Net in the professional-size spray can."

"Wow."

"But what about your family?"

"What about yours?" he countered.

"Mine doesn't want anything but my happiness. I understand that now."

"Then it will be okay?"

"I don't know. My dad can fight me. The whole lot of them can fight me over it."

"Hadleys have been fighting O'Malleys for a long, long time. They ain't as scary as they make themselves out to be." Granny Missus stood in the doorway, holding Sugar Anne by the sleeve. "Great Caesar's Ghost! You said you'd done something awful to Jolie's hair, Sugar Anne, but you never said you'd left it looking so danged *purty!*"

"It washes out," the girl said meekly. "And I just . . . I thought . . . I wanted to do something that would make you two mad enough to start listening to each other, okay?"

"You we'll deal with later." I glanced back at Ry. If I needed any sign that this was the right thing to do I saw it in the love reflected back at me in his eyes. "Right now there's something that I should have done years ago, but I lacked the courage and common sense to act on it."

"What are you going to do?" Sugar Anne asked.

I grabbed the handcuffs and Ry's arm and headed for the door. "Is that photographer still around?"

"You can't just go out there like that," Granny Missus anchored her feet.

"Oh, right. Right." Four or five quick swipes at my hair tamed the worst of the tangles. Then I turned to Ry, grinning like a total fool. "Shall we go?"

"Lead the way." He dipped his head, his eyes sparkling.

Be still my heart. But my feet went right on walking, right on past my solid, stalwart grandmother.

"Where the hell are you two headed?" Granny Missus called from the open doorway.

"Off the deep end," Ry answered back. "Come on with us, whatever happens. It should be one breathtaking show."

Chapter 22

The next day the headline in the paper read: FEUD OVER! HADLEY AND O'MALLEY TO TAKE THE PLUNGE!

Under the direction of the mayor's son, the story took a Blue Ridge Romeo and Juliet angle that got picked up by the news wires and sent out as a human interest story all over the country.

Tourism picked up after that, especially around the wedding date that following spring.

I wore my hair simple and short and in my natural, not purple, color. The lady minister conducted the ceremony held in the Flea Market barn—though *not* on the second Saturday of the month.

Dylan took the role of the best man quite seriously and Sugar Anne shared the maid of honor honors with Emma, both of them much less serious about it all but enthusiastic all the same. I wore my grandmother's ivory satin gown and carried a painted quarter for luck in my garter. Mama came home to walk me down the aisle—and to tell us she wanted to make the move permanent since she liked her job so well and everything in town had sorted itself out just fine without her.

I even got a card from Art sending his best wishes from Coeur d'Alene, Idaho!

Ry's parents did not attend, but his sister and her family did. I figure that's a start.

We drove away in the rebuilt Starliner and came home to a change of address. Bought an honest-to-goodness house—not one attached to one of our businesses—in Verbena proper, just across the street from the Sunshine Market.

Sugar Anne went off to beauty school in Atlanta—so she can support *herself* when she's ready to go back to college.

Emma has a new boyfriend, a cowboy who flies in once a month for the market from his very own cattle ranch in Montana. So she has added *Western Horseman* and a whole stack of *Sky Mall* catalogues to her reading repertoire, God bless her.

And me, every day I am grateful for the mixed bag of blessings that brought me to the life I lead today.

I have an adorable husband I can always count on. A sex life that, while it might not scorch any therapist's couches, is hot enough to keep me smoldering, thank you very much. A terrific son and stepdaughter and the cutest wash-n-wear haircut in the tri-county area.

Oh, and a picture that appeared in over a hundred papers all over the country taped to the mirror in the Combin' Holiday Salon. It's of me—my hair a total wreck—and Ry, looking tall and gorgeous—as always—standing in the middle of Highway 612. Our arms are raised, our hands are cuffed, and behind us, in her full, lighted glory, Esther performs her fearless high dive into the great unknown.

And I wouldn't change a thing.

Except my hair.

AVON TRADE...
because every great bag deserves a great book!

AIN'T NOBODY'S BUSINESS IF I DO
by Valerie Wilson Wesley
0-06-051592-9 • $13.95 US • $20.95 Can

THE BOY NEXT DOOR
by Meggin Cabot
0-06-009619-5 • $13.95 US • $20.95 Can

A PROMISING MAN (AND ABOUT TIME, TOO)
by Elizabeth Young
0-06-050784-5 • $13.95 US

A PAIR LIKE NO OTHA'
by Hunter Hayes
0-380-81485-4 • $13.95 US • $20.95 Can

A LITTLE HELP FROM ABOVE
by Saralee Rosenberg
0-06-009620-9 • $13.95 US • $21.95 Can

THE CHOCOLATE SHIP
by Marissa Monteilh
0-06-001148-3 • $13.95 US • $21.95 Can

THE ACCIDENTAL VIRGIN
by Valerie Frankel
0-06-093841-2 • $13.95 US • $21.95 Can

BARE NECESSITY
by Carole Matthews
0-06-053214-9 • $13.95 US

THE SECOND COMING OF LUCY HATCH
by Marsha Moyer
0-06-008166-X • $13.95 US • $21.95 Can

DOES SHE OR DOESN'T SHE?
by Alisa Kwitney
0-06-051237-7• $13.95 US • $21.95 Can

LOVE AND A BAD HAIR DAY
by Annie Flannigan
0-380-81936-8• $13.95 US • $21.95 Can

GET SOME LOVE
by Nina Foxx
0-06-052648-3• $13.95 US • $21.95 Can

Available wherever books are sold or please call 1-800-331-3761to order.

RTB 0803